DEAD WRONG

Also by Richard Phillips

The Ripper/Rho Agenda Novels

Once Dead

The Rho Agenda

The Second Ship

Immune

Wormhole

DEAD WRONG

A RHO AGENDA NOVEL

RICHARD PHILLIPS

47NORTH

This is a work of fiction. Names, characters, organizations, places, events, and incidents are either products of the author's imagination or are used fictitiously.

Published by 47North, Seattle

www.apub.com

Amazon, the Amazon logo, and 47North are trademarks of Amazon.com, Inc., or its affiliates.

ISBN-13: 9781477825532
ISBN-10: 1477825533

Cover design by Jason Blackburn

Library of Congress Control Number: 2014907523

Printed in the United States of America

This novel is dedicated to my loving wife, Carol, and to Sienna Farall and Jeremy Loethen, the most wonderful daughter and son-in-law a man could have.

CHAPTER 1

Tupac Inti leaned against the bars, his dark eyes drawn to the gathering storm in the Palmasola prison courtyard a dozen feet below his cell. In the eighteen months he'd been imprisoned awaiting trial, he'd seen lots of violence, much of it initiated by neo-Nazi gang members of the Unión Juvenil Cruceñista, or UJC. After all, they had access to money, and that meant the Disciplina Interna, the prison gang who ran Palmasola, left them alone. Real guards rarely entered Santa Cruz's notorious prison town, preferring to maintain a perimeter defense to prevent escapes, leaving the internal governance to the prisoners themselves.

Tupac had been lucky. Lucky to be as big as he was. Lucky to be one of the many Quechua people with muscles hardened by years swinging a pick in a Bolivian mine. As he watched the eight swastika-tattooed pricks converge on the newcomer, Tupac knew that this man had no such luck. The Disciplina Interna thugs were either too disinterested to intervene, or they were looking forward to the show. Tupac suspected the latter.

The object of neo-Nazi attention stood bare-chested in the filth-strewn exercise area, having just completed a vigorous workout that had left his upper body glistening with sweat in the hot, late-afternoon February sun. What he'd done to get on the UJC's bad side Tupac didn't know. It didn't take much. The man had no tattoos that would have placed him in a competing gang, and he was Caucasian, a definite plus with the neo-Nazis. But from the scars that crisscrossed the man's chest and back, he was no stranger to getting on someone's bad side. Whatever the newcomer had done, here in Palmasola, being on the UJC's bad side was the equivalent of a death sentence.

To look at the man, you'd never know he was about to die. He wasn't big like Tupac, who stood just over six feet, with lean muscle that rippled beneath his skin at every movement. But it was the man's eyes that fascinated Tupac. As those eyes surveyed the men closing in on him, they held no trace of fear. The sight triggered the memory of a black leopard he'd once spotted in the high Amazon. Hungry, hunting eyes, glistening with animal eyeshine. It sent a sudden chill up Tupac's spine.

When the UJC's champion stepped forward, it was no surprise. Clean shaven, with short blond hair, at six feet six he was almost as big as Tupac. Although most Bolivians of German descent were good, honest people, that didn't apply to Karl Liebkin. Until his arrest during an elite police unit raid on the UJC's headquarters, he had been a rising star in the neo-Nazi subculture, claiming more than two dozen personal kills. Being in Palmasola hadn't hurt his body count. Karl liked to keep his victims alive, handing their broken and bloody bodies over to his comrades for final disposition. Their screams often continued for more than an hour.

It was why nobody screwed with these guys. But from that look in the newcomer's eyes, he was about to.

When Karl made his move, it was as if the newcomer had seen it coming before it began. With an easy grace that wasted no energy, the newcomer shifted his weight, letting the shiv slash by the side of his neck with less than an inch to spare, using the motion to coil for the counterstrike that put all of his two hundred pounds into an open-hand impact. The blow connected with Karl's windpipe, dropping the bigger man to his knees, sending a bloody froth bubbling over his lips.

The newcomer's spinning side kick impacted the side of Karl's skull, directly over his right ear, the force of impact snapping his head to the side and dropping him on his face, with blood from the shattered eardrum leaking down. From the jail cells and the crowded alleys that surrounded the conflict, shouts and cheers rose up, growing in volume as the newcomer picked up the shiv and cut Karl's throat from ear to ear, sending a fountain of red neo-Nazi blood spurting toward his stunned companions.

Then, like the black leopard, the newcomer was among them, whirling and slashing, killing the first two before they realized their danger. The first of the survivors to regain his senses bull-rushed the red-eyed demon, but the attacker's attempted tackle was met with a judo flip that converted his momentum into a flailing arc toward an impact that would break his ribs. In the midst of the flipping motion, the newcomer slid his left hand up the Nazi's face from chin to eyes, his fingers thrusting, ripping, and tearing the blue and white orbs from their sockets, leaving them dangling down their owner's bloody cheeks as he writhed on the ground.

Then the shirtless man stood clear, Karl's shiv in his right hand. Though his breath panted out, it was clearly from battle lust, not exertion. Four down, four to go. And when those four backed away, the newcomer dropped the shiv and turned his back on them, stepping across Karl's body on his way back to his cell as wild cheers shook the red brick hell-town.

And as the newcomer made that walk, Tupac got a good look into the man's strange eyes. It was a look that left him cold.

CHAPTER 2

Jack Gregory stripped out of his blood-stained clothes, sluiced the gore from his body with brown water from the sink, and then slid beneath the sheet on one of the cell's three cots. From the look in his cellmates' eyes, none of them was inclined to challenge his right to it. When Jack closed his eyes, sleep came almost immediately, unleashing the dream that rode its wake.

~ ~ ~

There's no tunnel with a beautiful light to call me forward. I didn't expect one. But I didn't expect this either.

A pea-soup fog cloaks the street, trying its best to hide the paving stones beneath my feet. It's London, but this London has an older, Victorian feel. Not in a good way either. For some reason it doesn't really surprise me. If there is a doorway to hell,

I guess a gloomy old London backstreet is as appropriate a setting as any.

While my real body bleeds out somewhere in Calcutta, I don't suffer from wounds here. I step forward, my laced desert combat boots causing fog to swirl around me. Long, cool, steady strides. A narrow alley to my left beckons me. I don't fight the feeling. I didn't start this journey by running away, and I'll be damned if I'm going to end it running away from whatever's around the corner.

The fog isn't any thicker in the alley. The narrowness just makes it feel that way. I don't look back, but I feel the entrance shrink behind me as I walk. To either side, an occasional door mars the walls that connect one building to the next, rusty hinges showing just how long it's been since anyone last opened them. It doesn't matter. My interest is in the dark figure that suddenly blocks my path.

The man's face lies hidden in shadow, although it isn't clear what dim light source is casting the shadows. Still, I see his lips move, hear gravel in his voice.

"Are you certain you wish to walk this path?"

I pause, trying to understand the meaning of the question.

"Didn't think I had much choice."

"Not many do."

"I'm listening."

"You've thought about death?"

"Figured it was just a big sleep."

I watch as the shadowy figure standing before me hesitates. My uneasiness grows with each passing second.

"Nothing so easy."

"Heaven and hell then? Enlighten me."

"Keep walking this path and you'll find out. I offer you something different."

"Ahhh. My soul for my life, is it?"

The laugh rumbles deep inside this thing's chest, and the sound sends a chill through my body.

"I've been around a very, very long time, but I'm not your devil."

"Then what are you?"

For several seconds, silence.

"Think of me as a coma patient, living an eternity of sensing the things going on around me, unable to experience any of them. I know what's happening, what's about to happen, but I feel nothing. Such immortality is its own special kind of hell. Humanity offers me release from that prison."

"I'm not interested in being your vessel."

"I have limitations. I can only send back one who lingers on death's doorway, not someone who is beyond natural recovery. There are rules. My host must willingly accept my presence, and the host remains in control of his own being. His nature is unchanged. I, on the other hand, get to experience the host's emotions for the duration of the ride. I can exist in only one host at a time, and once accepted, I remain with that host until he dies."

I stare at the shadowed figure's face. Did I see a flicker of red in its eyes?

"No thanks."

"I don't deny that there's a downside. As I said, I don't change a host's nature in any way. But what he feels excites me and some of that excitement feeds back to my host. The overall effect is that he still loves what he loves and hates what he hates, but much more hotly. He's the same person he always was, just a little bit more so. And because my intuitions also bleed over, my hosts find themselves drawn to situations that spike their adrenaline. Because of that, few of them live to a ripe old age."

"So you ride these people until they die, then move on to the next person."

"I never said anything about this being a random selection. I have certain needs, and those can't be fulfilled by inhabiting some Siberian dirt farmer or his wife. With all my limitations, I have a very clear sense of those who stride the life and death boundary, fully immersed in humanity's greatest and most terrible events. I always choose a host from this group."

"Such as?"

"Alexander, Nero, Caligula, Attila, Joan of Arc, Napoleon, and hundreds of others, including another Jack who once roamed these London alleys."

"Not a great references list."

"It's not about your notions of good or evil. Whether you want it or not, you are a part of it."

"So my choice is to die now or to open myself to evil?"

"As I said, I can't make you anything you aren't. Hosting me merely amps up your inner nature."

"And you expect me to believe that?"

Again the dark figure pauses. "You pride yourself on your highly developed intuition, your ability to know if someone is lying to you. What is that inner sense telling you now?"

The truth is that, as I stand here, wrapped in damp fog, my intuition isn't telling me shit. Or maybe it is and I'm just too damn tired to listen. I stare at the shadowy figure, inhale deeply, can't feel real breath fill my lungs, and decide.

"I guess I can live with that."

~ ~ ~

Tossing away the damp sheet, Jack sat bolt upright on the cot, his naked body bathed in sweat. He rose to his feet, struggling to remember where he was and why he was here. Ignoring the startled cellmates that moved aside to give him a wide berth, Jack walked to the sink, turned on the faucet, and scrubbed his face with the muddy water, letting it wash away the dream that was more than a dream.

Shit. How long had it been since he'd awakened from a peaceful sleep? Jack couldn't remember. His dreams were so vivid that they seemed more than memories, a past re-experienced. In his sleep, the dreams leaked from the alien parasite that had accompanied him back across the life–death threshold on that awful night in Calcutta. Whatever dying had done to him, Jack couldn't recommend it. One thing was for sure; if he didn't find a way to control his post-deathbed adrenaline addiction, he wouldn't remain alive long enough for it to matter.

As he dressed, he regained some semblance of clarity and, along with it, the memory of yesterday's exercise-yard bloodbath. He'd known it wouldn't take long for the UJC goons to make a move on him. After all, he'd set it up. It was all part of the purpose that had brought him here. And the neo-Nazis had played their part, their deaths serving to introduce Jack "The Ripper" Gregory to the rest of the jailhouse population. Most important, it had introduced him to the one prisoner he'd come all this way to find.

But Jack still had to meet the man. And then he had to get them both the hell out of here. In this part of the world, bribery was the best option for making something like that happen. The trick was to find the right people to bribe, and then to make sure that they feared Jack more than they feared the UJC. He'd accomplished the first part before getting in here. Yesterday's violence had closed the deal. Now, if Jack could avoid being poisoned in the meantime, so much the better.

CHAPTER 3

Feeling all of his sixty-three years, Conrad Altmann stepped off the stairs into the concrete sub-basement, avoiding the dead bodies and pools of blood that might stain his Toscana crocodile shoes. These dead men, the last remnants of Klaus Barbie's personal guard, had taken their master's words too literally all those years ago when he'd ordered them to allow no one to enter this secret place. If they had realized that Klaus never intended that order to apply to his bastard son, they would still be alive.

Moving past the half-dozen submachine gun–wielding bodyguards that had preceded him into this secret haven, he reached for the German schrank mounted against the far wall, fitting his father's special key into the cabinet's keyhole.

The lock clicked open with a snap that echoed through the dark chamber. Despite his practiced calm, Altmann couldn't resist the urge to glance back over his shoulder. Dark echo chambers did that to you, squeezed those suppressed childhood nightmares from under your bed into your present. But this glance failed to reveal hell's demons. If they were out there, they cowered before him, as well they should. The long-dead Führer's rightful heir brooked no opposition, be it from heaven or hell.

Turning his attention back to the closet door, Altmann pulled it all the way open. The empty shelves that met his gaze cramped his gut.

Impossible!

After all the years he'd spent researching every facet of his family history, of Klaus Barbie's life, it couldn't end here.

Running his hand over the neatly trimmed beard that was the same graying blond as his shoulder-length hair, Altmann looked at Dolf Gruenberg. "Tear it out of the wall."

As the other men looked on, the big albino grasped the cabinet and tore it free from the bolts that secured it in place, toppling it onto one of the scattered bodies. Low on the wall where the empty schrank had stood, a crawl space opened into darkness.

Without having to be told what Altmann expected, Dolf crawled into the opening, Sig P226 in one hand and his flashlight in the other. Without waiting for the foot soldiers, Altmann followed him inside.

Resembling an extremely narrow mineshaft, the crawl space was braced by rotting four-by-fours and planking that leaked dust between the cracks each time the men bumped against them. Ignoring the damage the crawl was doing to his expensive shoes and clothes, Altmann let his anticipation pull him deeper underground.

Twenty feet in, a minor cave-in had blocked the passage. Not completely, but enough that it forced them to a stop. Dolf worked to clear enough of the rock to allow him to wriggle through the tight opening.

"Sir, let me have my men clear this. It'll only take a few minutes."

Altmann shook his head. "I'm not waiting for anything. Keep moving."

Ten feet beyond the collapsed section, illuminated by the narrow flashlight beam, the cramped tunnel opened into a much larger space. Seconds later, relieved to be standing, Altmann watched as Dolf's flashlight beam swept the room. At first, Altmann thought it was a small natural cave, but as more of his men entered the room, adding their flashlights to the illumination, it became clear that the crude shape was the result of hasty construction.

That, at least, made sense. In those final days leading up to Klaus Barbie's arrest and extradition to France, the Nazi mastermind had acted in desperation to hide Hitler's greatest artifact, one that Pizarro had captured as he conquered the Incan empire. It was ironic. Hitler's search for items of mystic power had yielded one that had been the real thing, but he had never recognized its true purpose. But in those last days, Klaus Barbie had figured it out. Throughout the years when he worked for the American intelligence services, immediately following the fall of Nazi Germany, he had carefully guarded his secret. And when the Americans had relocated Klaus to Bolivia to keep him out of French hands, he had brought the artifact with him, returning it to the land of its origin.

Now Klaus Barbie's heir was on the verge of claiming it for himself. Somewhere in this secret storage vault, it lay amid these stacks of boxes. Altmann could feel its presence. Standing to one side, he gave the order that put his men into action.

"Empty them all. Nothing goes untouched."

"And if we don't find it?" Dolf asked.

Altmann gritted his teeth. "Then we'll touch everything again, and then again, until we find it. I will not leave this place without it."

Dolf's eyes showed that he understood what Altmann had left unsaid. *And neither will anyone else.*

CHAPTER 4

Levi Elias walked into the NSA director's office knowing that Admiral Jonathan Riles wouldn't be happy with the information he was about to deliver.

The admiral looked up, his ice-gray eyes locking with Levi's. "Yes?"

"Sir, Dr. Jennings has informed me that Big John has a hit on a high-priority target in Bolivia."

"Tupac Inti?"

"Yes, sir."

Levi felt his boss's gaze intensify at this confirmation.

"I thought he was in Palmasola prison."

Levi nodded. "He still is."

"So what's the problem?"

"A new inmate."

The lift of Admiral Riles's left eyebrow indicated his loss of patience. "Your point?"

"Yesterday, the inmate, one Jack Frazier, killed a handful of neo-Nazis in a prison gang fight. Big John has placed a 0.984 correlation of this incident to Jack Gregory."

"The Ripper's in Palmasola?"

"Denise Jennings believes it."

"Do you?"

For a moment, Levi considered his answer. "I do."

The admiral paused, lost in thought. When he broke his half-minute silence, his eyes stabbed Levi. "Get Janet Price."

Levi hesitated. Since they'd enticed her away from the CIA, Janet Price had been the NSA's most valuable asset. Now, for the second time, Admiral Riles was about to launch her into action associated with the ex-CIA assassin known as The Ripper.

"She's in Mozambique."

"I don't care. For some reason, The Ripper's going for Inti. Christ, I don't know why we pay billions for a system like Big John when we could just plant a GPS tracker on Jack Gregory. That man has a missile lock on trouble."

"Anything else?"

"I want Janet on a flight out tonight."

"It's 2:00 A.M. in Mozambique."

Once again Levi felt the weight of his boss's gaze. "If she's asleep, wake her up and get her ass in the air. How long will it take to get a jet there from Pretoria?"

"I can have one at Maputo International Airport within three hours."

"Get Janet airborne thirty minutes after it lands. I want her in Bolivia, but by way of Athens."

"The Golden Dawn?" Levi knew the answer to his question, even as he asked it. The Golden Dawn was Greece's third-largest political party, one with very strong neo-Nazi ties. Those ties extended beyond borders to other such organizations, even Bolivia's UJC.

"Have her new identity waiting when she arrives. Turn the screws on our man inside the organization. Her background has to stand up to UJC scrutiny."

"It'll put him at risk."

"It can't be helped." The admiral paused. "And Levi . . ."

"Yes, sir?"

"I know Janet had a thing with Gregory. Make sure she understands exactly what's at stake here."

"She's a professional. I'll brief her in Athens."

But as Levi walked out of the NSA director's office, he knew Admiral Riles had a very good reason to worry. As much as Levi wanted to deny it, Jack "The Ripper" Gregory scared the hell out of him.

CHAPTER 5

Although outsiders believed that most Bolivian immigrants of German descent had Nazi connections, they were wrong. In the late 1930s, tens of thousands of Jews fled Germany to Chile and from there to Bolivia via a train dubbed the Jewish Express. Stefan Rosenstein's grandparents had been among them.

If not for his decision to hire The Ripper, Stefan would now be a broken and lonely man, a Bolivian senator robbed of his most prized possessions, the lives of his wife and twin daughters. The Ripper had not come cheap, but it was the best money Stefan had ever spent. Now, just over a year and a half later, Stefan had called on The Ripper's services once again.

Ironically, this move had been triggered by the very government Stefan had helped usher into office. It amazed him how paranoia could paralyze those in power, or worse, drive them to act in diametrically opposed fashion to the ideals that had put them there. In this case it was the Bolivian president's fear of one man, Tupac Inti.

Instead of supporting the charismatic shaman, President Cayo Suarez had ignored the neo-Nazi frame-up that resulted in Tupac Inti's arrest and had worked the judicial system to keep Tupac in jail, perpetually awaiting trial on trumped-up sedition charges. But what had triggered Stefan to hire The Ripper for one last job was his discovery of a planned neo-Nazi attempt to kidnap Tupac Inti from Palmasola.

"Stefan. It's after midnight."

Stefan looked up from his laptop to see his wife, Miriam, clad in her blue nightgown, standing in the doorway.

"I just need to send a couple more e-mails."

"I'm sure no one will read them tonight."

Stefan glanced down at his computer and hesitated, glad that she couldn't see that he had a news story open in his browser instead of his e-mail. When he raised his eyes again, Stefan nodded.

"I'll be along in a minute."

Miriam raised an eyebrow as if she was about to say something and then turned toward their bedroom, her bare feet producing soft swishing sounds on the hallway's tile floor.

As he reached over to put the laptop to sleep, Stefan's eyes were once again drawn to the headline from Santa Cruz.

"Palmasola Prison Fight Leaves Three Dead, One Horribly Blinded"

Switching it off, Stefan rose from his chair and followed in his wife's footsteps. Although he knew his mind was too busy for sleep, he could at least lie there and keep her company. Maybe her gentle breathing could lull the worries from his mind.

Undressing, he climbed into bed. As Stefan spooned up against Miriam's warm body and put his arm around her, the images of the dead men in that prison yard replayed in his head. But it was the image of the eyeless survivor that lingered. Although he knew that he should have been prepared for this, he wasn't. As he'd done once before, Stefan had knowingly unleashed The Ripper.

CHAPTER 6

Janet Price stepped off the bottom step of the NSA corporate jet onto the tarmac at Athens International Airport and paused to raise her hands above her head, stretching her lean, five-foot-ten-inch body in the cool February afternoon sunlight. Clad in form-fitting black jeans, blouse, and boots, she unpinned her newly blond hair. It cascaded onto her shoulders in a way that framed a face that somehow managed to draw men's eyes away from her dancer's body.

Nodding to the man who handed her the duffle bag, she smiled, the easy self-confidence with which she carried herself masking the danger behind those laughing eyes. As she walked toward the terminal, she breathed in the Greek air. Her last memory of Greece had been in Heraklion, Crete. She'd watched Jack Gregory turn and walk away along the beautiful inner harbor, the tail of his white cotton shirt flapping over his loose-fitting cotton pants, the wind ruffling his brown hair.

She remembered Jack's words after she'd tried to recruit him to the NSA.

"Believe me. Long term, you don't want me anywhere around you."

But Jack had been wrong about that. And now she might be forced to kill him, assuming that killing Jack "The Ripper" Gregory was even possible. Hopefully she wouldn't have to find out.

By the time she'd cleared customs and made her way via cab to the Hotel Amalia, Janet was ready to settle into her room, take a long bath, and catch a few hours of sleep. The hotel's modern atmosphere stood in stark contrast to the ancient Greek architecture that surrounded it. That Levi Elias had booked her a room this close to the Greek parliament building was surprising. Then again, sometimes the best-known locations were the least conspicuous.

But as she tossed her duffel on the green bedspread atop the king-size bed, her cell phone rang. Picking it up, she noted the caller ID. Levi Elias. Hearing the slight hiss associated with the encrypted call, Janet answered.

"Yes, Levi?"

"I see you've checked in."

"Yes. I was just about to take a bath and close my eyes for a while."

"Make it a quick shower. You've got a meeting with Ammon Gianakos an hour and fifteen minutes from now. I assume you read the packet."

"That's why I didn't sleep on the plane."

"He'll be waiting at the Acropolis Museum. Walk around, see the sights, and listen. He'll fill you in on everything else you need to know about Golden Dawn's relationship with the UJC and Conrad Altmann. One more thing. We had to play all our cards to keep him in line on this one. He's not happy."

"So long as he gives me what I need, I don't care."

"Just a heads up. Sometimes even someone you own can be pushed too far."

"I'll keep it in mind."

Arriving at the Acropolis Museum ten minutes early, Janet mixed with the tourists as she waited for her contact to arrive. Ammon Gianakos had risen to become the Golden Dawn's top enforcer, a position not usually associated with a NATO country's third-largest political party. But, far from being dead, neo-Nazi organizations across Europe and South America were in the process of reestablishing footholds within the halls of political power. Although the Golden Dawn attempted to maintain plausible deniability in its ties to the Greek neo-Nazi movement, those efforts were thinly veiled at best.

When Gianakos appeared, he made no attempt to hide his arrival. Twin black limousines pulled into the parking lot, disgorging a handful of muscular, dark-suited bodyguards, each sporting sunglasses and the earpieces that made such security details so visibly intimidating. Last to step out of the second car, clad in an elegantly comfortable beige sports jacket, open-collared white shirt, and pre-faded jeans, Gianakos scanned the crowd.

Ignoring the stares of curious tourists, he turned his prematurely graying head toward Janet. Having acquired his target, the man actuated a practiced, easy smile. Echoing the false greeting, Janet watched as Gianakos issued brief instructions to the head of his security detail and then left them to walk toward her.

Janet met him halfway, and like two close business associates, they turned to walk together around the exterior of the modern glass and concrete structure. As they passed out of earshot of nearby tourists, the casual small talk transformed into something else entirely. And though Gianakos's face maintained its pleasant expression, his gray eyes acquired an angry glint.

"I told your superiors that I don't like being threatened."

Janet met that gaze as casually as if he'd just commented on the weather. "I don't make threats."

"You are the threat."

"But you're not my target."

"Meaning what?"

"You do your part and you'll never see me again."

Gianakos stared at her for several seconds, hesitated, and then reached into his brown leather valise, extracting a large manila envelope and handing it to her. Without glancing inside, Janet nodded, smiled, and shook his extended right hand.

Together they turned to walk back toward the parking lot, once again engaged in pleasant conversation. Then, as Gianakos climbed into the second limousine, Janet slid into the backseat of the lead car, accompanied by two of Gianakos's bodyguards. Her car pulled out of the parking lot, turning south onto Mitseon, as the trail car carried Gianakos in the opposite direction.

Janet glanced back to watch the other black vehicle disappear around a corner, before turning her attention to the trip that lay ahead. A brief stopover to collect her bags and then she'd let these Golden Dawn thugs escort her back to the airport.

After all, she had a date in Bolivia. She could study on the plane. Sleep would have to wait awhile longer.

: CHAPTER 7

Tupac Inti had something that was extremely rare here in the crowded prison town of Palmasola—a private cell. Maybe it was because of some sense of guilt that President Suarez felt about imprisoning a prominent member of his own Quechua tribe. Or perhaps it was because someone feared that he might attract a local following that could challenge the existing criminal hierarchy in this prison town. But as Tupac watched the armed Disciplina Interna thug unlock his eight-by-eight cell and usher him out, he suspected that there was another reason behind his isolation.

Despite his leveled pistol, the gangster stayed well back from Tupac as he stepped onto the walkway outside his cell. A glance down into the junction of three alleys revealed more activity than normal for this early in the morning. Beneath an overhang in the alley that led off to the north, one of the many sanctioned drug dealers sold cocaine at a tenth of the street price to customers who had cash. A dozen feet beyond the drug dealers, ignoring the children who kicked a can down the alley, were prostitutes who had bribed their way out of Palmasola's women's section, actively engaged in satisfying the needs of their own customers.

Reaching the stairway, Tupac allowed himself to be ushered down and out among the other inmates who filled the courtyard. Aided by his great height, Tupac scanned the milling crowd, his eyes seeking those within the throng that meant to do him harm. The random crowd movement bothered him as much as being removed from his cell to join them. It meant that Tupac wasn't the only one who had been rousted from his cell, that others were even more confused than he was.

Moving south across the yard, he moved past the junction of two long brick buildings to look down one of the wider streets that passed through the prison town. Wherever he looked, inmates issued into the streets. Obviously this had nothing to do with Tupac. So why did he feel so certain that it did?

"If you want to live, come with me."

The voice at his side surprised Tupac, but not as much as his recognition of the speaker. It was the killer he'd watched dismantle the UJC death squad. Although the man's Spanish accent wasn't native to Bolivia, it could have been Argentine. Clad in stained jeans and a loose-fitting cotton shirt that hid the crazy quilt of scars Tupac had seen on his chest and back, the man had brown eyes that showed no hint of deception.

"Why?"

"We have very little time. Believe me or not. Make a choice."

Without waiting for an answer, the man turned down the street that led south. Making a decision driven by curiosity and instinct, Tupac followed. As he watched the man move through the crowd, Tupac marveled at the ease with which he passed through the inmates without drawing undo attention. Only a small fraction of the four thousand men, women, and children that populated the prison town of Palmasola had seen this killer in action, so it wasn't surprising that he could move about unrecognized.

The same couldn't be said for Tupac. As it did wherever he went, his great size drew stares from all those he passed.

The man he followed turned west on a side street, Tupac's long strides matching his increased pace.

Then a massive explosion rocked the north side of the compound.

For a second, the entire inmate population of Palmasola froze in place. What followed was a mad rush toward the sound of the explosion. A smattering of distant gunfire indicated that the outside guards were attempting to stop a flood through a breach in the north wall.

The momentary distraction almost caused Tupac to lose sight of the man he'd been following. When he located his guide, Tupac saw that he was twenty meters ahead, continuing on his previous path westward. Pushing against the flow, the shaman gradually closed the gap. By the time he caught up, the flood of inmates had become a trickle.

With the sound of distant battle increasing as yells, screams, gunfire, and sirens echoed down the alleys from the north, Tupac's guide stepped into a narrow gap between thick brick walls and signaled for Tupac to join him in the small alcove. The large man hesitated for just a moment as the unreality of this situation struck him. Then, twisting sideways to allow his broad shoulders to enter the tight space, Tupac ducked under the concrete overhang and joined the smaller man.

As the question rose to his lips, a much closer explosion ripped the air, sending a shower of bricks, flying metal, and debris down the alley they'd just left, followed immediately by a thick dust cloud that made breathing almost impossible.

"Stay with me!"

His head ringing from the explosion, Tupac had difficulty making out the smaller man in the swirling dust cloud, but he reached out and placed a hand on the guide's shoulder and allowed himself to be tugged along despite the coughs that wracked his body. Then they were through the damaged outer wall. Five meters in front of them, a white panel van waited. Beside the open side door, a native Bolivian man fired at the nearest guard tower. From the lack of return fire, it was clear that his aim had been good.

Tupac stopped.

The man who had led him out through the collapsed wall climbed into the back of the van and then turned to yell at Tupac.

"Come on. Get in the van!"

Behind Tupac, the sound of approaching yells and gunfire helped him decide. He hadn't wanted to make a prison break, but turning back now would be suicide. Tupac climbed inside, and the van's sliding door slammed closed behind him. The man who had been shooting dived into the passenger seat, and with the squeal of tires, the van accelerated around one corner and then another before slowing to merge with traffic, leaving the sirens and gunfire far behind.

Rubbing his eyes in an attempt to clear some of the dust that clogged them, Tupac leaned back against the wall of the panel van and looked at the dust-coated man across from him, meeting those strange brown eyes that held the same predatory gleam he'd observed the previous day.

A smile split the man's filthy gray face, his teeth appearing unnaturally white as he leaned forward and extended his right hand.

"Hello, Tupac. You can call me Jack."

CHAPTER 8

Jack Gregory extended his dust-coated right hand toward the huge, native man who leaned against the wall on the driver's side of the white panel van.

"Hello, Tupac. You can call me Jack."

There was no hesitation in Tupac Inti's response, and Jack found his hand enfolded in one twice the size of his own, a hand with the strength to snap his bones. But though Tupac's grip was strong, it held no malice. Neither did it show any warmth. The big man's dark-brown eyes stared at him out of a face caked with gray dust, giving them a mystical appearance, reminding Jack of an aborigine coated with clay-pipe mud. Considering the reverence with which most of the Quechua people regarded this shaman, that vision seemed appropriate.

As Tupac opened his mouth to respond, the van cornered hard to the right and then back to the left as it slowed to a stop.

The two men in the front hopped out, and the side door slid open to reveal the interior of a double-wide garage, the other space occupied by a black Ford Explorer.

Without hesitation, Jack stepped out and shook hands with the dark-skinned man who had opened the door, ignoring the Uzi which hung loosely in his left hand. Behind the van, the driver tugged a chain that lowered the garage door with the rattle and groan of metal.

"Nice shooting back there, Pablo."

Jack shifted his attention to the driver, a short white man with curly brown hair flattened on the top by a round yarmulke. "I can't say the same for your driving, Efran."

Efran grinned. "Looking like you do, you're lucky I let you in my van."

Tupac Inti climbed out of the van to tower over them. When he spoke, his deep voice rumbled.

"Maybe someone would like to tell me what is going on."

Jack nodded. "I owe you that, but not here."

Efran gestured toward the front of the garage. "There's a bathroom with a shower stall through that door. I've laid out a change of clothes for each of you. The fit for Tupac probably won't be great."

"You can go first," Jack said. "But don't take long. I want to be out of here in fifteen minutes."

Without a word, Tupac took him up on his offer. Five minutes later, he emerged from the shower wearing loose-fitting pants that were three inches too short, sandals, and a dark cotton pullover shirt that was tight across his chest. For the first time Jack took the time to study the man's face.

Dark-skinned with short-cropped black hair, Tupac had a high forehead; a broad, triangular nose; jutting cheekbones; a square chin and lips that curled up at the edges. It was a powerful face that exuded dignity. In better circumstances, Jack would have liked to know this man.

Pulling himself out of his reverie, Jack took his own turn at the shower, sluicing the dirt in a muddy clockwise swirl down the drain. Then, sliding into boxers, jeans, black Nikes, and a dark undershirt, he stepped back into the garage.

He accepted the small duffel bag that Pablo offered, set it on the floor, and unzipped it. Grabbing the H&K P30S, he slapped in a full 17 round magazine, chambered a 9mm round, and slid the weapon into the holster pocket of his undershirt. Slipping into a brown leather jacket, he pulled the key fob from its right pocket and clicked a button to unlock the Explorer.

Reaching inside the bag one more time, Jack grabbed the disposable cell phone and a second H&K, turning to offer this last item to Tupac.

The big man shook his head. "I quit using guns a long time ago."

"You might want to reacquaint yourself."

"I don't think so."

Tossing the H&K back in the duffel, Jack zipped the bag closed, walked to the Explorer, and set it behind the driver's seat.

"I'm driving."

"Are you going to answer my question?" Tupac asked.

"On the road. Climb in."

For a moment Tupac merely stared at him, his face a mask that showed no hint of what was going on behind those dark eyes. Then he walked around to the passenger side, slid the seat all the way back, and climbed in.

Turning back to the other two, Jack shook hands one last time.

Efran gripped Jack's hand in both of his. "Stefan says to be careful."

Jack felt the habitual grin split his face, even though he failed to feel any humor. "He knows that's not my way."

"Yes, but God gives us hope."

As Pablo raised the garage door, Jack climbed into the black SUV and started the engine. Five minutes later, he turned northeast on Av Santos Dumont, headed toward the Cuarto Anillo city loop and then took Highway 9 toward San Javier, intent upon getting out of the city before police roadblocks could be established. Nothing happened fast in Santa Cruz. The police were currently occupied trying to stop the massive riot along Palmasola's damaged north wall as they looked for one huge target within that mob.

After all, Tupac Inti was the sole reason the Bolivian government had orchestrated that explosion.

As their vehicle left the outskirts of Santa Cruz, headed northeast, Jack felt Tupac's stare as powerfully as the red dot of a laser sight. The voice that followed carried with it an implicit threat.

"My patience has reached its end."

When Jack glanced at the man's dark face, he had no doubt that he spoke the truth. Words were expected, and a judgment was about to be made. In Jack's experience, moments like this called for nothing less than the truth. Maybe not the whole truth, but a significant portion of it.

"My real name is Jack Gregory, although down here some people know me as Jack Frazier. A little over a year ago, I did a job for a senior member of the Bolivian parliament. He was happy enough with my work to rehire me to break you out of Palmasola."

Tupac's silence dragged out for a full minute, and Jack didn't interrupt the big man's contemplation, instead focusing his attention on weaving around the frequent potholes on the two-lane highway while dodging oncoming cars and trucks performing the same dangerous snake-mating ritual.

"So you chose to bomb Palmasola and trigger a riot just to get me out of jail?"

"No. The first explosion, the big one, was a UJC setup. Didn't you wonder why you and all the other inmates were herded out of the cells and into the common areas? During the subsequent chaos, you were supposed to be kidnapped. Because your benefactor learned of the plan, I was sent into Palmasola to make sure that didn't happen."

An oncoming pickup truck with a half-dozen women and children in the open bed swerved around a huge pothole and careened into Jack's lane, forcing him to swerve onto the right shoulder. The SUV's right wheels spun in the loose gravel, and the vehicle fishtailed until Jack managed to guide it back into its lane.

Tupac continued his questioning as if he hadn't even noticed the near collision.

"The second explosion was yours?"

"Yes."

"People may have been killed."

"Yes."

"And the men who waited outside the wall with the van?"

Jack weighed the decision of just how much to tell the Quechua shaman.

"Men I've worked with before."

"On the other job you mentioned?"

"Yes."

"Another job where people died?"

"Yes."

Once again, Jack felt the weight of Tupac's gaze. He couldn't blame the man for judging him harshly. Feeling the familiar adrenaline-fueled fire fill his veins, Jack readied himself. The moment of decision had arrived, and if Tupac made the wrong choice, this ride was about to get a whole lot more interesting.

: CHAPTER 9

Sitting in the second-floor office of his La Paz estate, Conrad Altmann stared across his desk at his lieutenant in disbelief, feeling his blood pressure rise so fast that it threatened to pop a blood vessel in his forehead. At these times he looked like one of the demons illustrated on the ancient Incan temples. In one of the fiery rages that had become more and more common of late, people quailed before him. But not Dolf Gruenberg.

Having delivered the latest bad news, the six-foot-seven albino just stared back at him.

"What the hell do you mean they can't find Inti?" Altmann asked.

"He's not among the dead or the living in Palmasola. After they reestablished control of the prison grounds, police conducted a complete search of the compound. They believe he must have escaped through a hole in the western wall as police battled the mob trying to get through the gap in the north wall."

"A second hole?"

"Several minutes after our car bomb rammed the north wall, there was another explosion along the west wall. Because police and guards had converged on the north wall following the planned attack there, only a single manned guard tower had visibility on the part of the western wall where the second explosion occurred. Unfortunately, both guards were killed before they could call for assistance."

Unable to stay sitting, Conrad Altmann rose to his feet and leaned forward, both palms planted on the massive mahogany desk that dominated the southern end of his office.

"Tell me there were witnesses."

"Three, for what it's worth. One reported seeing the explosion and hearing gunfire after he dived for cover. The other two saw a van driving away at high speed. Neither of them saw a license plate or any of the people inside. One of them said the van was white, and the other said it was gray. Useless."

As much as Altmann wanted to reach under his desk for the concealed gun and put a bullet through his lieutenant's head at this news, he gritted his teeth and restrained himself.

"Checkpoints?"

"The chief of police has ordered them set up throughout Santa Cruz, but because of the extraordinary police presence at Palmasola, it is taking longer than it should to disperse them to other parts of the city. He has ordered all vans to be stopped and searched."

"Why the hell do I pay so much to that stupid bastard? Inti will have switched vehicles. He could be anywhere by now."

Straightening, Altmann turned to stare out the curved floor-to-ceiling window, although he took no notice of the manicured grounds beyond the glass. Without turning back toward Dolf, Altmann took two calming breaths and gave the order.

"Get General Montoya. I want to see him as soon as possible."

"Yes, sir."

The sound of the door closing behind him told Altmann that he was alone. Walking back to his desk, Altmann seated himself, extracted a silver flask from his right drawer, removed the lid, and raised it to his lips. The long pull that followed funneled its glowing warmth into his belly, but rather than soothe his anger, the smooth whiskey fanned it. That was fine with him. Maybe his rage would provide the motivation that the Bolivian chief of intelligence would need to get people off their asses and deliver Tupac Inti, alive. After the years of work it had taken to retrieve the Sun Staff's crown piece, Conrad Altmann wasn't about to allow his father's project to fail for lack of the shaman's unique knowledge.

CHAPTER 10

The mind worm had been called by many names, among them, Anchanchu, the soul bane. Loosely translated, it meant "The Rider." Although humans thought of it as a demonic being from their various religious traditions, the truth was something far stranger. It was an entity beyond the four dimensions that compose space-time, able to observe all possible timelines but, until it had discovered the human race, unable to experience any of them, its existence a frustrating hell from which humanity's arrival on the cosmic stage had offered release.

Anchanchu had learned that as a human straddled the life–death threshold, it could establish a parasitic link to that person's limbic system. It required the host's cooperation, but once accepted, it could stimulate the human's physical responses far more effectively than a doctor's adrenaline injection or electric paddles. If the body was not too badly damaged,

Anchanchu could shove its host back across the life–death boundary.

The mind worm's limbic attachment enabled it to feel human emotion, to experience the world through its host's senses amplifying its host's feelings and bodily responses. But Anchanchu's lack of connection to the higher brain functions meant it was unable to sense its host's thoughts.

Anchanchu knew its hosts better than they knew themselves. It understood what drove them. And with its ability to sense what was coming, it was easy to see the paths along which their amplified passions would carry them. Breaking a new host was different in every case. With some it was as simple as amping up specific desires. Though some struggled to resist its siren call and maintain their sense of self-control, even the most strong-willed generally succumbed within months.

Yet, as difficult as it was for the mind worm to accept, in the months since Jack Gregory's deathbed acceptance, the man continued fighting to reestablish his self-control. It was a new experience, one that Anchanchu found both thrilling and terrifying.

It was time to apply the bloody spurs that would break this stallion to rein, once and for all.

CHAPTER 11

The black Ford Explorer bounced the last part of the thirty-mile dirt road that led to the Frazier Hacienda and rolled to a stop in the midst of the thatched-roof buildings, corrals, and barns that flanked the main ranch house. As Jack opened the car door, he was met by Rafael Morales, the native ranch foreman, and Yachay, the motherly Quechua woman who ran the household, empty though it had been for the vast majority of the time since he'd acquired it. These two had run the ranch long before Jack had inherited it, and he'd seen no sense in changing this arrangement. It had been one of his better decisions.

"It is good to see you, Señor Jack," Rafael said, the weathered skin of his face crinkling at the eyes in what was the closest thing Jack had seen to a smile on the lean man's face.

"It's good to be back."

Jack inhaled deeply through his nose, letting the clean, high-country air fill his lungs, holding it for several seconds before slowly exhaling through his mouth.

The main house was a long one-story building with a high-peaked thatch roof in the style of the native peoples of the area. To the west, a number of smaller thatched huts stretched out toward the corrals. Beyond them the beautiful rolling countryside spread out in all directions as far as the eye could see. Above this magnificent view, a spectacular sunset had just begun to bathe the western sky in fire.

He'd loved this hacienda the first time he'd set foot on it. It was little wonder that this was the same region that Butch Cassidy and the Sundance Kid had fallen in love with after they had fled to Bolivia. The rough hills with their many varieties of trees and grasses and the old soil that wasn't rich enough for farming but was perfect for raising cattle and horses smelled like what Jack thought the old west should have smelled like. It made him feel like just the latest in a line of infamous gunmen to savor this view.

When Tupac Inti stepped out of the car and rose to his full height, Yachay uttered a single syllable that she immediately stifled. Clearly she recognized the man, although, from the lack of recognition in Tupac's face, Jack assumed she must have only seen the shaman from a distance.

Without asking what Jack wanted, Rafael opened the Explorer's rear door, grabbed the duffel, and carried it into the main house through the door Yachay held open.

"Your place?"

The sound of Tupac's deep voice surprised Jack. After all, the man had barely spoken to him after posing his series of questions as they had left Santa Cruz in the SUV's rearview mirrors several hours ago. Jack had taken Tupac's previous silence as a positive sign, and he decided to take this break in that routine as another one.

"A gift from a client."

"Nice gift. I take it you were worth it."

"He thought so."

Tupac turned to survey the hacienda headquarters and the beautiful surrounding countryside.

"And you think it's safe to bring me here?"

"It's as isolated as any spot in Bolivia. You've seen my only two employees, both Quechua people like yourself. And with the fifty-gallon tank on this Explorer, I didn't have to stop for gas, so nobody saw you en route."

"President Suarez is Quechuan, but he's no friend of mine."

"I'm a pretty good judge of people. I trust Rafael and Yachay with my life. I see no reason not to trust them with yours. Besides, you won't be staying long."

"How is that?"

"As we stand here talking, someone is making arrangements for me to deliver you to a Quechua group who can help you disappear, assuming that's what you want. Other than a good meal, a hot shower, satellite Internet access, and a clean bed, it's the best I can do."

Jack felt Tupac's deep brown eyes search his face.

"How do you know I won't betray you?" Tupac asked.

"Like I said, I've got this thing. A really good sense of people is part of it."

"And the other part?"

Jack grinned. "Not something I want to get into."

Once again he felt the big man's eyes studying him.

"I can see what's inside you, to the bane that fills your mind."

Tupac's words left Jack momentarily speechless.

There was no way that this shaman could sense what Jack could barely bring himself to believe. But that's what a shaman did, wasn't it? Make a vague statement that hinted at deeper knowledge and then pause to let his subject's imagination fill in the missing details. At least Jack hoped it was.

"That might not be such a good thing."

Tupac shrugged and changed the subject.

"You mentioned something about dinner and a hot shower?"

"And a clean bed."

"Done."

As Jack turned to lead Tupac Inti through the door and into his ranch house, he couldn't shake the feeling that things were about to get a whole lot stranger.

CHAPTER 12

It was dark as the jet started its final descent to El Alto International Airport. Janet loved flying into cities at night, especially the mountainous locales of the world, where the city lights aligned themselves with the wonderful terrain features as opposed to the boring north–south, east–west grids laid out by a city planner. At night, the sky view of La Paz reminded her of looking at the night sky in the high desert of the American southwest. Simply extraordinary.

Her thoughts shifted to Jack Gregory. He was, without a doubt, the most dangerous and exciting man with whom she'd ever worked. For a few weeks, they'd been lovers. Not in the "I love you" sense. It had been a time of extreme and shared danger, followed by a few weeks of "Goddamn . . . we made it" sex.

But Jack had issues that she couldn't even begin to comprehend, an inner force that was simultaneously quasi-mystical and quite possibly psychotic. Of course, having killed her own father on her thirteenth birthday, who was she to make judgments about normalcy?

The bounce of the rough landing, followed by the squeal of tires and brakes, brought her thoughts back to the present. Having memorized and shredded all her background material that transformed her from Janet Price, she stepped off the aircraft into the chilly night as Janet Mueller, daughter of Friedrich Mueller and Karen Abercrombie, his American wife. With dual American and German citizenship, she had spent her high school and college years in Dortmund, Germany. Her path had led her to Greece, where she had become the Golden Dawn's most lethal assassin.

The big albino man who met her at the bottom of the steps offered her a hand three times the size of Janet's.

"Fraulein Mueller. I'm Dolf Gruenberg." He grinned, his white teeth shining in the bright lights that illuminated the aircraft steps.

Janet extended her hand but gripped down onto Dolf's fingers, preventing him from wrapping his huge hand around her smaller one, robbing him of the intimidation that handshake was intended to deliver.

"Herr Altmann?" she asked, taking pleasure at the angry glint in the albino's eyes.

"He sends his apologies that he could not be here to meet you in person. I will take you to his estate. Your bags?"

"I just have the one." Janet handed him her large duffel bag. "Will we need to transit customs?"

"No. Herr Altmann has made the necessary arrangements."

Dolf directed her to the waiting sedan, holding open the door as she slid into the leather backseat. Closing the door, he climbed into the passenger seat, sliding it all the way back, sending yet another, not so subtle message.

As the car started forward, Janet scanned the other two occupants as the big man returned the favor. The albino dwarfed the driver, his pink eyes pale lanterns in the interior vehicle lights, the ghostly effect amplified by the shoulder-length platinum hair that framed his face. There was no doubt about it; this car carried a very dangerous person.

As the car pulled out into traffic, Janet smiled and closed her eyes.

CHAPTER 13

Helmeted, clad in shining armor, I stand before my Spaniards as they force the once-mighty emperor to kneel at my feet. I reach out and take the elaborately engraved silver staff topped with a golden sun from his reluctant fingers. As he releases it into my grasp, something moves within me, as if this staff conducts a wondrous power. I almost fall to my knees, but manage to hide the moment's weakness from my soldiers.

With a wave of my gauntleted left hand, I give the signal. In one smooth motion, the executioner steps up behind the Incan emperor, wraps the garrote around his dark neck, and pulls it tight. Only dimly aware of the man's dying kicks, I gaze in rapture at this wondrous prize, knowing I should present it to my king, knowing that I cannot bear to part with it. And that knowledge fills me with dread.

~ ~ ~

Jack opened his eyes to a room cloaked in darkness, his heart hammering the walls of his chest. Remaining perfectly still, Jack inhaled deeply, holding the calming breath for a handful of seconds before breathing it out. Applying the skill he'd acquired through years of practice, Jack let himself relax, drifting deeper and deeper into peaceful meditation.

An hour and a half later, after a hard workout and a shower, Jack sat outside on the front porch, sipping a steaming mug of coffee as he watched the sun spread its peach-colored glow across the eastern sky. The creak of the screen door swinging open alerted him to Tupac's presence.

The sight of the big man wrapped in a white terry-cloth bathrobe that extended only to his thighs struck Jack so comically that he laughed out loud.

Tupac shrugged. "Yachay insisted on washing my clothes, even though I told her I'd only worn them yesterday."

"Sorry. We didn't outfit this place for visitors your size."

"You're up early," Tupac said.

As Tupac seated himself across from Jack, the robe opened at his chest to reveal a tattoo that caught Jack's eye. It was a man in a ceremonial robe and headdress. In his right hand, he held a staff with a golden crown piece.

"Interesting tattoo. What does it mean?"

"My father had it and his before him. For centuries, the eldest son in Manco Capac's direct line of descent has borne this sign. It marks the lore keeper."

"Manco Capac?"

"The first Incan Emperor."

"That's quite an honor."

"It's a pain in the ass."

Once again Jack laughed. He was starting to like this man.

"Can I get you a cup of coffee?"

"Gave it up after I left the army."

"You were in the Bolivian army?"

"Graduated from West Point as a foreign exchange student, then came home and did ten years of service."

The statement surprised Jack. The mental profile he was building of the shaman had just taken a hard right turn.

"Why'd you get out?"

"Got sick of the corruption. Decided to try to make a real difference."

"As lore keeper?"

"Or shaman. Whatever you want to call it. When that didn't pay the bills, I went to work in the mines."

"And Palmasola prison?"

"In case you missed it, I tend to speak my mind. Apparently someone didn't like it."

Tupac fixed Jack with a penetrating stare. "Your turn."

Jack nodded.

"I'm just a fixer for hire."

"A fixer?"

"People have problems. For a price, I make them go away."

"Sounds like a mercenary."

"If you like."

"Or a hit man."

Jack understood how someone could get that impression. But that didn't mean he had to like it.

"I don't kill for money."

"But you do kill people."

"Only if they get in my way."

"Like the people who scarred you."

"Yes."

Suddenly Tupac leaned forward and pointed a big finger right at Jack's forehead, an intense gleam in his dark eyes.

"How about what scarred you in there?"

Jack felt sudden anger boil up inside but tamped it back down. It was probably just something Tupac had pulled from the standard shaman's bag of tricks, but the man was hitting a little too close to home for comfort. Rising to his feet, Jack moved to the door, opened it, and then paused to look back at Tupac.

"That's on my to-do list."

CHAPTER 14

Conrad Altmann sat sipping coffee on his patio, gazing out over the infinity-edged pool at the lovely view of Mount Illimani on the southeastern horizon. As usual, this high in the mountains, the mornings were brisk, even in summer. Wearing tan slacks, a white button-down shirt, and gray sweater, Altmann felt comfortable in this place where he had lived his life.

His mother had come from old money, and for purely political reasons she had kept her years-long affair with Klaus Barbie secret. Nevertheless, she had been an ardent believer in the old Nazi's vision, so it was no wonder that Altmann had grown up sharing that view. Unable to accept Klaus Barbie's extradition, imprisonment, and death in France, Lisa Altmann had faded quickly. After her death, the entire estate had passed to Conrad Altmann.

For decades he had used his substantial resources to bring him to the point where he was today, so close to realizing Klaus

Barbie's vision that Altmann could almost reach out and touch it. He only lacked one thing—actually only a part of one thing. Unfortunately, the one person who could help him find it had been snatched from his grasp.

Movement to his left pulled Altmann from his reverie as his newest houseguest stepped out through the sliding glass doors onto the patio. Her blond hair fastened into a bun with a six-inch hair needle, she was clad in leather boots, tight black jeans, and a soft black leather jacket over a purple blouse. The woman approached with an easy grace and confidence.

Rising to his feet, Altmann leaned forward to gently kiss the back of her extended hand, noting the twinkle in her blue eyes as he straightened. Stunning. If Janet Mueller was putting on a performance, then she was a professional. Of course that was exactly what Ammon Gianakos had called her.

"Fraulein Mueller, it's a pleasure."

"Please call me Janet," she said with a laugh.

He gestured toward a chair adjacent to his. As Janet seated herself, a waiter offered her a cappuccino, which she accepted with a slight nod.

Sitting back down, Altmann watched as Janet sipped the froth from her cup and then turned her steady gaze upon him. Despite sitting in the presence of the godfather of Bolivia's neo-Nazi movement, the woman appeared completely calm. Indeed, she studied him as if she were the teacher and he the student.

"Ammon has told me a lot about you," Altmann said. "What he hasn't told me is why you're here."

"He sent me to kill Tupac Inti."

Feeling his temper rise, Altmann unconsciously yielded to an old habit, stroking his neatly trimmed graying beard with his left hand.

"Why would he care about Tupac Inti?"

"For the same reason that President Suarez has kept Inti locked up in Palmasola. Ammon Gianakos believes he is the one man that could potentially unite the indigenous peoples, not just of Bolivia, but of this entire region. If that were to happen, governments would fall, to be replaced with a communist alliance that would set back our movement for decades to come. Ammon's been very surprised that you haven't had Inti killed before now."

"He should have asked my permission before launching an operation like that on my turf."

"Maybe he didn't think you'd allow it."

"Damn right I wouldn't!" Altmann studied her face intently. "So why tell me now?"

"When I take an assignment, I do it my way."

"And if I say no?"

"Then we both know we've got a problem."

Once again Altmann was struck by this woman's utter self-confidence in the midst of a dangerous situation. Janet Mueller sat across from him, right leg crossed over left, sipping cappuccino, knowing full well that he'd killed people for far less. It was time to shake her tree.

Altmann reached into the leather valise that leaned against the leg of his chair, extracted a folder, and tossed it on the table, sending documents and a number of bloody crime-scene photos sliding into view.

"You know I've been a long-time supporter of the work the Golden Dawn is doing to advance the Nazi agenda in Greece, particularly that of Ammon Gianakos. So when he vouches for someone's skills, I take him seriously. He sent me that file as your introduction. But the funny thing is that every killing he attributes to you via that folder is officially listed as unsolved. I checked. Your problem is that I've never heard of an assassin named Janet Mueller."

"And you would have expected someone like . . .?"

"Carlos the Jackal or Jason Derek Brown—someone who can prove they've done what they claim."

Janet smiled. "The people you've heard of are either rotting in prison, hiding from the authorities, or dead. Didn't some of your *assassins* get themselves killed the other day in Palmasola?"

She leaned forward. "According to my sources, the man who killed your UJC thugs was the same one who helped Tupac Inti escape Palmasola before I could get here to make the hit. Guess what? The authorities don't know that guy's real identity either. I checked. So don't preach to me about the merits of getting caught."

The smile on Janet's lips had subtly shifted to match the mocking glint in her eyes. He'd thrown down the gauntlet, and she'd picked it up and slapped his face with it. And as furious as that made him, all doubt had been purged from Altmann's mind. Janet Mueller was even more dangerous than Ammon Gianakos had said.

A new idea took root in his head. Maybe if he handled this situation with appropriate care, Altmann could entice this woman away from the Golden Dawn.

If Dolf didn't kill her first.

CHAPTER 15

It was moving day. Late last night, Jack had received an encrypted e-mail message instructing him to take Tupac to a river boat where Highway 9 met Rio Mamore. The scheduled rendezvous time was just after sundown today, and despite being only a few hundred kilometers straight-line distance from Jack's hacienda, it would be an all-day trip.

Jack and Tupac had been on the road since long before sunrise. As the Ford Explorer made its way north of Trinidad on Highway 9, the nearness of the snaking Rio Mamore and the Amazon rain forest into which it fed became ever more apparent. The day was hot and muggy, so naturally the air conditioner was the first thing to break. Rolling down the windows helped, but not much.

Jack glanced over at the shaman and saw him staring back, leaving the impression that Tupac had been studying his face for some time.

"Something bothering you?" Jack asked.

"Maybe."

Once again Jack found himself mulling the comments Tupac had made back at the Hacienda. *Might as well get this cleared up right now.*

"You said you could see what's inside me. What was that about?"

Tupac shook his head. "It's your head. You tell me."

"I'd expect that from a two-bit carnival mentalist."

A low laugh rumbled from Tupac's throat.

"You can try to laugh it away, but you've got a problem and you know it. You just don't want to admit that I know it too."

Jack gritted his teeth. "Then how about telling me something useful?"

Tupac paused. Although his eyes remained locked on Jack's face, they acquired a distant stare, as if Jack had faded into thin smoke that the shaman's dark eyes easily penetrated. When Tupac spoke, the rumble in his voice sent a shiver along Jack's spine.

"You're not the first to have your problem, but you might be the last."

Attempting to shrug off the sudden sense of foreboding that Tupac's cryptic statement had imparted, Jack turned his attention back to the road. *Screw it. This conversation is going nowhere.*

When the right rear tire blew, Jack was hardly surprised. It was turning into that kind of day. Pulling onto the shoulder of the narrow highway, Jack killed the engine, opened his door, and stepped out into the sweltering afternoon sun. This close to the mighty Amazon rain forest, there was no escaping the heat.

"You need my help?" Tupac offered.

"No. We can't risk passing motorists recognizing you."

Luckily, the traffic on this section of highway was light. Ending on the eastern river bank of Rio Mamore, Highway 9 was truly a road to nowhere.

As Jack replaced the tire with the spare, a green pickup truck approached from the north, slowed, and pulled over. Ignoring Jack's attempt to wave them on, two young men that looked like foreign college students stepped out. *Probably a couple of save-the-rain-forest, eco-reengineering majors,* he thought.

"Can we lend a hand?" the taller of the two asked as he walked toward Jack, his Spanish intonation confirming Jack's guess.

Jack let go of the tire iron and straightened.

"No need. Two more lug nuts and I'll be done."

The man's blond friend glanced into the SUV. "Your companion didn't get out? Is he ill?"

Jack shook his head and grinned. "Juan has a bad back, which means I get to bust mine."

The other two laughed knowingly.

"Listen, I better get this finished and hit the road. Thanks for stopping, though."

"No problem."

As they walked back to their truck, both men glanced at Tupac, seated in the Explorer's passenger seat, then climbed into their vehicle and drove off. Jack watched the truck disappear around a bend in the road, feeling a seed of worry sprout in his gut.

Finishing up, he climbed behind the wheel and pulled back onto the worn two-lane highway, wishing there was an alternate route he could take to their destination. But this was Bolivia. Luckily, anybody that might pursue them would have to make the same, slow-ass trip. By the time anybody could get to where they were going, Tupac would be on a river boat into the Amazon, and Jack would be long gone, preparing to inform another satisfied client into which Cayman Island account to transfer his payment.

He glanced at Tupac, noting the grim look that had settled on the shaman's face. Despite what Jack had just finished telling himself, Tupac's look matched Jack's mood.

CHAPTER 16

Janet heard the two helicopters come in low and fast, the whup-whup of their rotors echoing throughout the Altmann compound as they settled onto the broad landing pad. Dolf Gruenberg's yells carried a note of excitement that lent speed to Janet's movements.

Sliding the Glock 19 into the elastic holster-pocket of her utility vest, she saw a grinning Conrad Altmann standing at the floor-to-ceiling living-room windows. He watched as a dozen men gathered around tables in the courtyard, arming themselves with machine guns and ammunition that had been spread out like a breakfast buffet.

"Tupac Inti?" Her question turned Altmann's head toward her.

"He's been spotted in a black Ford Explorer near San Ramon."

"I'm going too."

Altmann's expression darkened. "This is a capture mission. I need Inti alive."

Janet smiled. "That's fine. I'll kill him after you're done with him."

Seeing the smile return to Altmann's face, Janet walked back to her room, grabbed a three-foot-long hard-plastic case from her duffel, and laid it on the bed. Clicking open three clip fasteners, she opened the lid to reveal four separate pieces of the sniper rifle resting in separate foam compartments.

Her hands moved with loving familiarity, snapping and locking the components together, the last being the day-night scope. Slapping a 20 round box magazine in place, she tucked three more into utility vest pockets and then walked out of the room.

As she crossed the courtyard, Dolf moved to intercept her.

"You're not coming."

Janet nodded at the house. "Talk to your boss."

She watched as the albino looked toward the glass window through which Conrad Altmann observed their preparations. Seeing the muscles in his jaws clench gave Janet her first real moment of pleasure in what promised to be a very long day.

"Which chopper do you want me on?"

Dolf turned his icy gaze on her. "You're with me in that one. Two things."

"Yeah?"

"Don't do anything unless I tell you to, and stay the hell out of my way."

"Anything else?"

"Screw up and I'll put you down."

Janet smiled. "I'll keep that in mind."

Turning away, Dolf put two fingers to his lips, blasting out an ear-splitting whistle. As all heads turned toward him, he circled his right hand above his head and yelled.

"Mount up!"

Janet climbed into the rear of the lead helicopter, sliding onto the web seat that faced out the pilot's side. Dolf and another neo-Nazi slid in beside her as three others climbed in on the opposite side.

As the blades spun up and the two choppers simultaneously lifted from the helipad, Janet watched as Conrad Altmann stepped out onto his pool deck. The walled compound diminished in the distance as the aircraft banked away from the snowcapped Mount Illimani, heading toward a distant rendezvous with Tupac Inti.

Janet was sure of one thing. If Jack Gregory still accompanied the shaman, Dolf Gruenberg was in for a lot more excitement than he was counting on.

CHAPTER 17

Jack spotted the inbound helicopters as the SUV crested a small rise, two rapidly growing specks in the distance.

"We've got trouble. Helicopters."

"Where?"

"Coming in behind us from the southwest. Hang on."

Slowing, Jack shifted the vehicle into four-wheel drive and turned off the road, heading toward the tree line a hundred meters to the west, moving as fast as the rough terrain would allow without breaking an axle. Reaching a place where a finger of the rain forest reached out toward them, Jack picked a spot with the least amount of impeding vegetation and plowed forward. Twenty meters in, the trees closed in too tight for the SUV to continue.

Turning off the engine, Jack opened the door and climbed out, grabbing his kitbag from the back seat and throwing it over his shoulder. Tupac rounded the vehicle and stepped up beside him, his inscrutable face showing no sign of fear.

Jack plunged into the thick brush, and Tupac followed without having to be told to do so. They needed to get away from the vehicle, and they needed to do it quickly, but not in the same direction they'd driven into these woods. Jack turned south. Fifty meters in, he found what he'd been looking for, a place where a fallen tree provided thick concealment over a shallow stream bed.

Hearing the choppers for the first time, Jack pointed into the dark space. "Crawl in there and stay down."

Again Tupac followed Jack's directions without objection, wasting no time on argument. That was good, because time was a luxury Jack was quickly running out of. In the distance he could hear the helicopters come in low. They passed directly over the spot where the SUV had been forced to stop and then separated. One went southwest and the other northwest, heading toward the clearings on either side of the woods, intent on cutting off Tupac's escape route and surrounding them.

Jack ran south, racing toward the southern clearing as fast as possible through the dense foliage, his H&K P30S having filled his right hand automatically. Adrenaline flooded his blood stream, giving Jack a rush that heightened his senses to an animal level. Though he couldn't yet see his enemies, he could smell the danger they presented, and that sensation pulled him toward them.

Ahead he heard the helicopter drop close to the ground and hover, to let the men inside off. Jack dropped his kitbag. It was exactly what he wanted to happen.

Between tree branches and palm fronds, twenty-five meters away, Jack caught his first glimpse of it, a Chinese H425 capable of carrying a dozen armed men. This one carried six, all of whom leaped out as the three wheels touched the ground. Jack slid through the bushes on his stomach, looked over the gun sight, and squeezed the trigger three times.

A red mist sprayed the air as two of the men fell to the ground and the third staggered back against the chopper. On the opposite side of the helicopter, the other three men dived into the tall grass as Jack put his fourth bullet through the right lens of the staggering man's sunglasses. The dead man tumbled to the ground. On the far side of the chopper, wild machine-gun fire from the man's prone companions raked the woodline, making it clear that they had no idea where his shots had originated from. The whine of helicopter engines going full throttle accompanied the aircraft into a wheeling climb. Jack sent three shots into the helicopter's belly before turning his attention back to the spot where three men fired in panic from within the deep grass.

Holding his own fire, Jack listened as several new bursts of machine-gun fire echoed through the late afternoon. When the firing stopped, Jack let silence hang in the air as he counted down from thirty. In combat, silence was its own special kind of loud, rising in volume until many found it unbearable.

Seeing a movement in the grass, Jack squeezed off two more shots, heard a gurgling scream, and watched as the two remaining Nazis sprayed lead into the forest until their magazines were empty. In the field, two thin wisps of smoke marked their positions.

The four shots Jack placed into the grass just below that smoke were followed by silence. Without waiting to confirm the effectiveness of his gunfire, Jack melted back into the woods, slapped a fresh magazine into the H&K, grabbed his kitbag, and turned west.

The others would have heard the gunfire, and they would be coming in from the northwest. But they would proceed through the dense forest slowly and carefully, trying to keep their companions in sight as they moved. If they were good, they would maintain a ragged wedge formation that provided interlocking fires on three sides. But these guys weren't military, and Jack doubted they were that good. Inhaling the musty forest smell, Jack felt a fresh surge of adrenaline amp up his senses.

They were in his world now, and nothing here would save them.

CHAPTER 18

Heading directly toward the spot where the black SUV had disappeared into the forest, the helicopters descended to buzz the treetops. Janet caught a brief glimpse of the Ford at the same time that Dolf saw it. Doors open, it had been hurriedly abandoned. Turning her head, she saw the albino speak into the microphone of his radio headset, his instructions sending the accompanying helicopter banking toward the clearing to the southwest while their helicopter turned northwest toward a more distant landing spot.

Janet replayed the last image in her mind. Three of the SUV's doors had been left open, two on the driver's side and one on the passenger's side. Someone was still escorting Inti, possibly two people, although she doubted it. More likely Jack Gregory had been driving and had opened the back door to retrieve something after getting out. Knowing Jack as intimately as she did, that wasn't a good sign for his attackers. As they descended toward the landing zone, Janet raised her rifle, scanning the edges of the clearing through the powerful scope.

Dolf's plan was to surround Tupac and whoever was helping him, herding them back through the forest until they were trapped against open space or pinned between the twin neo-Nazi pincers. But Jack was a hunter, not the hunted. He wouldn't hesitate, and he couldn't be herded.

As the helicopter's wheels touched the grass, Janet released the buckle that belted her to the web seat and leaped to the ground. Without hesitation, she raced across the open space and ducked into the forest's edge, assuming a prone firing position. An angry Dolf Gruenberg crashed into the woods beside her.

"What the hell are you doing?" he asked.

"The same thing your people should have done. Clearing the danger area."

The sound of distant gunfire cut off his response, sending the other four neo-Nazi foot soldiers running toward the concealment offered by the dense bush. Machine guns from the southern clearing began firing, the sound painting a clear picture for Janet. These weren't the short, three- to five-round controlled bursts that would indicate the situation was going well. The guns were blazing away as if the gunners were being charged by an enemy rifle brigade.

Janet rose to a knee, half-turned to face Dolf.

"If you want to take Inti, we need to move now, before the other action wraps up."

"You hear that? The other half of my team has them pinned down."

"Does it sound like that to you? Because it sounds like panic to me."

To his credit, Dolf showed no hint of his earlier anger, listening carefully to the distant sounds of battle as he weighed her words. The machine-gun fire ceased, followed by four quick shots. When Dolf turned his gaze back on Janet, he nodded.

"Okay. Your plan. You lead."

"Fine."

Janet ducked under a branch and began moving rapidly through the undergrowth, angling back toward where she'd seen the black Ford. Behind her she could hear Dolf and his men working hard to keep up. The silence that draped this finger of rain forest was now broken only by the stamp of booted feet, the breaking of branches, and the hard breathing of men who sensed danger all around them.

Dolf spoke into his radio. "Rudy. What's your status?"

As they continued moving, Janet heard the hiss from the radio as Dolf turned up the volume. He repeated the question. "Rudy, do you hear me?"

Nothing.

Catching a glimpse of metal ahead, Janet dropped to a knee and raised her rifle to look through the scope. The jungle environment significantly limited the effectiveness of the sniper rifle, but the scope still had its uses, giving her confirmation that she had seen the Ford's front grille and hood. Janet scanned the surrounding area as best she could and then resumed her forward progress, walking up to peer into the car. Except for some empty snack-food wrappers and water bottles behind the passenger seat, it was empty.

"We've got tracks over here," Dolf said, bending low on the driver's side of the vehicle. "Two sets leading west."

Janet moved past him, following the tracks over the damp ground, Inti's large feet making the task easier than it otherwise would have been. In Janet's head a clock had started ticking, and she didn't like the feeling. As much as Janet liked having a plan, Jack Gregory lived by following his instincts. It wouldn't take him long to figure out that the second helicopter's occupants had acted very differently than their counterparts. Then he would come back for Tupac. Certainly, he would not have allowed the big shaman to follow him on his counterattack.

Janet hoped Jack wouldn't kill her, and she hoped she wouldn't have to kill him. But despite their past history together, it was still only a hope. And if she didn't want to find out, she needed to hurry.

A soft shuffling sound ahead brought Janet to a halt. Behind her, Dolf signaled his men, and they froze in their tracks. There it was again, as if something, or someone, was slipping through mud. Turning her head, she saw Dolf unclip a flash-bang grenade from his utility vest. When Janet pointed and nodded, he pulled the pin and tossed it over the bank into what looked like a stream bed.

Hitting the deck, Janet covered her ears and eyes. Though it kept the blast from incapacitating her, she found herself wobbling when she rose to her feet and rushed forward. On the far bank she saw Tupac Inti lying face up, a trickle of blood running from his left ear. Then Dolf was on top of him, cuffing his hands behind his back.

Two of Dolf's men grabbed Inti's arms and hauled him to his feet. Though the big man staggered, he managed to stand on his own.

Turning to the two men who weren't supporting Inti, Dolf pointed to the west.

"The other one will come back for Inti. When he shows up, kill him. Then meet us back at the chopper."

Nodding, the men moved into covered firing positions along the far stream bank. Dolf moved up face-to-face with Tupac Inti. To Janet, they looked like bookends, one dark-skinned and noble of countenance, the other ghostly pale and devoid of human compassion. The sight made Janet's trigger finger twitch.

Dolf reached out and grabbed Inti's throat.

"Come along, Indian. Someone important wants to meet you."

As Janet watched the albino shove the manacled shaman ahead, she stifled a desire to plunge her icepick hairpin through Dolf's right ear canal, repeating a mantra she'd repeated many times in the past.

Focus on the mission, Janet. Stay focused on the mission.

CHAPTER 19

The distinctive sound of a flash-bang grenade startled Jack. It had come from the east, from where he'd left Tupac. He'd assumed that there would be little difference between the two groups of neo-Nazis, that both lacked the kind of serious special forces training that would give him problems. Apparently, he'd been wrong about that. The leader of the second group had understood the meaning contained within the sounds from his encounter with the first group and had taken decisive action to move on Tupac.

Changing direction, Jack headed north toward the place where he thought the second helicopter had landed. The neo-Nazis would have to take Tupac there.

It turned out to be closer than he thought. With the sun a huge orange ball on the western horizon, Jack spotted the clearing. Setting his bag on the ground, Jack unzipped it, grabbed a grenade with his left hand, and then crawled forward to get a view of the entire clearing. The Chinese helicopter sat in the open, a mere thirty-five meters northeast of the spot where Jack lay prone in the bushes.

The pilot had remained in the chopper, ready to start it up as soon as his passengers entered the clearing. Jack rose to his feet, stepped out into the open, and began calmly walking toward the helicopter, the sinking sun casting a long and slender shadow that matched him stride for stride. Seeing the pilot shade his eyes, Jack waved, a movement that the pilot echoed. Then he reached up and began flipping switches. With a loud whine, the rotors began to spin up until Jack could feel their wash buffet him.

Keeping his gun hand at his side, Jack watched the pilot's face carefully as he approached. Five meters out, the man's expression changed and his hand darted down, almost reaching his gun, when two bullets smashed through the windscreen, one striking him in the forehead and the second, center of mass.

Jack pulled the pin, tossed the grenade inside the aircraft, and retreated to the tree line. The explosion ignited the fuel and launched the burning aircraft ten feet into the air. The spinning blades struck the ground first and broke free of their moorings, sending shards spinning away into the rain forest, backlit by the fiery glow.

Once again Jack retrieved his kitbag and turned toward the distant Ford SUV, drawn to the danger that awaited him in that direction. It was an old, familiar tug that he didn't try to resist.

With his vision misting red in the fading daylight, Jack disappeared back into the rain forest.

CHAPTER 20

Dolf heard the sound of the helicopter engine winding up, from two hundred meters away. "What the hell?"

The pair of gunshots that followed stopped him in his tracks, but the explosion and its accompanying fireball dropped him on his belly. It was an automatic reaction, one that was copied by all of those with him except for Tupac Inti and Janet Price.

The latter dropped to one knee beside him. "I hope you have a backup plan."

Ignoring her, Dolf climbed back to his feet and motioned to his two men. "Back the way we came. Bring Inti."

Moving as quickly as he could manage, Dolf plowed through the undergrowth they'd just trampled over. As angry as it made him, he had to admit that Janet Mueller had been right about the man who had accompanied Inti. He was some sort of special-operations commando, a highly trained professional who reacted with lightning speed to changing battlefield conditions. It might be different in a city, but if they were going to survive this encounter out here in the woods, Dolf had to match that reaction speed.

Shifting to the alternate radio frequency, he keyed the microphone.

"Escobar, where are you?"

There was a pause of several seconds before he heard the second pilot's voice over the rush of helicopter noise.

"Jesus. What the hell is going on down there? It looks like a war zone."

"Shut up and get back to your landing zone. We're inbound in five minutes."

"Are you crazy? That's where we were ambushed. I barely made it out. The others are all dead."

"Get your ass back there right now. We've got the gunman pinned down, and I've got Inti."

Hearing no immediate reply, Dolf felt the growl crawl from his throat.

"Escobar."

"Yes?"

"If I get there and you're not waiting, you'll wish you had died with the others."

CHAPTER 21

Jack moved in rapid bursts, separated by brief interludes of listening silence. Whoever his opponent was, the man was making fewer mistakes. The group that had taken Tupac had heard the helicopter explosion and had immediately reversed course instead of coming for Jack. That meant they must be going for the Ford. That wouldn't do them a whole lot of good. Jack had the keys, and bypassing the security system and hotwiring the vehicle would take too long. So where the hell were they going?

The distant sound of an inbound helicopter answered Jack's question.

Damn it. He'd thought the fleeing pilot would exit the area after his narrow escape. The fact that he hadn't meant the aviator feared going home as the lone survivor more than he feared hanging around. More than that, his sudden return meant that the leader on the ground had established radio contact.

Jack increased his pace as he moved through the deepening darkness. Suddenly he paused. Up ahead, the jungle had acquired a different feel, a watchfulness so full of tension and fear that he could practically taste it. Removing the second of his three grenades from his bag, Jack tossed it twenty meters to his left.

Immediately, two machine guns opened up, the flash of their muzzles clearly visible in the encroaching darkness. Avoiding revealing his own position by firing in the darkness, Jack pulled a knife from its ankle sheath and hurled it at the nearest shooter. The sound of a sharp blade burying itself in soft flesh was followed by a scream that trailed off in a wet gurgle.

With a curse, the other man quit firing and scrambled away through the undergrowth. Jack ignored the retreating man. Moving up to the dead man, Jack retrieved his knife from his throat, wiped it on the man's shirt, and returned the black blade to its sheath. He picked up the man's weapon, an AR-15, ejected the spent magazine, and inserted a fresh one. Then he moved on, staying well to the right of the path taken by this fellow's fleeing companion.

Ahead he heard the sound of a helicopter swooping into a hot landing zone, the RPMs kept high enough so that the aircraft never placed its weight on its wheels as it hovered just above the ground.

The yells of men climbing aboard spurred him forward, but as he reached the edge of the clearing, he could see the helicopter rise above the treeline and bank away. Seeing he had no shot that wouldn't risk killing Tupac Inti along with the others, Jack's frustration put a snarl on his lips. Then another sight shocked him to his core.

Seated next to an albino as big as Tupac Inti, with a sniper rifle cradled in her lap, sat a blond Janet Price. As their eyes locked for a full three seconds, Jack didn't raise his weapon . . . and neither did she.

Then Janet, and the helicopter that carried her, disappeared beyond the trees, leaving Jack rooted to the ground, with a storm of conflicting emotions buffeting him. Amid all the questions that boiled through his brain, one bubbled to the top.

What the hell was the NSA's top operative doing here in Bolivia?

CHAPTER 22

Rocked by the intensity of the feelings flowing from Jack Gregory into its being, Anchanchu hungered for more. The hippocampus was Anchanchu's playground, the place where short- and long-term memories converged with the human limbic system. In addition to Anchanchu's connection to its host's five senses, this limbic affinity provided the mind worm access to all of its host's memories and emotions. To have existed for an eternity without experiencing any human sensations or emotions made this connection oh so sweet. And Jack Gregory fed the mind worm so strongly that the pleasure was almost unbearable.

But Anchanchu had learned its limitations. Although it could interact with its host through dreams, attempting to communicate through conscious thought risked breaking a human mind, something that rendered its host worse than useless. That limitation had never before been a big problem, but Jack Gregory was different.

With the most probable futures shifting and changing with every significant action the man took, Anchanchu found itself in a panic to establish some level of control, anything that might prevent Jack from accidently toppling the temple of humanity. The normal method of rewarding desired action with adrenaline didn't work well with him. Sometimes Jack applied his iron will to resist that heady rush. Sometimes Jack went with his amped-up feelings so hard that his actions scrambled Anchanchu's future-timeline projections.

Even though the mind worm could invade Jack's dreams, there again it faced frustrating limitations, only able to replay memories experienced through previous hosts instead of something that might guide this man to that which needed to be done. Humans thought their history had a tendency to repeat itself. And that was true, but only generally, not precisely. What was coming demanded precise action.

The growing terror that filled the mind worm now had a face behind it. One previous host had brushed up against the very fate that once again issued its siren call. It was the only instance in which Anchanchu had been forcibly ejected from a living host. But if that happened this time, the odds of human survival were infinitesimal.

And a stampeding Jack Gregory was carrying Anchanchu on a path that led directly toward that destiny.

: CHAPTER 23

The start to this day didn't leave Levi Elias with a good feeling. It wasn't Friday, but it was February 13. An overnight earthquake, with a magnitude of 5.2 on the Richter scale, had forced the closure of the main NSA parking garage pending a structural integrity inspection. After passing through security at Fort Meade's "NSA Employees Only" gate, Levi had spent fifteen minutes trying to find a parking spot close to the organization's black-glass headquarters. He had finally given up, taking a parking spot at the far end of the huge lot. An unfortunate misstep as he exited his silver Acura had filled his right shoe with ice water. Now, with his overcoat collar turned up against the biting wind and sleet, he slogged a quarter of a mile through dirty slush before reaching the building entrance.

Passing through security, Levi walked to the elevator and pressed the call button. He pressed the button for floor five and watched it illuminate, glad to see the door slide closed before anyone else got on. Right now, he just wanted to get to his office, hang up his overcoat, take off his wet shoe, and wring the water out of his sock into the trash can.

When the elevator doors opened, he came face-to-face with Dr. Denise Jennings, her iron gray hair tied in a tight bun, a large android tablet in her left hand.

"Levi. I was just at your office, looking for you."

Levi stepped out of the elevator. "Is it important?"

"Yes."

Levi nodded. Of course it was.

When Dr. Jennings finished briefing him, Levi called Admiral Riles. He waited a minute as the NSA director's administrative assistant put him on hold, taking the opportunity to wring the muddy water from his sock.

"What have you got for me, Levi?"

"A Bolivia update. Have you got a few minutes for me and Dr. Jennings?"

"I'll make time. Come on up to my conference room."

Admiral Riles, already seated in his small conference room, waved them to their seats. It was a lack of formality the admiral had with his senior staff that Levi had grown used to.

Dr. Jennings seated herself at the keyboard and routed the computer display to the screen that took up the majority of the far wall.

"Sir, as you directed, we have targeted significant collection assets at Bolivia in recent days. Unfortunately, due to a limited high-tech infrastructure in much of the country, we have been unable to identify the location where Tupac Inti went to ground following his escape from Palmasola prison on Monday. However, we have breached the cell phone and computer data encryption used by Conrad Altmann's neo-Nazi organizations, including the Unión Juvenil Cruceñista. From those intercepts, we know that Janet Price arrived at the Altmann estate around 1:00 A.M. on Tuesday."

Admiral Riles leaned back in his chair. "Did she run into any problems?"

Levi took this question, trying not to let his concern creep into his voice. "We haven't had any direct communications with her, but that was expected. There's nothing else to indicate she ran into any trouble with her cover. From all indications, Ammon Gianakos came through for us. That brings us up to yesterday. Go on, Denise."

"Wednesday, just after 3:00 P.M. in Bolivia, we started picking up chatter on the UJC cell phones indicating that Tupac Inti had been spotted on Highway 9 in a black SUV, headed toward the Brazilian border. Later that evening, a major gun battle occurred near the Rio Mamore. We don't have any video, but one of our satellites did capture this."

The image on the wall monitor changed to a satellite photo of a finger of jungle that jutted away from the snaking Rio Mamore. In a clearing just to the north of the tree line, a bright orange spot showed clearly. With a gesture, Dr. Jennings centered that spot and zoomed in. Clearly visible, the burning wreckage of a transport helicopter dominated the scene.

Dr. Jennings continued. "Although police did not arrive on the scene until much later, they recovered eight bodies, including the pilot."

"Did they all die in the crash?" Riles asked.

"No, sir. The bodies of six men were recovered from what appears to have been a second landing zone farther to the south, all dead from gunshot wounds. Another man died in the jungle from a knife wound to the throat. By the way, the burning helicopter didn't crash. Someone shot the pilot in the face and chest, then tossed a grenade into the cockpit."

Riles clasped his hands beneath his chin. "Someone?"

Dr. Jennings met his gaze. "Big John has assigned a 0.935 correlation to Jack Gregory."

Levi watched the admiral shake his head as he spoke.

"I admit it looks like The Ripper's work. What I don't understand is how Big John can come up with that degree of correlation in a part of the world with so little electronic infrastructure."

Dr. Jennings shrugged. "I don't know. The system is a worldwide neural net that correlates a massive quantity of node weights for seemingly unrelated data. You either believe or you don't. Based on past history, I have to."

The admiral turned his gray eyes on Levi. "What do you think?"

"There's one thing Dr. Jennings didn't mention yet. Our latest electronic intercepts confirm that the UJC captured Inti. Based on everything, I think that Jack Gregory got himself thrown into Palmasola under a fake name, that he killed a handful of neo-Nazis in a prison gang fight, and that he engineered Tupac Inti's escape. Then, as Gregory tried to get Tupac out of Bolivia, I think the neo-Nazis paid a high price taking Inti away from him. Janet Price was probably right in the middle of the action."

Levi saw the admiral nod his head in satisfaction. "Good. The pieces are all in motion."

Admiral Riles rose to his feet, and Levi echoed the motion. As he watched the NSA director walk out of the room, Levi got the feeling that his boss knew something he wasn't sharing with his top analyst.

It was a feeling Levi didn't like. Not one little bit.

~ ~ ~

At six feet tall, Frederica Barnes, who everyone called Fred, had a soft Virginia drawl that matched her stunning face and figure. But she defended Riles's prized privacy like an NFL linebacker, and he regarded her as the best administrative assistant with whom he had ever had the pleasure of working. Much to the disappointment of the men around her, she was gay and attached.

Admiral Riles walked by her desk, issuing instructions as he passed.

"Fred, unless it's a national emergency, I don't want to be interrupted."

"Yes, sir."

Stepping into his spacious office, Admiral Riles walked to the floor-to-ceiling window that formed the wall behind his desk. With hands clasped behind his back, he looked out through the one-way, copper-infused glass that blocked all electronic transmissions from the massive building. It was probably the dismal weather that made the view of Fort Meade appear darker than normal, but it could also have been his mood.

To be this close to culminating a plan that he'd put into motion three years ago, only to have The Ripper throw himself into the mix, was worrisome. Too bad the NSA's recent attempt to recruit Jack had failed. Janet Price had come close, but for reasons only Jack Gregory knew, he had ultimately walked away. Now Jack was the admiral's problem.

Normally, he would bring Levi Elias in on this. But in this case, Riles had long ago made a decision to protect Levi from an operation that was based on an insane idea. Levi was the NSA's top analyst, blessed with a brilliant and meticulous mind that spotted connections that others missed. Levi was the human equivalent of Big John.

The thought brought a rueful smile to Admiral Riles's face. It was crazy to equate a man to a computer. Then again, Big John wasn't a computer, was it?

The system was a sophisticated data-mining cyber-structure; hence the name Big John, after the legendary miner in the old Jimmy Dean ballad. The truth was that even Dr. Denise Jennings didn't understand how Big John did what it did. No data center could hold the information that coursed through Big John's synaptic system, a system that encompassed an estimated two-thirds of the earth's computing power.

The fact that Denise, who had designed the software that formed Big John's core underpinning, didn't understand how it worked wasn't surprising. An outgrowth of the most advanced parallel computing research from Los Alamos and Lawrence Livermore National Laboratories, supplemented by work from MIT, Caltech, Carnegie Mellon, and others, Big John was a collection of genetic algorithms operating on a vast, polymorphic neural net.

It was fed by a software kernel Denise had developed in the latter part of the twentieth century under a secret government program designed to support and encourage the hacker subculture. With the rise of computer viruses, Trojan horses, and worms, along with their endlessly evolving variants, everyone found themselves needing antivirus protection. Unknown even to the companies that arose to fill that need, Denise's software kernel was incorporated into almost every one of the antivirus applications. And with each software update, her kernel got better.

Big John operated on too much data to ever transmit across the Internet to a central data center, not even the massive NSA facility in Utah. It needed to touch everything. The elegance of Denise's solution provided the answer. The antivirus software on each device scanned all of its local data and all data coming or going through its communications layers. And antivirus software needed to regularly update itself with the latest definitions.

When it did that, Denise's kernel updated itself and delivered its encrypted node weights using the same mechanism.

Her kernel didn't transmit raw data across the network. Each instance formed a synaptic patch of neurons, a tiny slice of a much larger brain, an insignificant piece of the vast neural net that was Big John.

Computers, cell phones, and tablets came and went, were turned on and off, were replaced by newer ones, and Big John shifted and evolved with that changing capability. The information that each synaptic patch analyzed acquired shifting weight patterns in Big John's correlative data web, a web so vast no data bank could store it. The world was Big John's data bank.

Admiral Riles turned away from the window, grabbed a clean cup from his shelf, placed it beneath the coffee nozzle, and pressed the "Mug" button. A minute later, seated at his desk, he sipped the delightfully stout brew, letting the flavor and aroma combine to spread a golden glow to his stomach as his mind reworked the current situation.

Three years ago, Dr. Jennings had brought him the Big John data that had put the NSA on the trail of the Sun Staff and the unsolvable algorithm that crawled up its silver shaft and into the golden crown piece. That had started all this craziness and, like Klaus Barbie, Admiral Riles had recognized its importance. Unfortunately, the NSA had neither the crown piece nor the staff, and it needed both if it was to crack the code.

So, despite the threat The Ripper posed, the operation would continue, and Tupac Inti would get the chance to play his part. Janet Price would make certain of that.

CHAPTER 24

Stripped naked, Tupac Inti stood on the damp concrete floor of the dark underground cell, his manacled hands and feet chained to the wall. The chains denied him rest, holding a promise of worse treatment yet to come. Tupac held no illusions of the humanity of his captors. Though Conrad Altmann needed Tupac alive, that didn't mean the neo-Nazi's UJC goons wouldn't hurt him. Just a taste at first, followed by an offer of relief if Tupac told Altmann what he wanted to know. After that, the cycle would repeat until Tupac's resistance finally broke.

But then Tupac had known this was coming since that day, three years ago, when he'd made his deal with the NSA. It was all part of the master plan. Though Admiral Riles hadn't anticipated that Tupac would be left in prison for eighteen months, no plan ever went exactly as intended. Apparently it had taken Altmann longer than the NSA had thought to find his father's hidden artifact. Whatever the cause, as long as Tupac got what he'd been promised, he was fine with it.

Tupac had watched his father die heartbroken that his son had abandoned his ancestral destiny for the military life. Now it was time to pay the penance the old gods demanded of him.

His thoughts turned to the man called Jack who had rescued him from Palmasola prison. Something about Jack had enticed Tupac to go off-plan and escape, even though he had intended to let the UJC capture him then and there. It had been a crazy risk, but the shaman had sensed an otherworldly energy in the man. And though Tupac did not know what role Jack would play in this, Tupac felt certain he would see him again. Destiny was about to come full circle.

Bracing his arms and legs, Tupac tightened his core, letting that tension seep outward into the muscles that powered his mighty limbs. Clenching his fists, Tupac increased the power his arms exerted on the chains, feeling his body lift from the floor until it was suspended in a close approximation of a gymnast's iron cross. When the bolts that secured the chains to the wall groaned and began to give, Tupac relaxed and let his body settle back to the floor.

Escape would come only after he had what he'd come for. In the meantime, Tupac would endure the worst these neo-Nazi bastards had to offer.

CHAPTER 25

Conrad Altmann looked up as Dolf Gruenberg rapped on the open office door to signal his presence. Leaning back from the large teak desk covered with the papers he'd been reviewing, Altmann motioned for his lieutenant to enter.

"Leave your cell phone outside, and close the door behind you."

"I left the phone in my car."

It was their routine, always the same reminder, always the same response. But with Altmann's knowledge of the worldwide extent of NSA snooping on all forms of electronic communication, there was no such thing as being too careful. It was the reason that, other than electric lights and a coffeemaker, he allowed no electronic appliances in his spacious private office or in any of the other designated black zones he sprinkled around each of his compounds. And whenever he and his people communicated via cell phone or e-mail, they only relayed information that Altmann wanted the NSA to get.

Dolf seated himself in an easy chair opposite Altmann.

"Inti has been secured in our compound outside Cochabamba."

Altmann grinned. "Good. I hope you made him nice and comfortable."

"Lap of luxury."

"What about Janet Mueller?"

"She's here. I told her to wait outside."

Altmann stood and leaned forward to rest his palms on his desk. Dolf had come to this meeting knowing his boss wanted answers to some hard questions, and Altmann would wait no longer to ask them.

"I send two helicopters, eleven of my best men, and one woman to get Inti, and here you come, limping back on one shot-up helicopter with only three men and the woman."

"And Inti," Dolf said, his face showing no emotion.

Grabbing a glass paperweight from his desk, Altmann hurled it past Dolf's head to shatter against the bookshelves behind him. The big man never flinched. Altmann doubted he would have flinched even if the paperweight had hit him.

"Would you mind telling me how one man managed to kill seven of my foot soldiers and blow up one of my helicopters, along with its pilot?"

Dolf's pale eyes remained locked with Altmann's as he spoke. "As we flew away, Janet Mueller recognized the man. He's an ex-CIA assassin named Jack Gregory. Now he runs a one-man mercenary operation, hiring out to the highest bidder. His clients know him as 'The Ripper'."

"The Ripper? What a pretentious ass."

"Maybe, but he's one dangerous son of a bitch."

"How does Janet Mueller know him?"

"She said the Golden Dawn had some trouble with him last year. I checked with Ammon Gianakos, and he said The Ripper killed one of their Polish business partners."

Altmann paused, stroking his beard as he considered this new information.

"Tell me, now that you've personally observed Janet Mueller in action, what do you think of her?"

Dolf's eyes narrowed slightly. "She's as cool and decisive as anybody I've ever seen. She was the one who first figured out the kind of man we were up against. I don't like saying this, but if she hadn't been there, I doubt any of us would have made it out of that jungle alive."

"So you trust her?"

"Not in the least."

Altmann felt a grin return to his face at the blunt answers from his lieutenant. It's what he liked about Dolf—straight talk, no bullshit. Good news or bad, Altmann could always count on Dolf to say exactly what he thought.

"Okay then. Here's how I want you to play it. Assume she's working someone else's agenda. I don't care whether it's the Golden Dawn, CIA, or NSA. Feed her just the information we don't mind them learning about, just enough to keep them from guessing we're onto their game. In the meantime, put her to the test."

"How do you propose to do that?"

"Let's find out just how far she's willing to go. Send her after Gregory. And get ahold of General Montoya. Give him Jack Gregory's name, description, and tell him I said to have his intel people dig into Gregory's background. I want a full-blown dragnet. Gregory is to be killed on sight."

Dolf nodded. "Anything else?"

"I want our people hunting Gregory too. I'm too close to success to let a rogue screw things up."

Dolf turned to walk toward the door, but Altmann stopped him, allowing his anger to edge into his voice.

"And Dolf?"

"Yes, sir?"

"Don't let The Ripper make me doubt you again."

This time Altmann saw it in the albino's pale eyes. A barely contained killing rage. For a moment, Altmann gripped the pistol holstered beneath his desk, wondering if he'd pressed his lieutenant too far. Then Dolf turned on his heel and walked out of the office.

CHAPTER 26

Janet Price didn't like inactivity. She didn't like being cut out of the loop either. It was no great surprise that Conrad Altmann didn't trust her. He didn't want to do anything that would strain relations between his neo-Nazi groups and the Golden Dawn. So instead of directly opposing her, Altmann was keeping her at arm's length. Despite having been allowed on the capture mission, she hadn't been informed where Inti had been taken after their return. That just meant she'd have to work harder.

On this cool, misty morning, seated alone on the patio as two of Altmann's native household staff served her breakfast, Janet played her part, offering a "no thank-you," dismissing their excellent efforts as one of their betters would be expected to act. It made her want to pull the Glock from beneath her black leather jacket and shoot the next neo-Nazi bastard she saw.

That person turned out to be Dolf.

"Finish your meal. Herr Altmann wants you to do a favor for him."

Janet lifted her cappuccino, sipping it casually before setting the cup back in its saucer.

"I don't do favors. If he's offering me a job, I need to hear what it is. Then, if I like it, we can discuss price."

Dolf smacked his huge right hand flat on the table in front of her, and Janet stuck a knife into the wood surface between his two middle fingers.

When he jerked away, a thin trickle of blood wept down his hand. Dolf's jaw muscles clenched as the veins in his temples bulged.

"Do something like that again and I'll break your pretty little neck."

Janet pulled her knife from the table and wiped its blade on the white cloth napkin.

"Next time I'll cut something off."

Leaning back in her chair, she continued, "But you're not going to do it again, are you, Dolf? Because my boss wouldn't like it. That means your boss wouldn't like it. So, I recommend you knock off the bullshit and get down to business."

Looking into those cold, dead eyes, Janet found herself hoping that Dolf would yield to temptation. Instead, he sat down across from her, the change in the man so dramatic that, except for the blood that continued to seep from the webbing between his fingers, a passing stranger would think they had been amiably chatting.

"Herr Altmann wants you to kill Jack Gregory."

"A dangerous job," Janet smiled. "It carries a dangerous price."

"Name it."

"Eight hundred thousand euros, payable after the job is done."

Dolf laughed. "Give me a serious number."

"I gave you my number. Altmann can take it or leave it."

"No man is worth that much."

"Then you kill him."

Dolf grabbed a napkin, wiped the blood from his hand, and stood.

"I'll tell him. You might not like his response."

"I'll take my chances."

Dolf grinned.

"You already are."

Janet watched him walk away, the tension in the big man's back threatening to split the seams of his tailored jacket. One way or another, she was about to get back in action.

CHAPTER 27

Even in the dark hour before dawn, Jack could tell it would be a warm Friday here in the Bolivian lowlands. It had been two days since Jack had watched Janet Price fly away in that helicopter full of neo-Nazis, two days since he'd lost Tupac Inti. After ditching the Ford Explorer, Jack had purchased a used Honda Shadow motorcycle and then paid a month's rent for this small house on the outskirts of Santa Cruz.

Being back in the city where this all started was good for a couple of reasons. The authorities didn't expect pursued individuals to return to the town from which they'd just escaped. More important, it was one of the biggest cities in Bolivia, which made it easy to go unnoticed.

Jack had spent the last two days outfitting himself with the supplies he would need in order to start fixing the mess he'd made of this mission. First, he needed answers. He knew people who could get him what he needed, but they were only available via very secure communications links and didn't come cheap. But, unlike back in his days with the CIA, money was no longer one of Jack's problems.

He would have to arrange transfers from one of his Cayman Island accounts into other numbered accounts. To do that he needed to make use of one of the satellite Internet accounts of his Shell Corporation. The small satellite dish he'd attached to the north-facing back wall gave him part of that capability. The software he was installing on the laptop would do the rest.

It was slow work, but necessary. Having seen firsthand the NSA's involvement in this, Jack knew that he would need to take extraordinary precautions.

He physically disconnected the new laptop's internal microphone and camera and then performed a multipass wipe of its solid-state drive. Now Jack booted the system from a special USB dongle and installed a clean version of the Linux operating system, a bare-bones Internet browser, and an encryption package that he was confident even the NSA couldn't hack, at least not until they managed a major breakthrough in quantum computing.

Waiting for the lengthy installation to complete, Jack stood, walked over to the coffee pot and poured himself a brimming cup of Bolivia's finest. Taking a slow sip of the strong black liquid, he leaned back against the old counter and examined his new abode. Its eight hundred and fifty square feet consisted of two rooms. This one served as living room, dining room, and kitchen, with no divider between any of the rooms. At one time, the obscured pattern on the worn linoleum floor might have been floral. The years of water stains from the leaky roof had combined with general wear and tear to make such a judgment no better than a guess.

But the place had electricity to power the stove, a refrigerator, his laptop, and this newly purchased coffee pot.

This room's meager furnishings consisted of a sagging brown couch, a metal-legged table, and two dining chairs, one of which was stable enough to allow Jack to sit without fear of it tipping over or collapsing. There was a phone jack in the wall next to the couch, but no end table or phone. The entry door and a four-foot-square window occupied the south wall. Another door on the east wall stood open, granting access to the bedroom and its small bathroom. The north wall had no windows, only a door that opened into a tiny, overgrown backyard surrounded by a high chain-link fence that a thick growth of vines had rendered opaque.

All in all, adequate accommodations.

Walking back to the table, Jack glanced at the installation progress bar on the laptop's display . . . thirty-seven percent complete. Christ. He hated waiting. But like his daily meditation and workout routine, patience was one of the many disciplines he'd enforced on himself over time.

For more than a year, he'd worked harder than ever on imposing self-discipline, hoping it would quiet the fire that raged within. Always gifted with an uncanny intuition after that Calcutta night, Jack had experienced an amped-up state of consciousness. In combat, it let him anticipate an opponent's move as his enemy decided upon it. If that had been the only side effect, it would have been fine. But Jack sensed danger, and he hungered for it with a ferocity that threatened his self-control, threatened his sanity. And each time he yielded to those impulses, whether from necessity or weakness, the greater that hunger became.

It was the reason Jack had rejected the offer Janet Price had made in Heraklion, Crete. It was the reason he'd walked away, leaving her seated at that harbor café, when he'd really wanted to stay. Seeing her again had brought those suppressed memories flooding back, and right now, that was a distraction he didn't need. What he needed to know was why the NSA had sent her here. Why was she helping the neo-Nazis?

Jack knew that Conrad Altmann ruled Bolivia's neo-Nazi organizations with an iron fist, that the man's corrupt tentacles extended into the Bolivian police, military, and even parts of the government. The combination of high intelligence, big money, and ruthlessness generally yielded those results, even in the countries of the first world. These were traits to be expected of Klaus Barbie's bastard son.

These were the traits that had led American intelligence to protect the Butcher of Lyon after he'd been captured at the end of World War II. The United States had done much more than protect Klaus Barbie; they'd hired him and set him up with a secret house and support staff in Germany, all because they knew how exceptional the Nazi was at infiltrating foreign intelligence organizations. And the Americans had been well rewarded for their efforts as Barbie identified secret Soviet operatives throughout the eastern and western European countries.

It was the reason why, when the French discovered that the U.S. was protecting Barbie and demanded his extradition, the American government helped him escape to Bolivia. Little wonder that he'd seeded the neo-Nazi movement in this new land with his capabilities. Little wonder that Barbie's son had mastered his father's techniques.

What Jack hadn't figured out was why Altmann hadn't had Tupac killed. He could have ordered it done in Palmasola prison. His men could have killed Tupac instead of loading him onto a helicopter and flying him away. If Altmann needed information from the big Quechua shaman, why had he waited a year and a half to grab him from Palmasola? Why now?

A glance at his laptop showed that the installation had completed. Good.

Having established the link that logged him onto his satellite Internet service, Jack launched the encrypted voice-over IP chat session. It was time to get some high-priced answers.

Two hours later, having shut down the laptop, Jack slipped into his brown leather jacket, grabbed his helmet, and walked outside, locking the front door behind him. At a little past 8:00 A.M., the jacket already felt too warm. But where he was going, it wouldn't be.

Pulling on his dark-visored helmet, Jack started the motorcycle, gunned the 750cc engine, and let the black bike carry him away from Santa Cruz.

CHAPTER 28

Stepping off his personal helicopter, Conrad Altmann felt the rotor wash blow his hair against his neck and face before he moved away from the whirling blades to the open-handed greeting of Renaldo Rodriguez, the foreman of Altmann's fortified Cochabamba estate.

"So good to see you, Herr Altmann."

Altmann nodded. "I hear all is well."

"I think you'll find it to your liking."

The son of mixed parents, Renaldo had his mother's fair complexion and his father's work ethic. Those traits combined with a genial nature to yield a man that Altmann genuinely liked, to the surprise of some of his fellow neo-Nazis. Altmann's devotion was to the National Socialist Party, not to the white race. Although he would never have admitted it to other party members, he knew, as had his father, that Hitler's vision of the master race had been wrong. There was certainly a master race; it just wasn't human.

For the thousandth time Altmann questioned his decision to live at his La Paz compound as opposed to this lovely spot with its ideal, year-round temperatures. Inhaling the clean air, Altmann shook his head. There was a price to be paid for staying close to the country's political epicenter. Bolivia's government demanded the frequent and intimate touch of his deft hand. Nevertheless, it was nice to get away, if only for an afternoon.

"Show me to our guest."

"Yes, sir."

Although not as large as his La Paz house, the five-thousand-square-foot, single-story home was elegant in its simplicity. Passing through the twelve-foot iron and glass doors held open by a pair of the household staff, Altmann found the open, tiled spaces inviting. Two more men joined Renaldo as he ushered Altmann into the narrow stairwell that led to the basement and then down to the old dungeon. By the time Altmann stepped off the last of the steps, he had entered a different world.

This dungeon had originally lain below the two-hundred-year-old manor house that Altmann had torn down in order to build his compound atop this spot. But he'd fallen in love with these musty tunnels, with their old iron and stone cells, their lingering smell of ancient blood, sweat, and death, so Altmann had incorporated it into the new plans. Down here, he'd avoided all but the essential renovation required to restore structural integrity and to route electrical power for a new generation of torture devices and a line of naked ceiling bulbs that illuminated the main tunnel. To do more would have been to violate the spirit of this sacred place.

In recent years, these cells had been freshened with new blood, with screams that echoed through these tunnels, never finding their way to the surface. Today, the gift of new screams would feed this edifice, and Tupac Inti would be the giver.

Stopping in front of the fourth cell on his right, Renaldo removed a key ring from his pocket and fitted a large skeleton key into the keyhole. The clank and rattle that followed sent an electric and chemical thrill of anticipation through Altmann's nervous system. When the door creaked open, he got yet another thrill when he saw the naked shaman chained to the far wall.

Two days without food or water and only the sleep he could manage while dangling by his cuffed wrists had already taken their toll on the big man. But Inti's eyes didn't show it.

Altmann nodded at Renaldo, and he motioned for his two assistants to get the apparatus Altmann would soon be needing. As they moved to comply, Altmann stepped up close to Inti and smiled.

"Hello, Tupac. Welcome to my Cochabamba estate."

When Inti failed to respond, Altmann continued.

"Despite your peasant appearance, you're an educated man. West Point. I suppose congratulations are in order on your early attempts to better yourself. Too bad it didn't stick."

Hearing the rumble of hard rubber wheels on the rough stone floor, Altmann turned to watch the two men wheel an apparatus that looked somewhat like a fully outfitted welding cart up beside him. Then, unwinding a long, thick extension cord, one of them walked out of the room to plug the other end into one of the electrical sockets that had been installed on this level.

The other man unrolled an inch-thick rubber mat and Altmann stepped aside to let him roll it out in front of Inti. Then, as Renaldo powered on the machine and began arranging its various attachments for easy access, Altmann pulled on a large pair of gun-metal-gray rubber gloves and turned to face Inti.

Most of the people who'd stood in Inti's place were already begging by the time Altmann got this far in his setup. Not this man. Altmann had to admit that he was impressed. But it just added to the fun.

"Of course you have heard of the Marquis de Sade. He wisely said, 'It is always by way of pain one arrives at pleasure.' My father showed me the truth of that, both in the giving and in the receiving."

Like a surgeon expecting his nurse to hand him a scalpel, Altmann reached back to take the wire brush that trailed an electrical cord from its wooden handle. Altmann squeezed the device's rubber trigger, heard the familiar crackle as thin blue lightning bolts crawled between its many bristles.

A hopeful glance at Inti's dark eyes as Altmann extended the wire brush toward Inti's chest failed to yield the hoped-for trace of fear.

"Behold the truth."

As the wire bristles scraped into Tupac Inti's skin, his body arched in agony so intense that it pulled a scream of pain and rage from the massive lungs. The pleasure that flooded Altmann's soul was so intense it threatened to bring him to orgasm.

Then, with the sound of breaking iron and stone, the wall shackle binding Inti's right hand gave way.

CHAPTER 29

Altmann reacted instinctively, throwing himself backward as a sliver of rock sliced his left cheek, just below the eye.

Seeing his men go for their guns, Altmann scrambled to block their line of fire.

"Don't kill him, you idiots!"

Glancing back, Altmann saw Inti on his knees, head hanging, his left hand and feet still chained to the wall. As he watched, Renaldo stepped clear, aimed a tranquilizer gun, and fired a dart into Inti's right thigh. As if in slow motion, Inti lifted his head, locking his gaze to Altmann's. Then his eyes rolled up in his head and he slumped to the floor, his chained left arm raised high along the wall.

As Altmann stared down at Inti, feeling the blood run down his cheek from the inch-long cut, frustration burned him. Shit. The tranquilizer dart would put Tupac out for at least twelve hours. With critical meetings planned for tonight he couldn't wait for the man to revive. And Inti was far too important to let someone else do the interrogation. The questioning would just have to wait until tomorrow.

Altmann turned to Renaldo.

"Clean him up, move him to a new cell, and chain him seated in a corner. When he comes to, give him food and water. It'll make it that much harder when we take it away again."

"Yes, sir."

As Altmann turned and walked out of the cell, he gave one last order.

"And this time, Renaldo, use more chains."

CHAPTER 30

If she had been at a high-end hotel, Janet would have expected an area like this for its business center, where guests could go to use hotel-owned computers to access the Internet to check e-mail or print boarding passes. But this loft area that overlooked the den was a courtesy where Conrad Altmann offered his guests the use of laptops that his security people could monitor and that were isolated from his private network. It was just one more security layer implemented by the ultra-paranoid neo-Nazi godfather. Janet approved of his efforts.

Altmann had returned to his La Paz compound a half hour ago, stepping off his helicopter into a cold late-afternoon drizzle. Janet had walked out with Dolf to meet him, but he'd been in a foul mood, pausing just long enough to tell her he wanted Gregory dead, and he'd pay the eight hundred thousand euros to the first person that got it done. Janet had noticed the butterfly bandage on his left cheekbone but had avoided commenting on it. Apparently someone had strapped on the huevos it took to strike Altmann in the face.

More important, she'd gotten a glance at the helicopter's fuel gauge. The mental calculations that followed totaled up to a round-trip distance of approximately five hundred kilometers. Assuming he'd taken no side trips and hadn't refueled at the far end, his destination had been approximately a hundred and fifty miles away. When she had some privacy, she'd take the time to identify all the cities that lay on that arc. Off the top of her head, she could only think of two of significance, Oruro and Cochabamba.

Finding herself alone in the guest computer loft, she chose the leftmost of four laptops, followed the Guest Log-in instructions, traversed to her dummy Gmail account, and began composing a message to Ammon Gianakos.

SUBJECT: Trip Report

As anticipated, primary mission on hold awaiting conclusion of your partner's interest in this business opportunity. Have agreed, on a time and materials cost basis, to lend my expertise to assist in overcoming competitors for this opportunity. Will be available for safe online access until tomorrow A.M. *Out of office for several days after that.*

JM

Janet reread the message, especially the code phrase that would trigger a critical NSA alert for Admiral Riles's eyes only. Satisfied, she clicked *"Send."* Logging off, Janet rose and walked back to her room to pack for tomorrow's travel. In coming days she'd be needing all her playthings.

Assuming she didn't get herself killed tonight.

CHAPTER 31

"Sir, we've received a high-priority alert from Janet Price, for your eyes only."

Admiral Riles looked up to see Levi Elias standing in his door, an irate Frederica Barnes at his elbow.

"It's alright, Fred, I'll see him."

Giving Levi a look that showed her displeasure, Riles's gatekeeper returned to her desk. Levi stepped inside, closing the door behind him.

As Admiral Riles awoke his computer, he saw the alert that Levi had forwarded, entered the additional password the message required, and read Janet's e-mail message. Although there was no likelihood that anyone other than himself would have recognized the trigger, Riles refused to take any chances that might endanger the operation.

There, toward the end of the e-mail message was the keyword phrase, *safe online access*, followed by a timeline, *until tomorrow A.M.*

Looking up, Admiral Riles met Levi's expectant look and shook his head. As much as he trusted and relied upon his top analyst's expertise, and despite the desire he could see in Levi's face, Riles was determined to keep him out of this. If this went wrong, or possibly even if it went right, it could place everyone responsible for this operation in jeopardy.

"Thank you, Levi. I'll take it from here."

Riles noted the fleeting disappointment that crossed Levi's face before the man masked it, nodded, and departed. When he had gone, Riles pressed the button that connected him to his admin.

"Fred, notify Dr. Kurtz and Dr. Jennings that I want to see them in Dr. Kurtz's lab. Tell Kurtz to clear out any staff working in there."

"Anything else?

"The classification is Top Secret and the need-to-know is restricted to the three of us. I'm on my way now."

When Admiral Riles reached the computer lab, he found Dr. David Kurtz and Dr. Denise Jennings waiting for him, curiosity clearly etched on their faces. As the door closed behind him, Riles saw the wild-haired Dr. Kurtz push a button that locked the door and illuminated its "Classified Meeting in Progress" sign.

"Please sit," Riles said. "I'll make this as succinct as possible. First of all, Dr. Kurtz, I apologize for bringing you into this, but let me be clear. If, at any time, you feel uncomfortable about what I have to say, you are free to go, and I will not hold it against you. You may note that I make no such offer to Dr. Jennings since she first brought this matter to my attention three years ago.

"At that time, Big John identified an anomaly in communications between the top neo-Nazi figure in Bolivia, a man by the name of Conrad Altmann, and a number of research organizations. Over the course of several e-mails, some hitherto unknown Klaus Barbie writings came to light, papers in which he revealed the existence of a golden crown piece from an ancient Incan artifact known as the Sun Staff, purportedly the staff given by the gods to Manco Capac, the first Incan emperor."

Admiral Riles paused to study Dr. Kurtz's face before continuing.

"Centuries after Manco Capac's death, as civil war ravaged the Incan Empire, Pizarro captured the new emperor, took the staff, and had him executed. The Sun Staff's golden crown piece was separated from its silver shaft and sent back to Spain as tribute to the king. The shaft was then presented to the Incas' newly installed puppet emperor as a symbol of Spanish good faith.

"Other than legend, there is no documentation that tells what subsequently happened to either the crown piece or its silver shaft. Not until the Barbie papers I just mentioned.

"As you know, you can find all sorts of craziness in old Nazi documents, and the reference in Klaus Barbie's papers wouldn't normally attract Big John's attention. However, the papers contained a single photograph of Klaus Barbie holding the crown piece. Barbie's age and the quality of the photograph indicate that the picture was taken in Bolivia not long before Barbie was extradited to France in 1983."

Dr. Kurtz shook his head. "How is any of this relevant?"

"That was my question. The answer lies in the picture of the crown piece and in shaman lore passed down through the centuries, lore that includes detailed three-dimensional drawings of the silver staff."

Admiral Riles nodded at Dr. Jennings. "Denise."

The scientist turned to the nearest computer, logged in, and typed a sequence of commands that brought the far wall monitor to life, displaying a series of drawings showing a complex fractal pattern of symbols that weaved its way around the staff-like vines climbing a tall tree trunk.

Dr. Jennings spoke as she continued to manipulate the imagery. "As Admiral Riles mentioned, Big John first alerted me to the patterns in these shamanic drawings of the staff and their relationship to the image in the newly discovered Klaus Barbie documents. I then created a 3D model of the staff and a partial model of the spherical golden crown piece. I say partial because we only had a single picture of it, so I was unable to deduce what was on the other side.

"What I have been able to determine is that the symbology that snakes its way up the staff forms is an extremely complex mathematical algorithm, one that I haven't yet been able to solve."

Dr. Kurtz frowned. "How much computing power have you assigned to it?"

"I've had a number of our best systems working the problem."

"For how long?"

"From the beginning."

Dr. Kurtz's features acquired a look of disbelief, the same feeling that Admiral Riles had experienced for the last three years whenever he and Dr. Jennings broached this subject.

"Perhaps the algorithm has no solutions."

Dr. Jennings pursed her lips. "I've considered that, but based on the picture, we believe the answer lies in the crown piece."

"We?"

"Big John does, and I agree."

Admiral Riles interrupted. "Dr. Jennings, you know it distracts others when you refer to Big John like a person. Stay focused."

Running her hand over her hair as if she wanted to undo the tight gray bun, Dr. Jennings took a breath and then continued.

"Look at this."

The image on the wall changed to a tight zoom of the spherical crown piece.

"Note these perfectly straight horizontal cuts in the surface of the sphere. We . . ."—she glanced at Riles—". . . um, I have determined that the globe is divided into circular rings, each containing symbols like those on the shaft. By twisting each ring independently, the symbols align with the topmost fractal patterns on the staff in ways that produce different variations in the equations."

Dr. Kurtz nodded in understanding. "Like a Rubik's Sphere."

"Yes, but infinitely more complex."

"Would you mind telling me how the ancient Incans were able to design something like that?"

Admiral Riles stepped up to the wall screen, pausing to stare at the image. "Now, David, you know what got my attention. More important, over the ensuing months, while Dr. Jennings was unable to solve the algorithm, we came to believe that if we attained pictures of all sides of the crown piece, our new, experimental computation system might be capable of cracking the code."

Dr. Kurtz let out a low whistle. "Sir, you're talking about using the quantum computer to solve this, delaying the critical tasks you've already assigned to it."

"If we can get a complete set of pictures of the crown piece."

Admiral Riles watched his top computer scientist lean all the way back in his Herman Miller chair as he looked up at the ceiling. When Kurtz returned his gaze to the admiral's face, all doubt had departed.

"I'm in."

"Good."

Riles smiled, feeling the relief that came from knowing Denise Jennings wouldn't have to attempt this alone. As good as she was, David Kurtz was better, and Janet Price was about to put her life on the line.

"I need you and Dr. Jennings to remotely bypass an extremely sophisticated security system. And I need it done before midnight."

"We'll get on it."

"One more thing," Riles said. "The system is probably shielded and isolated from external networks."

Dr. Kurtz grinned and turned to his keyboard. "If it's plugged into an electrical outlet, it's not isolated from us."

CHAPTER 32

Stefan Rosenstein sat in the back of the sedan as his driver wound his way through the moonlit La Paz streets toward the outskirts of the city and home. It had been another cold, damp summer day, but what could he expect at twelve thousand feet above sea level? Tonight, although it had gotten colder, the clouds had cleared. As the sedan passed out of the city proper, Stefan saw the beautiful full moon illuminate the distant, snow-capped Mount Illimani. On the plus side, he had that view.

Considering how badly things had gone wrong two days ago, he'd better enjoy it while he could. It was only a matter of time until Conrad Altmann found out who had engineered Tupac Inti's failed escape. That was the reason that Stefan was going home to an empty house. It was the reason he'd put his beloved Miriam and his two daughters on a plane bound for Israel yesterday. His family would keep them safe, and even the long arm of the neo-Nazis had limitations. The Israeli government made sure of that.

The sedan stopped at the front gate and waited as it swung open, before entering the circular driveway to deposit Stefan at the front door. Although he preferred to let himself out, he waited for his security chief to open the door, nodding to the compact ex-Mossad agent as he climbed out.

"Thank you, Jacob. Any issues tonight."

"All quiet, Senator."

As Stefan climbed the steps, he was met at the front door by Ricardo, his Bolivian butler. Stepping past the slender, gray-haired man who had served Stefan's family for more than half of his sixty years, Stefan held up a hand, anticipating the man's question.

"Nothing tonight, Ricardo. I'm headed for bed."

Ricardo nodded. "Should I pour your bath?"

Stefan started to say no, but then reconsidered.

"That would be good, thank you."

Ten minutes later Stefan slid into the hot water and felt it ease muscles tightened by a long day sitting and listening to his illustrious colleagues pontificate. Of course, when it came to pontificating, Stefan could hold his own. It was the worry that had drained him.

Donning his warm pajamas, he climbed into bed and turned off the light. It seemed that his head hadn't even hit the pillow when he awoke. A glance at the cyan numerals on his bedside clock gave him the bad news. 12:00 A.M. The witching hour.

The moonlight streaming through the bedroom windows bathed the figure sitting in his reading chair in an appropriately ghostly light.

"Hello, Stefan."

The familiar voice broke the spell which had held Stefan breathless.

"For God's sake, Jack. You scared the shit out of me."

“These are scary times, Senator. Others are watching your house. And not just Jacob Bensheim.”

Pushing the remnants of sleep from his head, Stefan sat up and swung his legs off the side of the bed. “Jacob already warned me. It’s why I sent Miriam and the girls away.”

“You should have gone with her.”

“I have responsibilities here.”

“Is dying one of them?”

Stefan rose to his feet, walked to his liquor cabinet, and poured himself a glass of Chivas 25, straight up. He thought about offering Jack a drink, but why waste his breath? Instead, he carried his drink to the sitting area and took a seat across from The Ripper.

“What do you want Jack? Payment?”

“You know I never take payment until the job is done. I’m not finished.”

“Then why are you here?”

The silence that followed heightened Stefan’s discomfort, something he hoped a couple more swallows of the twenty-five-year-old scotch would alleviate.

“When you hired me to free Tupac Inti, you told me the neo-Nazis were going to murder him. I want to know why you lied to me.”

Feeling sweat bead on his brow despite the coolness of the room, Stefan took another drink and swallowed. It didn’t seem to be helping. It was strange how he feared this man more than he feared the neo-Nazis who wanted to kill him.

“It’s complicated.”

Stefan thought he saw a red glint in The Ripper’s eyes, but it must have been a trick of the moonlight.

“What I’m trying to say is that some things are easier to believe than others. I told you what I thought you could accept without laughing in my face.”

“Why would I do that?”

Stefan's laugh came out like a hiss. "Because I hate Nazis! Because I'm a crazy Jew who believes Klaus Barbie's bastard son is on the verge of accomplishing what his father's beloved Führer failed to do."

Again The Ripper fell silent. Stefan wasn't surprised. That outburst hadn't been something he'd planned, and it wasn't likely to inspire confidence in his mental or emotional stability. Then again, why would someone with mental and emotional stability hire The Ripper? Stefan started to take another drink but felt his stomach rumble and set it aside.

When Stefan started talking, he found he couldn't shut up. The story bubbled from his lips as though he'd just kissed the Blarney Stone. He told The Ripper everything he knew about Klaus Barbie and Conrad Altmann. He told Jack about all the things he believed but had no proof of. All the crazy bullshit poured from his lips in a rush that left him breathless.

When Stefan finally stopped talking, he looked at the moonlit killer sitting across from him, trying to spot some shred of evidence that he hadn't just torpedoed his only hope of salvation.

When The Ripper stood, he spoke softly.

"I'll look into it."

Stefan watched as The Ripper walked to his cabinet, picked up the half-empty bottle of scotch, and then looked back at him.

"I've taken the liberty of booking first-class seats for you and Jacob on the 4:45 A.M. Avianca flight into Miami, with a connection to Tel Aviv. Make sure you're on it."

Stefan felt a sudden rush of hope tinged with guilt at the thought of abandoning his parliamentary position. But letting Altmann's people kill him wouldn't fulfill that position either. As he looked at The Ripper standing there in the semi-darkness, holding the Chivas bottle in his left hand, a new worry assailed him.

"But the men watching outside?"

The Ripper nodded and then turned toward the bedroom door.

"I'll have a word with them on my way out."

CHAPTER 33

Janet opened her eyes and turned her head to glance at the glowing numerals on her bedside clock. 1:59 A.M.

Throwing off her covers, she climbed out of bed, fully clothed. Slipping on a thick pair of dark socks, she decided to forgo putting on her boots. There was too great a chance they might squeak on the smooth tile floor. After sliding her hands into a pair of black leather gloves, she lifted her Glock from the nightstand and slid it into the elastic holster pocket in her black undershirt. No need to check it. She already knew the compact had a full magazine and one in the chamber. Even if she hadn't checked it before going to bed, the weight of the familiar weapon would have told her.

Outside her window, the light of the full moon lit the courtyard, but it was too high overhead to cast direct light into her room. Janet took that, along with the fact that the clouds had cleared, as a good sign. It was funny how someone who lacked all superstition looked for good signs at a time like this. She preferred to regard it as positive thinking.

Pulling her double-edged black knife from its sheath, Janet checked its custom haft and then returned it to its side sheath. Stepping to her door, she paused several seconds to listen. Hearing nothing, Janet opened the door and stepped out into the large loft area that overlooked the family room below. The indirect moonlight that leaked in from the family room's twenty-foot-tall, floor-to-ceiling windows provided just enough illumination for her to see the nearest of the ceiling-mounted reflective glass bubbles that housed Altmann's security cameras.

As Janet stared up at it, she hoped that the eyes looking back at her belonged to Jonathan Riles and his team of NSA hackers. If so, Altmann's security guards were watching loopback video of an empty loft area instead of preparing to trigger the estate's alarm system. The small green LED on the adjacent networked smoke detector blinked several times. Dash dash dash . . . pause . . . dash dot dash. Janet recognized the Morse code for "OK" and smiled up at the camera.

Janet turned left, passing the elevator and the open spiral staircase on her left, her footsteps so soft on the tile that she couldn't hear herself move. Just beyond the door to Altmann's theater, she entered a short hallway that led to Altmann's second-floor office. Right now that door was closed. Janet ignored the hand scanner, reached for the handle, and heard a click from its electronic lock.

Nice to know the home team was on its game.

Twisting the doorknob, she felt the latch release and pushed the door inward. Stepping inside, Janet softly closed the door behind her. Janet knew that this office was one of Conrad Altmann's black zones, a space where he allowed no electrical devices that weren't already hardwired in. His security system was designed to detect any such device that crossed that threshold. The fact that there was no response to her entry further confirmed that the NSA now had total control of the Altmann estate's security apparatus.

The curving glass walls at the south end of the office backdropped Altmann's desk, providing a magnificent view of the distant Mount Illimani, its glacier-capped peak reflecting the moonlight.

Janet pulled her knife from its sheath, gripped the haft with both hands, pressed two different places on the grip, and twisted. The rubber haft separated, revealing a two-inch device that vaguely resembled a memory stick. Unclipping it from its mount, Janet reassembled the knife and returned it to its sheath. Approaching the east wall, she pressed the topmost of three buttons on the device, an action that lighted a tiny red LED.

Starting at the north end of the room, Janet moved slowly south along the wall, moving the device up and down over the paintings and the bookshelves. Nothing.

Moving across the room to the west wall, Janet repeated the process with no better results. Crap. She'd been sure that Altmann would want to keep the crown piece close. She'd assumed she'd find it in an office safe. That presumed that Altmann had a safe in his office.

Shifting her attention to the floor, Janet bent low, working her way across the room in a back-and-forth pattern that cleared one six-foot-by-six-foot square at a time. Fifteen minutes passed, then twenty. Her frustration continued to grow.

A noise from the hall was followed by a soft click from the office door. The NSA had remotely locked it again. Not good.

Moving silently across the room, Janet curled her body into the footspace below Altmann's desk. Pulling her Glock from its holster, she pressed her back against the teak front panel, stilled her breathing, and waited.

The sound of the lock disengaging told her who was outside. Conrad Altmann had pressed his hand against the scanner to unlock it. She heard the door open and Altmann step in. A second later the ceiling lights came on.

Altmann's slippers made soft scuffing sounds on the tile as he walked directly to the east wall bookshelf and stopped. Her hearing tuned to the slightest sound, Janet heard a book being pulled from a shelf, heard it returned, and another extracted. The sound of Altmann licking a finger. The sound of turning pages. The slap of a hardcover closing. The sounds repeated, then repeated again.

"Damn. Where the hell did I put it?"

Janet looked across the gunsight, past Altmann's chair, and let her index finger creep inside the trigger guard. From this angle she couldn't see the bookcase or Altmann, but he'd have to cross her sightline if he walked behind his desk.

Suddenly, she heard more footsteps, followed by Dolf's voice.

"Herr Altmann, is everything alright?"

"Couldn't sleep. Busy mind. Thought I'd pick out something to read."

"Something you didn't have in your downstairs study?"

Janet heard Altmann laugh.

"Odd, isn't it? I found myself craving a tome I keep up here."

"Anything I can do to help?"

"No. I've found what I was looking for. If Karl Marx doesn't put me to sleep, nothing will."

It was the first time Janet had heard Dolf Gruenberg laugh. She didn't care to hear it again.

The two men walked to the door, the lights went out, and Janet heard the door close and lock. Sliding the Glock back into its holster pocket, Janet grabbed the small device she'd been using prior to the interruption, switched it on, and started to crawl out from underneath the desk. Two green LEDs stopped her.

Sweeping the device around the floor beneath the desk, she saw three green lights come on as she neared the right panel. Tapping the panel, she found no means of opening it. Instead she moved back to the front of the desk and reached for the lower drawer handle, expecting to pull out a file drawer. Instead, a door made to look like two file drawers swung outward. She found herself staring at a safe, illuminated by the dim moonlight.

An old-fashioned dial combination lock occupied the center of the steel door. Knowing Altmann's aversion to electronics, that didn't surprise her.

Pulling a pen light from her pocket, Janet switched it on, placed it in her teeth, and aimed its narrow beam at the dial. Janet pressed a switch on the small device she'd previously used to detect the safe's presence, magnetically attaching it to the safe, just above the combination lock. Spinning the dial clockwise several times to clear it, she stopped on zero and then began slowly turning the dial counterclockwise. Four complete turns later, when she reached eleven, the first red LED illuminated. Three clockwise turns, and a second red LED brought her to a stop on sixteen. Another two turns counterclockwise produced another red light as the dial reached fifteen.

Janet removed her right hand from the dial and paused to pop her knuckles. Realizing what she'd just done, Janet chuckled at the subconscious act. She must have been watching too many movies.

She spun the dial clockwise one complete turn as she watched for the fourth LED to light up, something that happened at thirty-two. A final counterclockwise spin brought the dial to a hard stop. Janet reached for the lever and twisted, rewarded by the feel of the locking bars sliding into the open position. She pulled and the door smoothly swung open.

The sight that greeted her gaze brought a gasp to her lips. The size of a large Fabergé egg, the intricately etched golden sphere reflected the soft penlight in an almost magical way. No matter what equations this thing might hold the solutions to, Janet knew she was staring at an item of unimaginable value.

Pausing a second to memorize its exact location and orientation, Janet reached into the safe and carefully lifted the Incan orb from the cushion on which it rested. It was lighter than she imagined and, as she examined it more closely, she could see why. Mostly hollow, it was formed of stacked rings, between which she could glimpse intricate inner workings that reminded her of what she'd once seen on a tour of a Swiss watch factory. The symbols etched into and around each of the rings connected to different symbols above and below, the bottommost of these seeming to vainly reach for something that had been lost, no doubt the symbols on the missing silver staff.

Janet started to set the orb on the desktop and then reconsidered, reaching instead for its cushion, setting that on the desk before setting the crown piece atop it. Removing the penlight from her mouth, Janet switched it off and twisted its shaft to reveal the pinhole lens of a digital micro-camera. The low-light camera needed no flash, and she began taking a series of pictures as she moved slowly around the orb. After taking several more from above, Janet set the camera on the desk and turned the orb upside down. Then she took another complete set of pictures.

Satisfied, Janet stowed her tools and replaced the golden Incan orb on its cushion in the safe, taking care to return it to its original position. Closing the safe, she spun the dial twice, leaving it set on seventy-eight, just as she'd found it.

Janet closed the door that hid the safe within the desk, rearranged Altmann's chair, and then took a final look around the office, just to verify that nothing was out of place.

As she reached the door, she heard the soft sound of the electric lock opening, mouthed a silent thank-you to her NSA fairy godmother, and walked silently back to her room. As she slipped beneath the covers, consciously releasing the tension that had accumulated in her shoulders, Janet started to place her Glock on the nightstand, but then reconsidered.

Tucking the 9mm pistol beneath her pillow, Janet lay her head down and closed her eyes. Tonight she would snuggle up with the only lover she'd had since Jack Gregory. Tomorrow she would set out to find him.

CHAPTER 34

"Gone! What the hell do you mean, *gone*?"

Setting his coffee down on the table, Altmann felt the blood rush into his face as he rose to his feet. Dolf Gruenberg towered over him, as inscrutable as if he'd just informed Altmann that the kitchen was out of eggs for breakfast.

"Sir, according to Avianca Airlines, first-class passengers Stefan Rosenstein and Jacob Bensheim departed El Alto International Airport at 4:45 A.M., bound for Miami, Florida, with connections through Atlanta to Tel Aviv."

"Where the hell were Lars and Thomas while this was going on? Sleeping?"

"In a manner of speaking. Police found them in Lars's car this morning, both dead with gunshots to the head. There was a half-empty bottle of scotch sitting on the console between them."

Altmann cursed, turning his back on Dolf as he moved to stand by the pool. He looked out toward the city but beheld the mental image of the dead men and the bottle of scotch.

"Were they drunk?"

"Police don't have the blood tests back, but unless they suddenly decided to splurge on a twenty-five-year-old bottle of Chivas, I wouldn't bet on it."

Pacing slowly back and forth, Altmann rolled this new information around in his head. Stefan Rosenstein was known to favor that brand and vintage of scotch. Add that to the senator's hasty departure in the company of his ex-Mossad bodyguard, and the pieces of the puzzle started to fall into place. Although Jacob Bensheim was good, it was a safe bet that he hadn't killed Altmann's men. Someone else in Senator Rosenstein's employ had done that. The Ripper.

Altmann stopped pacing and turned back to face Dolf.

"Where is Janet Mueller?"

"She packed a few of her things in a small backpack and left before sunrise. It looked like she was headed out to collect the bounty on Gregory. The funny thing was she didn't take her fancy sniper rifle."

"How did she leave?"

"She asked for a car, and I gave her one of ours."

"And where is it now?"

"According to the GPS tracker, it's parked a block from the police headquarters. The man I assigned to follow her reported that she parked the car on the street and then boarded a downtown city bus. Somewhere along the bus route, he lost track of her."

Altmann nodded. He'd come to expect nothing less from Janet Mueller. At least that part of this was going as he intended.

"That's okay. Let her go about her business."

A scowl darkened Dolf's pale features.

"And if she's dirty?"

Returning to his seat, Altmann took a sip from his coffee cup and allowed himself a grin.

"I'm counting on it."

: CHAPTER 35

Levi Elias noted the receipt of the specially encrypted message from Janet Price, once again tagged "Top Secret, NSA Director's Eyes Only." The large message size meant that she had attached images, or possibly even video. Damn it. Levi had been the one who had brought the talented and deadly young CIA operative to Jonathan Riles's attention. He was the reason the NSA had recruited her. Now, as far as Levi could tell, she'd been sent out on a mission where she was being denied one of the NSA's most important resources: Levi's analysis.

Clenching his fists, Levi made a potentially career-ending decision. Dialing Admiral Riles's admin, Levi started speaking as she picked up.

"Fred, this is Levi. I need to see Admiral Riles right now."

"I'm sorry. He's in a meeting with Dr. Kurtz and Dr. Jennings."

Levi felt his jaw muscles clench. "Tell him it's absolutely critical that I see him right now. This won't wait."

After a moment's hesitation, Frederica Barnes responded. "Hold, please."

A minute later, she spoke again. "Admiral Riles will see you now, in his office."

Levi hung up. Two minutes later he stepped into the NSA director's office and closed the door behind him.

"What's this about, Levi?"

"Sir, this is about Janet Price."

Admiral Riles's gray eyes narrowed. "Yes?"

Levi swallowed but continued. "I've noticed a number of the best NSA computing resources have been redirected from critical tasks and assigned new priorities. As with recent Janet Price activities, I have been denied knowledge of what those systems are now working on. I demanded this meeting because I want to know why I have been excluded from the inner circle on Janet's current mission."

This time there was no doubt about the irritation that had crept into the admiral's voice. "Demanded?"

"Yes, sir. You know that I'm the best analyst you have. The fact that you placed me in my current position confirms that. Yet you have reassigned the NSA's most important field operative to a mission in Bolivia that involves Tupac Inti and multiple neo-Nazi organizations, only to cut me out of the operation after I set up Janet's Golden Dawn cover. That tells me a number of things.

"This has nothing to do with my initial assumption that her mission is associated with fears that a free Tupac Inti might lead a native revolution that could topple a number of corrupt South American governments. This is about something else, something in which you don't trust me to be involved. The only reason I can come up with is because I'm Jewish."

Now Riles's eyes held real anger. "I'm not in the habit of justifying my operational decisions to subordinates, even one as important as you."

Levi's gut cramped. This was it. "Sir, I'm not asking you to justify your decision. I'm asking you to change it. In the past, you've relied upon my skills and loyalty, including a recent operation that ensured our nation's survival. If I've lost your trust at that level, then I'm here to submit my resignation."

Levi watched as the anger slowly drained from Admiral Riles's face, replaced by a look of deep sadness. Levi felt his own mood darken. Apparently his gambit was about to be accepted. All he had to look forward to now was participating in the required human resources and security out-briefings and signing the required paperwork.

Admiral Riles leaned back in his chair, and Levi took what might be his last look at the NSA director, framed by the view through those copper-infused black windows. God help him, but he loved this place.

"Levi, I wanted to avoid this, but you've forced my hand. I'm going to give you what you've asked for and bring you in on this. You might not thank me for it."

As relief flooded his mind, Levi had to restrain himself from grinning. Not trusting his voice, he only nodded.

Admiral Riles continued. "You've heard of the rumors of Adolf Hitler's ties to the Thule Society?"

"Yes, but it's bullshit. The Thule Society disbanded in the mid-1920s. Even though many of its members joined the Nationalsozialistische Deutsche Arbeiterpartei, otherwise known as the Nazi Party, Hitler himself despised occultism."

"True. But some of his lieutenants maintained their fascination and used Hitler's quest for priceless art and historical artifacts as an excuse to search for items of mythic power. As the allies closed in, their search became more and more desperate, like a dying prayer."

Levi snorted. "A complete waste of time and resources."

"Yes it was. That brings me to Klaus Barbie."

"I'm pretty sure the Butcher of Lyon never associated with the Thule Society or its followers," Levi said. "He was a sadist whose only gods were pain and suffering."

"He had one other. Barbie was a true believer in the Nazi Party. During one of the brutal interrogations he conducted in Lyon, he learned of an object among the thousands in Hitler's stolen art trove, one that had attracted the attention of three of the Führer's top scientists—not because it held some mystic power, but because of the intricate symbols inscribed on its surface, symbols on rotating rings that could form a myriad of mathematical equations."

Seeing Levi's confusion, Admiral Riles paused. "Let me show you something. Come around so you can see my monitor."

As Levi walked around the desk to stand by his boss's chair, he saw a set of images tiled across the admiral's thirty-inch display. All of the pictures showed a stunningly beautiful golden orb made up of concentric rings with detailed symbols etched into their surfaces. The orb sat atop a black cushion, and it had been photographed from all angles. In the last few photographs, the orb had been turned upside down to allow the bottom to be captured.

Admiral Riles continued. "You're looking at photographs of the object I mentioned. They were taken last night by Janet Price."

Levi found himself unable to take his eyes from the captured images. To think that last night Janet had held it in her hand boggled the mind.

"Where? How?"

"Conrad Altmann's private office. Drs. Kurtz and Jennings managed to remotely bypass Altmann's security measures. Janet did the rest."

"It's beautiful, but I still don't understand its significance. I'm assuming you don't believe it has some sort of mystical power."

"Of course not. And that wasn't what fascinated the German scientists. The mathematical equations formed by the symbols on the orb and its silver staff did that. Despite more than two years of study, they were unable to solve them."

"How old is the orb?"

"The first references to the object come from a set of Incan stone carvings carbon-dated to the thirteenth century AD."

Levi found himself struggling to make sense of this revelation.

"You're telling me the German scientists couldn't solve a set of equations from the thirteenth century?"

"Yes. And although we didn't have pictures of the orb, we did have complete images of the symbols carved into its silver staff. For the last three years, I've had some of our best systems continuously working on finding solutions for the fractal patterns that wind around its length."

Levi felt his anticipation rise as Admiral Riles paused.

"And?"

"And despite all of our advanced technology, we've come no closer than the Germans. We're hopeful that by using these new images of the orb to generate a 3D model of the completed staff and feeding it to the quantum computer, it will find the solution."

Levi studied the images on the screen, feeling his fascination grow as he looked. A new question found its way to his lips.

"The solution to what?"

Admiral Riles leaned back in his chair and met Levi's questioning gaze.

"That is a very good question."

CHAPTER 36

Jack needed sleep, but he didn't want it. Sleep meant dreams, and lately his dreams had left him more exhausted than when he'd gone to sleep. He had two mutually exclusive cures for that need. Self-discipline and adrenaline.

Today he chose adrenaline. As the morning sun began to burn off the mountain fog, Jack leaned the Honda Shadow motorcycle into curves so narrow and tight that they flooded his body with his drug of choice. The steep, densely-wooded cliff face on his left and the two-thousand foot drop on his right amplified the feeling a hundredfold.

The unpaved, single-lane North Yungas Road, commonly referred to as the Bolivian Death Road, was generally regarded as the world's most dangerous highway. Jack could have taken Highway 1 and then Highway 4 to Cochabamba and avoided the perilous mountain route, but where was the fun in that?

Seeing an oncoming truck, Jack hugged the right edge, the Honda Shadow sending a cascade of small rocks and gravel over the precipice as he accelerated past the lumbering vehicle. The road pulled him forward along its twists and turns like an anaconda swallowing a rodent. Jack could no more fight the feeling than he could stop breathing.

He knew his life should be flashing before his eyes, but it wasn't. Janet Price had once accused him of having a death wish, but she was wrong. Jack hungered for life, especially the thrill he got out there on life's edge, knowing full well that someday the edge would take him. But not today.

Jack put the high Andes behind him, passed through the city of Cochabamba, and rode Highway 7 to Santa Cruz. By the time he reached his rental house, afternoon rain clouds hid the sun, leaving the muggy air heavy with portents of the coming storm. Jack dropped the kickstand, stepped off the black motorcycle, and removed his helmet, feeling the first fat raindrops spatter his face.

As he retrieved the house key from his pocket and reached for the doorknob, a feeling of wrongness caused him to set his helmet on the doorstep and shift his keys to his left hand. Pausing to listen, Jack heard only the swish of branches in the gathering wind, the patter of rain, and the rumble of distant thunder. It was the familiar scent of danger that caused him to shift his H&K from its holster to his jacket pocket as he unlocked the door with his left hand. Vaguely familiar, like an unremembered dream, the feeling pulled him forward.

With his right hand gripping the pistol, Jack pushed open the door. The sight of Janet Price, relaxing on his ragged couch, froze him in his tracks. As her eyes met his, an easy smile parted her lovely lips.

"Hello, Jack. Did you miss me?"

CHAPTER 37

"Hello, Jack. Did you miss me?"

Janet looked into Jack's surprised face and was rewarded by a fleeting look that answered her question in the affirmative. Then he picked up his helmet and stepped inside, shutting the door behind him. When he turned back toward her, she saw him take his gun from his leather jacket's right pocket and return it to its shoulder holster.

Jack set his motorcycle helmet on the kitchen table and then walked over and sat down opposite her on the couch, his eyes glassy and tired.

Janet laughed. "Not exactly what I expected, Jack. Anger, yes. Bewilderment, maybe. Wild-eyed joy, hopefully. Collapsing on the couch next to me, not so much."

Jack managed a thin smile. "Actually, you should be flattered."

"Really?"

"I think so. Sort of like an old married couple."

"Such a smooth talker. You're sweeping me right off my feet."

Then, to her utter amazement, Jack Gregory closed his eyes, took one deep breath, and fell sound asleep.

CHAPTER 38

It was night when the smell of pork chops frying on the stove brought Jack back to consciousness. For the first time in recent memory, he'd slept a peaceful and dreamless sleep. As he looked at the back of the deadly NSA agent cooking dinner on the far side of the room, he experienced a brief déjà vu moment that passed before he could make the mental connection.

Hearing him move, Janet glanced back over her shoulder. "Good, you're awake. I hope you're hungry."

"Starved," Jack said, stretching and rising to his feet.

"It's nothing fancy—just chops and mashed potatoes."

"Smells great. Where'd you get the food?"

"I made a quick run to the market. Just the basics."

Janet served her own plate and took a seat at the kitchen table. Jack followed her example.

"How did you find me?"

Janet cut into her pork chop with knife and fork. "Eat first. Then we'll talk."

Feeling his stomach growl, Jack didn't argue.

Janet finished her meal before he did, and then sat and watched as Jack cleaned his second helping from his plate. When Jack finally pushed back from his plate and raised his eyes to meet Janet's, it seemed a shame that he was about to spoil the mood.

"Thank you. Best meal I've had in quite some time."

Janet smiled, although Jack thought he detected a sharp edge that hinted at the conversation to come.

He repeated his earlier question. "How did you find me?"

"Apparently, you've forgotten whom I work for."

"I've taken the standard precautions, wiped the laptop, advanced drive encryption, spoofed satellite uplink with anonymous Internet access—the works."

"A few months ago, that would have done the trick."

"But not now."

"The NSA continues to evolve. You have no idea what the organization is on the verge of accomplishing."

Jack felt a scowl tighten his face. "Sounds wonderful."

"You may be glad I found you."

"Why don't I get that warm, fuzzy feeling?"

Janet stood and walked over to sit on the couch. Leaving the dishes on the table, Jack moved to sit opposite her.

The ceiling's bare lightbulb fought to push back the shadows that had crept in near the room's corners, but it was a poor match for the bright flashes of lightning outside. As thunder shook the house, it began to rain much harder than before, the wind driving the fat drops hard enough to rattle the glass pane in its frame.

Jack continued to press her. "What are you doing with the neo-Nazis? And how is Tupac Inti involved?"

"Admiral Riles hasn't authorized me to answer that, but I'm going to anyway."

Her statement didn't surprise Jack. Since he'd first met Janet Price, he'd come to know that in the field she made her own operational assessments and acted on those judgments as she saw fit, regardless of the risk.

"Tupac Inti contacted the NSA first. He volunteered for this mission."

"You're trying to tell me that Tupac works for the NSA?"

"No. I'm saying that, in this specific instance, Tupac's goals aligned with those of Admiral Riles."

Jack looked at her as he analyzed her words. The way Janet had phrased her response struck an odd chord.

"You say that as if Admiral Riles is acting outside of his role as NSA director."

Janet shook her head. "Riles and the NSA are synonymous. He seeks out cyber-threats to our national security and neutralizes them."

"Which is how he justifies a field operative like you?"

"After 9/11, in addition to the Patriot Act, a number of presidential findings were issued to provide the United States government's intelligence agencies greater flexibility in identifying and combatting our nation's enemies. Admiral Riles believes one of those findings provides the NSA director with the authority to form an operational team that can confirm and augment electronic intelligence. As you know, I'm part of that team."

"And President Harris is fine with Admiral Riles's interpretation?"

"Occasionally, it's the job of our president's key subordinates to provide him with plausible deniability."

Jack laughed. "So what are you trying to tell me? That Tupac Inti volunteered to be locked up in Palmasola prison for a year and a half? That he wanted to be captured by the neo-Nazis?"

"That's part of it."

"What's your part? Why did Riles send you to Bolivia?"

"Because you came charging in to screw up his operation."

"Just doing the job I was hired to do."

"Who hired you?"

"You're NSA. You tell me."

Jack watched as the small muscles tightened at the corners of Janet's eyes.

"Damn it, Jack. Not everything is a contest."

"Isn't it? Isn't that what brought you here? To take me out of the game?"

"This isn't your game, Jack. Not unless you want it to be."

As he looked at Janet, her expression changed so subtly that Jack almost thought he imagined it. Staring at this amazing woman, he felt the old fire stir within. Damn, she was good.

Trying to keep the heat from his eyes, Jack focused on his response.

"I told you in Crete that I'm not interested in working for the NSA."

"Actually, you told me that I wouldn't want you anywhere around me."

"You should have listened."

"Admiral Riles's offer still stands."

"And I'm still not interested. Besides, I'm on a job."

Janet paused in her staccato delivery, her contact-blue eyes searching his face like synthetic aperture radar penetrating dense rainforest canopy.

"Tupac doesn't want to be rescued."

"That's funny, considering he came along willingly when I busted him out of Palmasola. How do you explain that?"

Janet shrugged. "I can't. But let me ask you something. When we took Tupac away from you, he was just sitting in a stream bed under a deadfall, just like he was waiting for us. Why would he do that?"

"Because I told him to stay put."

Janet laughed. "Tupac Inti isn't the kind of man who takes orders. He's a West Point grad who quit the Bolivian army because he didn't like the kinds of orders he was getting. Didn't you ever wonder why Bolivia's President Suarez, a member of Tupac's own Quechua tribe, never lifted a finger to help him get a fair trial? It's because Suarez fears Tupac. And with damn good reason."

As Jack thought back on it, he realized that Tupac's reaction had bothered him. But at the time, Jack had been too busy to worry about it.

"So I'm supposed to let a bunch of neo-Nazi pricks kick my ass, then just walk away?"

"I wouldn't call what happened in that jungle 'kicking your ass.'"

"They took someone I was hired to protect away from me. As I remember it, you helped."

Janet rose to her feet, crossed to the kitchen chair where she'd draped her leather jacket, slipped it on, and walked to the door. When she turned back to look at him, her face held a trace of disappointment.

"This is more important than one man. I'm not proposing that you abandon your job. All I ask is that you give me two weeks before you make your move. Jack, I need you to trust me on this one. Can you do that for me?"

As Jack watched Janet stare back at him, he found himself wishing that he wasn't so damn stubborn. Maybe then she'd be staying with him instead of preparing to step out into the night, with only a leather jacket to shield her from the tropical squall. But Jack couldn't change who he was, so he gave her the best he had to offer.

"I'll think it over."

CHAPTER 39

As the bitter winter wind howls through the night, attempting to prevent me from entering the cavern housing the Altar of the Gods, its chill pulls my breath forth in smoky puffs that I barely notice. I crawl through the opening, light a torch that I take from its wall sconce, and allow my feet to carry me through the passage that leads to the Altar. There my footsteps halt.

The beautiful golden orb that graces the end of the Incan Sun Staff captures my gaze. Its intricately carved rings and the gears and shafts that form its inner workings hold me in a spell. With my gaze locked to the symbols that cry out to be rearranged, a slow boiling fear floods my soul. Even as I stand alone, frozen in terror, in thrall to this wonder of wonders that rests atop the altar, I feel my hands move toward the orb of their own volition.

If the touch of the staff sends a mystic current through my body, the feel of the golden metal beneath my fingertips shifts my perspective and causes the cavern to shrink around me until I can see myself. It is as if I have become the cavern and everything within it. The thing in my head screams in a way that I have only heard in my dreams, and my body shakes like the boughs of the trees out in that howling wind. Yet my hands continue to stroke the orb.

Now they twist it, first the bottom ring, aligning the symbols with new counterparts on the silver staff, before skipping up several rings to repeat the process. And as my hands turn ring after ring in a seemingly random order, the intricate engravings grab the torchlight so that its flames crawl across the golden surface and into the orb's interior.

Shaking uncontrollably, my hands nevertheless turn the next-to-last ring until all the symbols feel wrongfully right, so much of the torchlight now absorbed by the orb that the cavern grows dark around me.

My right hand now wraps the last of the circular rings in a death grip as my left hand clutches the silver staff; the muscles in my hands and arms bulge and slither beneath my skin as they war with each other for control. Cold, more deadly than ice, slides through my veins and into my chest, cramping my lungs on its way to my heart. Then with a final convulsion, my fingers twitch, imparting to the topmost ring one final shift. As the golden orb comes free from the staff, my undying scream echoes from the cavern walls.

~ ~ ~

The wind-whipped rain drenched Jack's naked body as lightning crawled through the night sky overhead. With a sound like ripping cardboard, the leading edge of thunder crackled and then shook the ground with its fury, its reverberations shaking him awake. Jack felt the H&K hanging at his side, in his right hand, his thumb telling him that he'd flicked off the safety, his index finger having invaded the sanctuary of the trigger guard.

Jack stood in the midst of the raging storm, struggling to comprehend how he had gotten here. Having never sleepwalked in his life, he had apparently grabbed his pistol from the nightstand, gotten out of bed, and walked outside to stand in the rain. Judging by the amount of water sluicing off his body, he'd been standing here for several minutes.

As he stood alone, trying desperately to wrap his mind around what had just happened, a single thought filled Jack's head.

Not good!

CHAPTER 40

Despite the late hour, Dr. Priscilla McCoy, or Bones, as everyone but her mother called her, sat at her terminal. Her nickname had been based on her snarky personality rather than on any physical resemblance to the *Star Trek* doctor. She stood five foot two in boots and had a serious face, framed by shoulder-length blond hair. Men thought her pretty, but she had no time for relationships. Though she'd gotten her last name from her Scottish father, she'd gotten her physical appearance from Anna, her Austrian mother. But Bones had long known that she'd inherited her brilliant mind from her mother's secret lover. It was a secret that she and her mom had shared together.

Having graduated at the tender age of thirty with a triple doctorate from Caltech, some would call Bones a late bloomer. They would be wrong. Bones was about to change the world.

Staring at the digital package that Dr. David Kurtz had pushed to her workstation, Bones felt a thrill straighten the fine hairs on the back of her neck. Mathematics was her god, quantum theory her goddess, computer hardware her Olympus. Bones could do in her head differential equations that stumped some of the world's best mathematicians.

Grand mistress of the world's most advanced computing environment, Bones needed no monitor, mouse, or keyboard. The 3D motion capture field before her precisely recorded the movements of her hands and fingers, letting her issue instructions and evaluate data far more efficiently than she would have been capable of using the archaic tools. Her right hand touched the holographic projection of the golden orb. With a flick of her fingers, she spun the image, first about the *Z* axis and then through the *Y* and *X* axes before bringing it to a stop.

Bones began manipulating the stacked rings, rotating each independently so that she could study the interplay of the engraved symbols as they moved in relation to each other. Something became immediately apparent within the simulation. The symbols were not only moving, but they were transforming due to the movements of the orb's internal mechanism. *Fascinating.* Although the 3D model Dr. Kurtz had delivered was very good, its internal model was incomplete, having been based on the limited views the available pictures provided of the device's inner clockwork mechanism. No matter. Bones had at her disposal the colossal computing power necessary to infer the missing parts.

Spreading both hands, she made a tossing motion, and fifteen more copies of the orb appeared, arranged in a plane before her. As if she were playing cat's cradle, Bones drew her hands apart, creating a sixteen-by-sixteen cube of the golden orbs. Her motions as smooth and precise as those of a Tai Chi master, she shrank the cube of orbs until it was no larger than a six-sided die. Then she duplicated that into a line of cubes, and then a plane, and then a new cube of cubes. Judging the assigned computational priority to be sufficient, Bones initiated the processes that would compute all of the golden orb's possible internal solutions.

Having recently moved from experimental laboratories into use here at the NSA, quantum computing was a relatively new capability. Bones had engineered the breakthrough that enabled large-scale quantum stability at room temperature, thereby bringing herself to the NSA's attention. It was the only place she'd ever wanted to work. The NSA was the goal that had made her continue her Caltech research while all her classmates were being snapped up by Google and its competitors. But even though the commercial sector offered far more money, the NSA was the only organization that operated without limits. And for what Bones had in mind, *she didn't need no stinkin' limits.*

Quantum computing was as close to magic as anything modern technology provided. Traditional computers solved problems one instruction at a time, limited by the speed of the processor. Those limitations on computing speed had been attacked by spreading the computation across multiple processors, with the most advanced machines throwing thousands or even millions of processors at the most complex problems. There were also limitations on this approach, the most important being the physical hardware requirement for each of the microprocessors and its associated connections.

But by taking advantage of the quantum mechanical properties of superposition and entanglement, it was possible for a single quantum computer to perform calculations many orders of magnitude faster than all of the world's supercomputers combined. Most so-called authorities on the subject thought quantum computing was still in its infancy, but the NSA's QB4096 was no baby. If anything, it was a baby killer.

Not a particularly pleasant analogy, but Bones thought it appropriate. The NSA's enemies whined about invasions of personal privacy, but personal privacy had been extinct long before the turn of the millennium. It was only a matter of time until new machines picked up and interpreted people's thoughts as they walked around the shopping mall.

As Aldous Huxley forecast, the human race stood at the door to a brave new world. And Dr. Priscilla "Bones" McCoy was about to take her size-six leather boot and kick that door off its hinges.

CHAPTER 41

The darkness that draped Tupac Inti was complete. If he squeezed his eyes tightly closed, he could see the ethereal flashes that the mind and optic nerve created, but those wandering ghost lights provided him no comfort. The darkness did that.

In his years working the notoriously dangerous Bolivian mines, there had been many times that he and his fellow miners had been temporarily stranded due to minor cave-ins or the loss of power routed down from above. In the last of those incidents, Tupac had waited twelve days in the darkness for the drills to break through. Although he and the seven others trapped with him had taken turns using their headlamps to provide some cheer for those who had needed it, the final battery had failed on day six in the depths.

But darkness had never terrified Tupac. The overabundance of carbon dioxide and the lack of oxygen had done that. When the drill had finally punched an airhole into their small chamber, Tupac's yells of joy had echoed through that space along with the others. When he'd finally been pulled up through the narrow rescue shaft to emerge into the night air, Tupac had spread his arms wide as if to embrace the star-filled sky. He'd had no urge whatsoever to kiss the ground.

Tupac heard the grinding squeak of rusty hinges announce the arrival of his host in the dungeon. Then the light from the naked bulb outside his cell knifed through the bars and into his eyes, forcing him to turn away as his pupils reacted to the unaccustomed illumination. The sound of footsteps on damp stone drew close and then stopped outside his cell. Keys rattled and then clanked against the lock.

Squinting up at the backlit figures that stepped inside, Tupac saw the neatly brushed, shoulder-length, gray-blond hair and beard of Conrad Altmann more clearly than he saw the man's face. Altmann walked up close to the corner where Tupac sat chained to the floor, staying just far enough away to avoid entering the filth that had accumulated around Tupac's naked form.

When Altmann spoke, his voice was filled with false sympathy.

"Hello, Tupac. Have no fear. Today I bring only questions, not pain. If you answer my questions satisfactorily, you can shed these chains. Think of it. I offer you a hot shower, clean clothes, and a room with a real bed and toilet. You'll get good food and water instead of the disgusting gruel you've endured these last few days."

Although Tupac had prepared himself for this ordeal, he couldn't stop the visualization Altmann's words created in his mind, couldn't keep the want out of his eyes. But he managed to keep it out of his voice.

"I can only tell you what I know."

Altmann's grin held no mirth. "That will do nicely. What do you know of an artifact known as the Incan Sun Staff?"

"Never heard of it."

The neo-Nazi's cold eyes narrowed. "You see why I have such trouble treating you in a civilized fashion? You promise me truth and deliver only lies."

"Maybe you could describe it to me."

"I hardly think that is necessary. You have it tattooed on your chest."

Tupac glanced down at the bold image that emblazoned the left side of his chest. "Ahh. You mean the Staff of Manco Capac."

"Whatever you prefer to call it."

Tupac paused. The longer he could drag this out, the less torture he would have to endure. He had promised Admiral Riles that he could endure anything the neo-Nazis could put him through for two weeks. That two weeks had been part of his deal. Then he could tell Altmann what he wanted to know, but not before. That meant he had to make it through eleven more days of this.

Looking up at Altmann's face, at his perfectly groomed beard and hair, Tupac had an almost overwhelming desire to puke all over the bastard's leather shoes. But he restrained himself.

"Where have you hidden the silver staff?"

"What makes you think I have it?"

Altmann chuckled, a sound that reminded Tupac of the clicking of crab pincers.

"Legend says that when Pizarro separated the golden orb crown piece from its silver shaft, he sent the orb to the King of Spain, but he presented the staff to his puppet emperor, Manco Inca II. The true keepers of Incan lore thought Manco Inca II unworthy, and subsequently stole the silver staff. Its hiding place is said to have been passed down from generation to generation of lore keepers. There the silver staff awaits the day when a worthy successor will reunite the silver staff with its golden crown piece and use the restored Sun Staff to resurrect the Incan Empire."

Altmann bent down, extended a finger, and poked Tupac on the left side of his chest. "In each generation, the next lore keeper in the line of succession is marked with this tattoo."

Now it was Tupac's turn to laugh, although it hurt his dry, cracked lips to do so.

"Actually, after I graduated from West Point, a couple of my buddies took me to New York City to celebrate. Apparently I had a very good time, because I woke up with this. Until right now, I had no idea what it meant."

Altmann straightened, his grin transforming into a grimace that allowed the hate to leak from his blue eyes.

Turning to the three men who waited outside the cell, Altmann issued his instructions in a clipped tone. "Get him cleaned up, and strap him down to the cart while I change into some work clothes. Strap the rubber plug in his mouth. I don't want him biting off that forked tongue before I straighten it out."

CHAPTER 42

Janet Price signed her name as Janet Schuster, checking into the Los Tajibos Hotel and Convention Center at noon. A fifty-dollar tip to the uniformed front desk attendant ensured that Janet didn't have to wait for her second-floor, pool-view room, despite her early check-in. Having outfitted herself in a three-button black blazer over a sleeveless white shirt, straight-legged black trousers, and sensible but sexy black platform shoes, she fit seamlessly into her role as a successful woman visiting Santa Cruz on business.

Janet let the bellhop ferry her suitcase to the room, but kept her laptop case with her as she made her way upstairs. The four-star hotel was one of the nicer business travel locations in Santa Cruz, and Janet found her spacious room more than adequate.

Another twenty-dollar bill accompanied her request to the bellhop that he notify the front desk that she didn't want to be disturbed until tomorrow morning. Janet reinforced this by hanging the "Do Not Disturb" sign outside her door and engaging the security lock.

Moving to the desk, Janet opened her case and removed the laptop she'd purchased two hours ago, turned it on, and ran through the process of establishing her log-in, password, and preferences. She knew this laptop wasn't secure and would be accessing the Internet through an unsecure WiFi connection, but that didn't matter.

When she logged onto the Internet, Janet navigated to one of the many sites that appeared benign but were actually NSA portals; such a site allowed someone who knew how to navigate it to download the specialized tools that could turn any computer, tablet, or cell phone into a digital fortress. Although the software equivalent of a Swiss Army knife could be downloaded and installed in a matter of minutes, the applications Janet wanted took just over two hours to retrieve, install, and configure.

Thirty minutes into the process, Janet removed her jacket and hung it in the closet. She left her shoulder holster in place, so used to the weight and feel of the Glock beneath her left arm that it was distracting to remove it. Stepping to the window, Janet looked out over the beautifully landscaped pool area with its majestic palms and the appealing gentle curves of the deck. The hotel had managed to avoid the overcrowding of deck chairs that turned many such pool areas into a close approximation of the worst Las Vegas had to offer.

Just after three o'clock in the afternoon, Janet sent the message that requested an encrypted video chat session with Admiral Riles. She didn't have to wait long; the active session available notification popped up on her screen eight minutes later. When she clicked the "Connect" button on the video chat application, Janet was surprised to see Levi Elias's serious face looking out of the screen at her.

"Hello, Janet."

"Hi, Levi. I was expecting Admiral Riles."

"He's delegated this to me."

Janet paused. She'd been told that the NSA director had limited this operation to a very tight group that didn't include the NSA's curly-haired chief analyst. Although that had raised a lot of questions in Janet's mind at the time, she'd known her role and hadn't asked a follow-up question. Having always valued Levi's take on situations, she was glad to accept this change. Based on the way she'd routed this chat request, it had gone first to Riles and then been assigned to Levi, so she had no reason to go over Levi's head with her questions.

"I wasn't informed of the change."

She heard irritation worm its way into Levi's voice.

"I've just informed you."

True enough. Besides, internal NSA politics were well above her pay grade.

"Understood."

"What's your situation?"

"I've made contact with Jack Gregory."

"And?"

"I've asked him to give me two weeks before making a move to free Tupac."

Janet noted the flash of concern on Levi's face before he wiped it away.

"What did you tell him about our operation?"

"Only that Tupac had volunteered for this and doesn't want to be rescued until he has completed his part of the mission."

"Why two weeks?"

Janet didn't like the answer she had for him, but Levi needed to know.

"It's how long Riles told Tupac the NSA needed to get pictures of the orb and break the codes it contains."

As she watched Levi's face over the video link, she saw the realization of what that meant hit him.

"So Riles bet the farm that we could solve it in that amount of time."

"And that Tupac could hold out that long."

"Telling Jack what you did just added another big risk."

"The only other way to stop Jack is to kill him. All things considered, I think my way is far less risky."

Levi paused to consider her words. "Okay, but now that Jack knows that Tupac is cooperating with us, the information could be exposed to Conrad Altmann."

"Jack may not do as I asked, but there's no chance that Altmann could extract any information from him, even in the unlikely scenario that he managed to capture Jack."

Janet switched subjects. "Any update on cracking the orb's codes?"

"It's taking longer than we anticipated, so Admiral Riles has assigned the task top priority on our newest supercomputer."

"Tupac won't complete his part of this unless I get him the answer. If he breaks under Altmann's torture before that happens, the operation is blown."

"I'm well aware of that."

Once again, Janet changed topics.

"I haven't been able to learn where Altmann's people are holding Tupac. Based on Altmann's helicopter's fuel usage, it probably lies on an arc approximately two hundred and fifty kilometers from his La Paz estate."

Without bothering to consult any reference material, Levi responded. "Altmann has a second compound on the outskirts of Cochabamba. The distance is right. I'll send you the layout and any other information we have on it."

Janet smiled. There was a reason Levi had the reputation for being one of the world's best intelligence analysts. She was glad he'd been added to the list of people who Admiral Riles had read-in on this operation.

"I'll watch for it."

Janet found herself staring at the "Connection Terminated" dialogue box and closed the application. It looked like her planned stay at the Los Tajibos Hotel was going to be a lot shorter than she had thought. Knowing how efficiently Levi Elias normally operated, knowing how good he would feel about driving a stake through a significant part of the worldwide neo-Nazi movement, especially a part that was commanded by Klaus Barbie's bastard son, Janet expected the promised electronic package within minutes, not hours.

As she pushed back from the laptop and rose to make herself a cup of coffee, her thoughts turned to Jack. Although they'd both been exhausted in Kazakhstan, she'd never seen him as played out as he'd looked yesterday. She was pretty sure that no amount of fatigue, by itself, could do that to Jack Gregory.

The look in his eyes had worried her. When she'd first met Jack in Germany, he'd displayed an inner fire that had both thrilled and concerned her. Ever since she'd known him, Jack had been religious in his self-discipline, only giving in to his violent nature within the context of doing the job he'd signed on for.

It seemed like she'd known Jack for years, but they'd only shared one mission, Jack having been brought in as a reluctant security consultant. A few weeks had launched them through Germany, Austria, the Czech Republic, Kazakhstan, and finally Crete. It was funny how shared mortal danger could pack so much living into such a condensed window.

Something about Jack Gregory attracted him to danger in ways that, at times, seemed almost supernatural. His CIA records revealed that he had always displayed a highly developed intuitive sense. Janet worried that he was now starting to lose himself to that pull. And if Jack Gregory went into an out-of-control death spiral, there was no telling what—or who—else might be pulled across the resulting black hole's event horizon and swallowed up.

Unfortunately, Janet had once again entered Jack's gravitational pull. And despite the anger she felt at her inability to fight the feeling, she found herself questioning her own decisions. Levi was right. Going to Jack's house had been a stupid risk with little prospect of success. She had a bad feeling that despite what she'd asked of him, Jack was going to go for Tupac as soon as he found out where the man was being held. And with Jack's connections and resources, it wouldn't take him long.

Then why had she done it? Had it been just to see Jack again, to feel the heat of his inner flame? Well, she'd felt it. Now, how the hell was she going to get it out of her head?

Maybe she would have to kill him after all.

: CHAPTER 43

Jack liked Cochabamba. When it came to picking an ideal location, the founders of the self-proclaimed City of Eternal Spring had chosen wisely. With the perfect combination of latitude and altitude, Cochabamba split the difference between twelve thousand feet above mean sea level of La Paz and the fifteen hundred feet of Santa Cruz. At an elevation of a little over eight thousand feet, Cochabamba maintained a year-round daily average high in the mid-seventies on the Fahrenheit scale. Apparently that and the views had inspired the architects of Bolivia's fourth-largest city as well.

Having already been found by the NSA, Jack had spent Sunday relaxing in the same house, occupying his time with collecting information from his well-paid sources about Conrad Altmann's extensive Bolivian holdings and any helicopter activity near those areas last Wednesday night. The two prime candidates were the Altmann mountainside estate at a half-dozen kilometers outside of Cochabamba and a larger compound overlooking La Paz. Cochabamba was closer, so it was his logical first stop.

He wasn't concerned that the NSA would monitor his Internet activities. The information providers had used a standard method of embedding the encrypted information he had asked for within jpeg photographic files posted on a variety of public Facebook pages and porn sites. By using a custom decryption algorithm, Jack had extracted the embedded data from the images, and though the NSA could detect his access, nothing he did revealed his sources, masked as they were by the millions of hits those sites received daily.

He'd left the motorcycle and laptop in Santa Cruz. After purchasing a primer-gray, eight-year-old Toyota Camry, Jack had swapped plates and then paid a visit to Diego Vega, an old acquaintance with whom he'd done business during his last visit to Bolivia, the first time Jack's services had been contracted by Senator Stefan Rosenstein. A Shining Path Maoist rebel fighter in his younger days, Diego's rotund body had long been ill-suited for active combat, or even for short hikes. Although Diego had never liked Jack, he liked the money Jack paid him, and after all, business was business. Altogether, this morning's business had cost Jack one hundred seventy-five thousand Bolivianos, roughly twenty-five thousand American dollars.

Now, with the late afternoon sun having just sunk below the Andes, Jack had settled into a hide location in the deep brush on the mountain ridge that overlooked Conrad Altmann's Cochabamba estate. The Dragunov sniper rifle he had wasn't his favorite, but in a situation like this, where extremely long shots would not be required, it would get the job done. Having stopped in the middle of Bolivian nowhere on his way from Santa Cruz to Cochabamba, he'd zeroed the scope to his satisfaction and loaded a half-dozen of the 10 round box magazines with 7N14 rounds.

But unless his luck was far worse than usual tonight, he wouldn't be firing the weapon, just using the night-vision sight. Still, it never hurt to be ready to bite back if the dogs of war came sniffing around.

With the onset of twilight, the temperature began to fall, on its way toward the mid-fifties if the weather forecast was to be believed. For a man about to spend the night nestled into the trees and thick brush, looking through a night-vision scope, you couldn't ask for much better. The waning full moon didn't hurt either.

Five hundred meters of steep slope separated Jack from the southwestern corner of the Altmann compound. From where he lay, he could see the main house and the much smaller foreman's quarters, surrounded on the east, south, and west sides by an eight-foot-high, concrete outer wall topped with triple-strand concertina razor wire, the type of fortifications you would expect to see around a custom wheels-and-rims shop in east Los Angeles.

A paved driveway entered through an electronic gate on the south side of the compound. Once inside the gate, a three-car garage jutted out of the southeast side of the main house, and a helipad and a small foreman's house occupied the southwestern portion of the compound.

The north side of the Altmann house formed a U-shape that enclosed a large pool area, complete with hot tub. The open end of the U dropped away in a hundred-foot cliff that provided rear security and a beautiful view across the valley to the mountains northwest of the city.

Jack could see a total of six guards outside, two at the gatehouse manning the double-wide electric gate that allowed cars in and out of the compound. The other four were split between two towers positioned at the southeast and southwest corners of the outer walls. He had read that an eighteenth-century Spanish landowner's mansion had once occupied this spot, but Jack couldn't quite envision it. Taking in the guard towers, high walls, and razor wire, the Altmann compound had more of a high-end, white-collar prison look about it.

As the night progressed, Jack nibbled on some surplus military rations, mixed a packet of freeze-dried instant coffee into his canteen, and watched the Altmann compound's night routine. The guard shift change arrived in a van on a rough six-hour interval, the actual replacement happening at 9:00 P.M., then again at 3:24 A.M., with some agitation displayed by the crew awaiting replacement. The morning shift change took place at 9:00 A.M. and had only been on duty for thirty minutes when Jack heard the inbound helicopter.

As it flew in from the northwest, Jack recognized it as the same Chinese H425 model that he'd seen before. Letting the scope reticle follow the chopper all the way down to the helipad, Jack watched as a well-dressed man walked out to meet it. Conrad Altmann stepped off the aircraft, wearing a dark sports jacket, tan shirt, and khaki slacks. The man from the compound walked through the rotor wash beneath the spinning blades, extending his hand and wearing a welcoming smile.

Altmann accepted the greeting as he continued walking toward the main house. As Jack tracked the neo-Nazi crime lord away from the aircraft, new movement drew his attention back to the helicopter. Shifting the scope to the person rounding the front of the helicopter from the pilot's side, duffle bag in hand, he felt his pulse jump up a notch. There, centered in the reticle, her dyed blond hair secured in a tight bun with the icepick-sharp hair needle she favored, was the beautiful face of the NSA's Janet Alexandra Price.

CHAPTER 44

Conrad Altmann hadn't been pleased when Janet Mueller arrived at his La Paz estate, asking to accompany him on this morning's flight to Cochabamba. He'd been less pleased when he'd learned that she knew that he had Tupac Inti imprisoned there. But her insistence that Jack Gregory would learn where Tupac was being held and come for him made sense. So did her desire to be waiting when The Ripper showed up, so he'd agreed to let her and her duffel bag hitch a ride on his helicopter.

As Altmann walked toward the main house, with Renaldo Rodriguez at his side, he let Janet catch up as best she could. Chatting with his estate foreman, Altmann spared Janet a glance. To see her strolling along behind them as casually as if she were enjoying a walk through the park shouldn't have surprised him, but it did. If Dolf hadn't been able to rattle the Golden Dawn's assassin then he had no right to expect that a bit of impoliteness would do the trick. What awaited her in the dungeon below the house just might.

By the time Renaldo opened the door to the descending stairwell, Janet Price had set her duffel bag down and caught up, having done so with no apparent effort. Once more Altmann found his eyes drawn to her. Ah, to have young legs again. Even better, to have young legs wrapped around him. It was a thought that put a real smile on his face. After all, he was a man of power, and she was clearly an ambitious and capable young woman. Assuming she didn't force him to have her killed, such a liaison would make sense.

The steel-bound wood door at the bottom of the stairwell sent an echoing groan through the dark tunnels as Renaldo pushed it open and flicked on the light switch just inside on the right. Other than their own noises, Altmann heard no sounds, not even the squeaking of rats or the periodic drip of water from the damp ceiling. The silence didn't worry him. Except for when he tickled Tupac Inti's flesh with electrical current, the Quechua shaman made no sound.

Altmann expected to see a hint of shock in Janet's eyes at the sight of the bedraggled, filthy, and starving Tupac Inti, with the electric scratch and burn marks on his chest, stomach, and thighs, but he was disappointed. Instead she laughed, as if the sight were one of the funniest things she'd ever seen.

"Oh my God," she croaked. "You can't be serious."

"You find this funny?"

"Well, yeah. You told me not to kill this man until you're done with him, and now I see you're about to kill him yourself. Don't worry. So long as he's dead when I return to Greece, I get paid regardless of how it happened."

Altmann gritted his teeth. This bitch had a real talent for pissing him off. Gianakos had probably sent her to Bolivia just to get her out of the country. He found himself tempted to have his men chain her down beside Tupac. But Dolf wasn't here, and he doubted that the three men who accompanied him could pull that off. Altmann made a mental note to make sure Janet Mueller didn't make it out of Bolivia alive. In the meantime, he still wanted to see if he could get some use out of her.

"I've been doing this long enough to get pretty good at it. Some would say very good."

"So what has he told you?"

Altmann stifled an urge to slap her.

"Sometimes these things take time. You think you can do better?"

She smiled. "I guarantee it."

"You willing to bet your life on it?"

"I do that every time I get out of bed."

Altmann stared at her. Then he stepped back, motioning her toward Tupac with a wave of his arm. "Okay. He's all yours."

When Janet didn't move, he frowned. "You have a problem with it?"

"If I do this, I do it my way, one hundred percent."

Altmann shrugged. "So long as I get my answers and he's still mobile and able to talk when you're done."

"Fine. And when Gregory comes for Tupac, you'll have a twofer. I'll need a list of questions you want answered."

Nodding his agreement, Altmann watched Janet shift her attention to Renaldo, issuing instructions in a tone that indicated that Altmann had just fired Dolf and made her his new number two. It actually sent chills up his spine.

"I want this cell scrubbed and disinfected. I don't work standing in piss and shit. Get Inti properly cleaned up, and put some clothes on him. This Abu Ghraib bullshit doesn't work for me. Give him some good food and water, and make sure he gets a good night's sleep. For what I'm about to do to him, he's going to need his strength. In the meantime, if you'll show me to my room, I'll put together a list of items I'll be needing."

Renaldo glanced at Altmann and, seeing no objection, echoed her instructions to his two men. Then he turned and led Janet Mueller out of the dungeon. Altmann watched her depart, the sharp shadows cast by the bare incandescent bulbs serving to accentuate her lithe form.

As Altmann followed her, a worm of doubt wriggled its way from his subconscious mind into his conscious thoughts. Maybe he'd been wrong about this woman being dirty. If so, Dolf might have good reason to worry about his position in Altmann's organization.

At the stairwell, Altmann turned and looked back toward Inti's cell. One way or another, the next few days would tell.

CHAPTER 45

Tupac Inti felt the cold water splash him as one of his two guards used a spray nozzle to hose the filth from his body while the other man squeegeed and mopped the floor. After finishing their cleanup, one kept a tranquilizer gun trained on him as the other removed the shaman's wall chains. Then they closed and locked his cell and departed. It should have felt good to stand erect, but the last few days had taken such a toll on his body that Tupac barely managed it.

The clank and grind of the stairwell door opening interrupted his efforts at stretching out some of his cramped muscles. The man who pushed the tray through the chuck hole in the bottom of the cell door barked at him and tossed a set of dark gray sweat clothes and boxers at him.

"Put these on."

Tupac complied, surprised that they were large enough to fit him. He guessed that they must have belonged to the big

Albino man who'd commanded the team that had captured him. Apparently shoes or sandals weren't a part of the bargain.

The smell from the food tray pulled him to it. The plate was piled high with beans and rice, fried yucca, and a large hunk of bread. There was no silverware, but he wouldn't have used it if it had been provided. Lest they take the food away from him before he finished, Tupac shoveled it into his mouth and then mopped the plate with the bread. He washed the last of the meal down with a liter of water from the large plastic bottle.

Watching him finish, the guard pointed at the now-empty tray. "Push it all back out here."

Tupac shoved the tray and empty bottle through the slot and watched the bald man carry it away, switching off the light as he departed.

In the darkness his thoughts turned to the blond woman he'd only seen once before. She'd been with the neo-Nazis when they had recaptured him in the rain forest. She'd laughed in Conrad Altmann's face, and he'd done nothing about it. Tupac wouldn't have believed it if he hadn't just witnessed it. Now she was giving orders as if she was running the whole show. What in the name of the old gods was going on?

For the time being, he'd have to leave it alone. The food in his belly was pulling the blood from his head, and he was just so damn tired. He lay down and curled up on his right side, head resting on his arm, and gave thanks for the soft, warm sweat suit. More badness awaited him on the other side of sleep, but for right now, he'd try to stay awake and enjoy this feeling.

In the pitch-black dungeon cell, Tupac blinked once, then twice. The third time he closed his eyelids. They fluttered briefly but did not open again.

~ ~ ~

Tupac didn't hear his cell door open, but he felt rough hands roll him onto his stomach and cuff his hands to a belly chain. By the time he had struggled back to wakefulness, his feet had been shackled together with only a foot and a half of slack between them. When he was pulled to his feet, he noticed the steel operating table outside his cell. Beyond it, the blond woman stared at him, her blue eyes showing no hint of emotion. Beside her stood a grinning Conrad Altmann, expectation shining in his face.

Then a black cloth hood was pulled over his head, shutting out the view entirely. The two guards tugged hard on his arms and he shuffled forward, stumbled, and was roughly pulled back to his feet, before being thrown face up atop the table. Tupac felt thick leather straps bind his feet and upper torso so tightly that movement was impossible. The next strap locked his head in place, leaving him with the claustrophobic feeling of being in traction.

A soft, warm breath caressed Tupac's right ear, her whisper so soft that only he could hear it.

"This doesn't have to happen. Just answer one question. Where is the silver staff?"

Something about that warm breath and soft, sexy voice filled Tupac with a dread that he had difficulty suppressing. He hadn't seen any surgical instruments before the hood had been pulled over his head, but the table had blocked much of his view.

"I don't know what you're talking about."

Tupac's hearing was so finely attuned that he could hear a roach crawling across his cell floor. He found himself listening for the zing of surgical steel being removed from a case. Instead he felt a latch click and the table tilted back so that his head was lower than his feet.

What the hell?

The bucket of ice-cold water that splashed into his face and neck, soaking and compressing the cloth sack against his nose and mouth, surprised Tupac, causing him to gasp and cough. Worse, as the cloth absorbed water, it cut off his airflow. More water was poured down onto the sack that covered his head, more slowly now, just a steady trickle. Tupac's muscles spasmed, and his chest heaved as his body's natural drowning response kicked in.

As he fought to free himself, the metal surgical table shook, and the leather straps creaked and groaned. But they held. The bitch was waterboarding him. Tupac struggled to calm himself, but the claustrophobic grip of the straps combined with his inability to draw a breath thrust him into a mindless panic of coughing, sputtering madness. It was as if his conscious mind and his body had become disconnected. No matter how well he understood what she was doing to him, no matter how much he told himself he wasn't really drowning, his body bucked against the straps as it fought its way toward the imaginary surface of this death pool.

It took two minutes for him to realize that the water had stopped and that air was flowing back through the pores in the cloth again. It took another minute and a half before his breath stopped whistling in and out of his throat.

Then the warm breath was back, that soft voice whispering.

"Where is the silver staff?"

"Screw you, Nazi bitch!"

This time Tupac braced himself, but it did no good. He tried to draw a breath and failed, felt a scream climb out of his throat, but only managed a coughing fit that threw his body into another convulsive panic attack. He wanted to die and yet fought for life. In his despair, Tupac tried to yell, "Stop!"; tried to tell her where the staff was hidden; tried to offer to take her there. But the hell-bitch wouldn't let up, and he couldn't get the words out through the suffocating sack. When she finally stopped the flow of water, the moment of weakness had passed.

Again he heard her question, but this time Tupac met it with silence.

For the next hour the water torture continued, until Tupac was too exhausted to struggle.

When two small hands pulled the sack off his head, Tupac found himself looking into her face barely two inches from his own, felt a strand of her blond hair cling damply to his cheek. For the briefest of moments, he thought he saw sadness in those eyes, but decided it was just a trick of his fevered brain.

The woman straightened. "Put him back in his cell, and remove his chains. We'll start again in the morning."

CHAPTER 46

For the second day in a row, Jack Gregory remained in the sniper hide, getting a feel for the rhythms of Altmann's compound. Yesterday, when Conrad Altmann departed, Janet Price had not gone with him. She had remained inside throughout the remainder of the day and the night. When Altmann arrived aboard his helicopter again this morning, Jack had his confirmation. Tupac Inti was being held somewhere inside the main house, probably in the basement.

Janet was here to make sure that Jack didn't try to bust Tupac out. Because she was deep cover, she would be taking steps to protect Tupac while making it appear to Altmann that she was doing exactly the opposite. Whatever was happening in there, Jack figured that the big Quechua shaman was having some bad days. Jack only wished he knew more about what the NSA and Altmann wanted from the man.

Three hours after Conrad Altmann had climbed off his helicopter, he reappeared, and Janet stepped outside with him. The two faced each other, exchanging words. Jack let the scope reticle steady just above the bridge of the neo-Nazi's nose. Altmann's expression was a curious mix of excitement and frustration. Jack shifted his aim to Janet but could only see her back. Her gestures reminded Jack of a hostage negotiator calmly trying to talk a perp into releasing a hostage.

Again Jack shifted views. Altmann listened, nodded, then turned and walked to his helicopter. From the pool deck, Janet Price watched the chopper lift off and then turned to face up the mountainside toward the spot where Jack lay hidden. He watched her eyes carefully as she scanned the hillside. Jack lay in shadow, so there would be no telltale reflection from his scope, but she was doing exactly what he would have done had he stood in her place, seeking out the best spots for a sniper to hide. Her eyes looked directly at him and stopped, shifting ever so slightly as she studied the dense brush that provided an optimal view into the compound.

Just as he was beginning to wonder if he'd been made, she shifted her eyes to a spot higher up and to Jack's right, studying it just as carefully.

A minute later, she dropped her gaze and walked back into the house.

Jack crawled backward into a covered position, rose to his feet, and began working his way through dense brush to the spot he'd left the hiker's backpack. Removing the scope and custom stock, Jack disassembled the Dragunov rifle into three pieces, sliding them into slots on the tall backpack between the main compartment and the frame. Stowing the spare magazines inside an inner backpack pocket, he slipped the backpack over his shoulders, adjusted the straps, and began working his way through the steep woods toward a distant hiking trail.

By the time he reached it, he was just one more dirty ecotourist making his way out of the mountains, looking forward to a beer and a good night's rest at a cheap hotel. As his long strides carried him closer and closer to Cochabamba, Jack decided that, before he finalized his plans, he would take advantage of both of those luxuries.

Janet Price was an unwanted and dangerous complication, but she'd dangerously complicated his life once before, and he'd enjoyed it. The memory of a cool Mediterranean night, her warm body moving against his, stoked a hunger he'd been doing his best to repress. But as he hiked into Cochabamba and neared the hotel where he'd prepaid for a weeklong stay, he just couldn't get her out of his head.

CHAPTER 47

The afternoon cloud cover continued to lower over La Paz as Dolf began to wonder whether Bolivia's chief of intelligence would show. Based on the weather forecast, he had chosen to meet at this scenic outlook, knowing full well that nobody wanted to visit a place that normally provided a beautiful panoramic view of La Paz on an afternoon when visibility was limited to a few hundred meters.

As the meeting time came and went, Dolf felt his patience wane. He didn't have a lot of faith in General Esteban Montoya's competence, but he did count on the man's loyalty. After all, Conrad Altmann had long since bought and paid for it, and Altmann had enough blackmail material on the man to ensure his imprisonment if revealed.

Montoya did have one thing that interested Dolf Gruenberg: a high-level contact within Cuba's Directorate General of

Intelligence, or DGI. And that man, Chumo Garcia, had excellent connections to the Russian FSB. Like Conrad Altmann, Dolf hated the communists, and the current Russian government was a kissing cousin to its Stalinist ancestor. But under Klaus Barbie, Conrad Altmann had apprenticed and mastered the art of infiltrating intelligence services. In that world, the line between friends and enemies was loosely drawn based only on your current interest.

The sound of a shoe scraping gravel caught Dolf's attention, and he turned to see the heavyset general appear out of the thickening fog. General Montoya paused long enough to say something to the two security personnel who accompanied him and they stopped thirty meters from where Dolf waited, turning to look back down the hill in the direction from which they'd just come.

Dolf applied the fake grin that others found so winning, and shook the general's extended hand, resisting the urge to squeeze the flabby palm like a damp sponge.

As the general spoke, he stepped up to the edge of the low stone wall that surrounded the scenic lookout, and Dolf stepped up beside him, as if they were merely two tourists gazing out at the beautiful view. The fact that they couldn't see shit through the fog didn't seem to matter to General Montoya. It was stupid, but Dolf understood it. Few men felt comfortable looking up into Dolf's face as he gazed down at them. And only Conrad Altmann made Dolf feel that he was the one looking up.

"Perhaps you wouldn't mind telling me what is so sensitive that it requires pulling me out of my office to this lovely spot?" The general's voice was heavy with annoyance.

"There is someone whom Herr Altmann is interested in checking out. He would like you to have your DGI contact perform an extensive background search on her."

General Montoya turned toward Dolf. "Who is this person?"

"She goes by the name of Janet Mueller." Dolf handed the general a large manila envelope. "This is all the information we have on her. It includes background material from our European contacts, a photograph, and a set of prints I pulled from a drinking glass."

General Montoya undid the metal clip that secured the envelope and removed the contents, pausing to stare down at the full-page photograph that topped the sheaf of documents. A low whistle escaped his lips.

"Quite a looker."

Dolf said nothing.

Pushing the stack of papers back into the manila envelope, General Montoya nodded. "I'll notify Señor Altmann when I have his answer."

Dolf shook his head. "The packet is to be delivered directly to me."

The general's dark brown eyes narrowed. "Directly to you?"

"Herr Altmann would not like his European friends to think that he is questioning their information."

A knowing grin curled General Montoya's lips. "I see. If it should come to light that you did some unauthorized digging on your own, it would merely be an embarrassment instead of an affront."

Dolf nodded. "When I get the background file, twice the usual fee will be deposited into your account. If your DGI man's response also includes Fraulein Mueller's FSB file, there will be a matching bonus. But I need it in the next two days, three at the latest."

General Montoya's grin grew wider, revealing a mouthful of yellow, tobacco-stained teeth. "Any information my Cuban friend can find will be in your hands by Friday."

Then the general turned and walked back to where his men waited, disappearing in the fog without a backward glance. Dolf waited until he saw the military sedan's headlights slice through the fog and then turn to descend the hill.

Alone again in the gathering darkness, the image that filled Dolf's mind was of Janet Mueller's face as she'd stabbed her knife between his splayed fingers. When he cut those pretty lips off her face, he'd give her a grin to die for. But before Altmann would give him permission to do that, Dolf needed ammunition.

With the fog swirling about him, Dolf started down the hill toward his car. The FSB would get him what he needed.

CHAPTER 48

"Tell me what you've got, Levi."

Levi Elias stood beside the big screen in the NSA director's private conference room, a red laser pointer in one hand, a Bluetooth remote control in the other. Looking at the concern on Admiral Riles's face didn't help alleviate his own worry. Seated on the admiral's right, Dr. Denise Jennings was the only other participant in this briefing.

Levi pressed a button on the remote, and the picture of a man wearing a Cuban military uniform appeared on the big screen.

"This is Colonel Chumo Garcia, a senior intelligence figure in the DGI. Early this morning we picked up a series of queries initiated by this man, seeking information about Janet Mueller. Principal among the recipients of his queries was General Alexandr Prokorov, head of the Russian FSB."

Levi changed the image to a balding, distinguished-looking man in a civilian suit seated at a large conference table.

"Included in the packet was this picture and an almost complete set of fingerprints from Janet Price's right hand."

The screen changed to show Janet Price, her hair dyed blond, her eyes contact-blue, staring directly into the camera. It was a German passport photograph issued to Janet Mueller.

Admiral Riles turned to Dr. Jennings.

"Denise, has Big John picked up how Colonel Garcia became interested in Janet?"

"So far Big John has only identified one other person in the request chain, General Esteban Montoya."

Levi changed the image to show the portly Bolivian general standing in review of new graduates at the Bolivian police academy. Levi pointed a red dot from the laser-pen at the general's face.

"Obviously, this is not the brains behind the query. But it isn't difficult to guess who is, considering that we've known for a long time that General Montoya is on Conrad Altmann's payroll."

Admiral Riles leaned back in his chair, his left hand rubbing his chin as he paused to consider this information. Levi met his intense gray eyes.

"Do you think Janet has been compromised?"

"No, sir. We expected them to have suspicions, and we know Janet can get under people's skin with her directness. I think this is probably just Altmann's due diligence."

"Contacting the head of the FSB seems like a bit more than due diligence."

"Normally I would agree. But you know how much the neo-Nazis hate the communists. Even if Altmann wanted to use them, he would never do so directly. And I doubt that he would trust General Montoya to make such a query on his behalf."

Levi paused, hoping that his analysis was correct. If not, his words might get Janet killed.

"I think Altmann told General Montoya to dig into Janet Mueller's background and that General Montoya was hoping for a nice bonus, so he contacted his old friend in the DGI and, without mentioning Altmann, offered him a piece of the action. If Colonel Garcia didn't have anything on Janet, it's reasonable that he would have asked the FSB for help."

"Can we get word to Janet?"

"No, sir. She's gone dark."

"What about The Ripper? Do we know his current location?"

"Not with a high degree of confidence. He ditched the laptop and hasn't returned to the house in Santa Cruz. However, Dr. Jennings tells me that Big John has noticed a series of large payments to construction, plumbing, and electrical contractors in the Cochabamba area for information about previous jobs. The only thing all of them have in common is that they were each involved in the construction of Conrad Altmann's Cochabamba compound."

"Where we believe Altmann is holding Tupac Inti?"

"Yes, sir."

Admiral Riles nodded and stood. "Okay. Stay on this, both of you. I want to know the second anything changes."

CHAPTER 49

Standing at the base of the cliff, with the three-quarter moon showing dimly through the high clouds, Jack felt more alive than he had since last week's battle with the neo-Nazis at the southern edge of the Amazon. Over the past two years he had learned one thing. Only by staring directly into the face of death could you truly appreciate life's wondrous beauty.

Checking his utility vest, Jack pulled tight on the straps that bound his equipment to his back and began the night climb. He moved up the vertical face, wasting no motion, relaxing any muscle not currently in use, exerting the bare minimum of effort where such effort was required.

Sixty feet up, a broad ledge protruded outward from the wall, blocking his path toward the top. Jack considered a sideways traverse, but his current path took him directly to the water collection trough at the infinity edge of Altmann's pool. Jack loved people with a taste for beauty. When they opened themselves to a view, they created a window of vulnerability. It was a vulnerability that Conrad Altmann relied upon this vertical cliff face to block. Tonight that wasn't going to work out for him.

Releasing his right hand and leaning back, Jack felt along the base of the overhang. Finding a crack in the surface, he thrust his palm up inside and balled his fist. Satisfied with the handhold, he released his left hand and dangled free. Rotating his body, Jack managed to get his right toes into the same crack and levered his body outward until his left hand found a new handhold on the overhang's lip.

Releasing his right toe hold, Jack dangled beneath the ledge, both arms spread wide. Jack released his right hand from the crack and used the momentum of the swing to establish a toe hold for his left foot. Pulling himself up with his left arm, Jack managed to find a firm handhold for his right hand. Two more moves carried him up the wall to a place with two decent footholds where he could pause to let his ragged breathing slow to normal.

At the moment, he wasn't loving the sixty-pound pack on his back. But he'd damn sure like it once he got all the way to the top.

It took him another ten minutes to reach the bottom of the stone and concrete wall that marked the back edge of the pool. Just above him, the splash of water pouring over the infinity edge and into the recycling catch basin sounded abnormally loud. The scent of chlorine wafted down on the cool night breeze, but he heard no late-night bathers. Not that he'd expected any. Apparently, here at Altmann's torture compound, 2:00 A.M. on a Thursday morning wasn't pool party or hot tub worthy.

Jack moved higher, grasped the edge of the catch basin, and began working his way to the right, toward the spot where the hot tub rose up above the level of the pool deck. Once more Jack paused to rest. A glance at the pale cyan numerals on his wrist watch confirmed the time: 2:06 A.M.

There was a problem with six-hour guard shifts, especially this time of night. They were two hours too long for all but the most highly trained and motivated individuals to maintain focus. And long, boring stretches in the wee hours of the night made people groggy, even if they were deployed in pairs. This shift had come on duty at 9:00 P.M. and was due to be relieved in just under an hour. Exactly as Jack had planned it.

Reaching the spot he wanted, Jack hauled himself up, letting the side of the hot tub and the night shadows hide him from any guard who might happen to glance this way. Removing his backpack and setting it to the side, he took the H&K from its slot on his utility vest. Jack checked to ensure the linear inertial decoupler and suppressor were still screwed tight to the threaded barrel. Satisfied, he removed a wire-thin, fiber-optic periscope, adjusted its angle, and looked into the eyepiece, letting the tiny far lens poke up over the rim of the hot tub. Sweeping it slowly side to side, both low and high, he saw no sign of the roving guards.

His senses amped up with a fresh adrenaline rush, Jack wasn't surprised. If the guards had been closer, he would have sensed them. But the real danger inside this compound was Janet Price. He would rather have had her at his side on this one, but he didn't, so he'd just have to deal with it.

Having spent the last two days gathering and committing to memory the blueprints, along with the electrical wiring and plumbing plans for this facility, Jack was as ready as he could be.

Unstrapping the fifty-meter rope from the side of his backpack, Jack secured it to one of the decorative boulders beside the hot tub with an end-of-the-line bowline knot and a couple of half hitches. Jack gave it a stout tug. Satisfied, he tossed the length of rope out over the cliff and laid a thick pair of rappelling gloves on the ground next to it. Then he fastened a black tactical rappelling harness around his legs and waist, and attached a carabiner to its left side. It wasn't comfortable to move around in, but when he needed to get out of here, it would be a hell of a lot faster to already be wearing it.

Jack made one final inspection of his utility vest: two flash-bang grenades, two high-explosive grenades, a half-dozen spare magazines for the H&K, infrared goggles, infrared flashlight, flexible fiber-optic periscope, two throwing knives, and his SAF survival knife. Except for a pouch containing a few additional tools, the silenced H&K in his right hand, and the specialized electrical kit in his left, it had all the extras that he'd be carrying when he made his move.

When Jack moved, he slipped from behind the hot tub and alongside the house's west wing. Staying below the level of the windows, he moved along the wall and then across the narrow space that separated it from the three-sided shed that housed the electrical and pool equipment. Spotting the breaker boxes, the telephone, and alarm wiring cabinets, Jack knelt beside them.

Setting his electrical kit on the ground, Jack slipped on the infrared goggles and grabbed his IR flashlight. Opening the alarm panel, he switched the flashlight on. A quick scan of the wiring brought a smile to his lips. It was a perfect match for the wiring diagram for which he'd paid such an inflated price. That was good. It meant there was one less person Jack would have to hunt down and teach why it wasn't a good idea to double-cross The Ripper.

Clipping four bypass leads into the patch panel, Jack switched on the device that would make everything in the security center look normal, and then snipped two wires. Expectantly, Jack tilted his head, listening for the alarms that should have blared throughout the compound. But he heard nothing.

As he closed the alarm panel and prepared to move back into the shadows, Jack felt the familiar call of danger. When the guard stepped around the corner, his form ghostly white in the IR goggles, Jack's H&K spit two bullets. The slap of the man's body hitting the ground was louder than the spit-spat of silenced gunfire. But as he dragged the corpse deep into the moon shadow, Jack felt a new danger awaken inside the main house.

It was a feeling he'd missed for far too long.

CHAPTER 50

In her dream, Janet stood in sunlight atop a high pinnacle, her gaze directed far out over pastoral farmlands. Somehow she knew this was a wizard's trap, set to ensnare the mighty black dragon. On the horizon, she saw . . . something. In the distance, clouds boiled up in a supernatural profusion, as if they danced to a tune that only Beelzebub could play. But this time, a dread minstrel stepped forth, his fingers strumming a flashing lute, his melodious voice humming forbidden chords.

"Jack!"

The name slipped from her lips as she sat bolt upright in bed.

Swinging her legs out from under the covers, Janet rose to her feet, naked. She didn't know why it surprised her. Whenever she wasn't on a mission, she'd always slept naked. But she was on a mission, so why the hell had she stripped down for bed?

Then she remembered. Tupac. For the second day in a row, she'd tortured a man whose mere presence made her want to be a better person. All in the name of her mission. It made her want to throw up. It made her want to get clean. So Janet had showered for so long that she thought she might shed her wrinkly skin. But when she'd crawled naked beneath the sheets, Janet had still felt dirty.

But now, although she didn't know how, Janet felt Jack somewhere out there in the night, burning white-hot. It was more than a feeling. It was a certainty. Her ex-lover had come here to free Tupac Inti or die trying. She'd seen it in his eyes at the house in Santa Cruz. But in her presence, he'd slept, peaceful as a lamb. The lamb of God.

The idea struck her as funny. Jack Gregory might be many things, but he would never be God's lamb.

Janet dressed in the dark, her movements so quiet that even Jack couldn't have heard them. With her Glock in her right hand, Janet moved to the closed door and paused to listen. The post-midnight silence was unbroken. But some small sound must have awakened her. Either that or Jack had infected her with some of his crazy voodoo. Right now, Janet really hoped it was the former.

As she gripped the brass doorknob, she froze. She'd heard something, the faintest of sounds from outside. It had been a soft scraping noise, possibly the dragging footstep of a roving guard, but Janet didn't think so. Taking a long, slow breath, Janet readied herself.

Time to go find out.

CHAPTER 51

Looking to make sure he didn't have more company, Jack lifted the guard's body from the ground and carried it into the electrical shed, laying it down next to the pool pumps. He'd been quiet, but not completely silent. If someone had heard him, that person would be coming to investigate. But anyone who came looking would soon be dead.

With the IR goggles still in place, Jack risked a glance outside the shack. Seeing no sign of infrared body heat, he ducked low and moved rapidly past the hot tub and pool, reaching the east wing. As he rounded the corner, he heard a sliding glass door open on the far side of the pool, along the west wing that he'd just left behind. That wing held the two guest bedrooms, and Jack had a pretty good idea who had just stepped out of one of them to scan the pool deck for signs of an intruder.

If Jack was right and it was Janet Price, he didn't want to engage her in conversation. And he damn sure didn't want to get into a gun fight with her. She might be good enough to kill him, or even worse, he might kill her. What he wanted was to get inside the east wing, take the stairs to the basement level, find Tupac, and get them both the hell out of here. Hopefully, Janet wouldn't walk all the way to the back edge of the infinity pool and look down to see his pack and the climbing rope he'd left hanging down the cliff face. If she did that or if she checked out the electrical shed, Jack would be moving to plan B real fast.

Jack listened and waited, his mental clock ticking through four minutes before he heard the quiet, booted footsteps retreat back into the house, followed by the sound of the sliding back doors closing. Jack remained still and silent for another minute, knowing that just because the 3:00 A.M. shift change had been late on both nights he'd watched them didn't mean he could rely on it. If it came right down to it, he'd prefer to finish what he had to do under the sleepy eyes of tired guards than deal with fresh ones. And the shift change would result in the discovery of the missing guard's body.

Moving to the window on the north side of the east wing, Jack removed the screen and attached a suction cup device that anchored a specialized glass cutter, designed to quietly cut a hand-sized circle in the pane of glass to which it was attached. Applying just enough pressure to keep the glass from chattering, Jack gave the handle two 360 degree turns followed by a gentle tap with his palm. The glass circle came free, clutched in the grasp of the suction cup.

Jack reached through the hole, undid the latch, and slid the window open. He had no worries that the room might be occupied. This was Conrad Altmann's master bedroom, and he would never allow others to sleep in his bed while he was gone. And because the neo-Nazi godfather hadn't had a meaningful long-term relationship for the last three years, any encounter that brought someone here to share this bed would be of the one-night-stand variety.

Moving the closed curtain aside, Jack stepped into the dark room. Through the infrared goggles everything took on a green tinge. Though there was nobody to give off that white-hot body glow, all of the objects in the room, from the floor to the ceiling, were at slightly different temperatures. The different materials all conducted heat with different efficiency. And the house was kept warmer than outside, so the walls, windows, and tile floor looked cooler than the furniture or throw rugs.

The bed was positioned against the wall on Jack's left, bracketed by an open closet door and the opening to the master bath. On his right, the sliding glass doors that offered access to the pool area were currently covered by a heavy sliding curtain. With no desire to go through Altmann's dresser drawers, Jack walked across the room to the closed door on the south wall.

Once more, Jack paused to listen to the rhythms of this sleeping house. Except for the hum of the central heating, he heard nothing. But something sure as hell called to him—multiple somethings. It wasn't as if Jack could see through walls, like some of the new tech gear let you do. The sensation was more akin to his sense of smell. It was as if he were hungry and suddenly caught a whiff of Aunt May's hot turkey dressing, fresh from the oven. Knowing where the kitchen was, it was easy to arrive at the smell's origin. Absent that knowledge, tracking down the source took considerably more effort.

When Jack opened the door, he found himself at the junction of an L-shaped hall. The part that led to his left ended at a door that Jack knew opened onto a stairwell that led to the basement. Tupac Inti was imprisoned somewhere down there. And though Jack felt a tug from that direction, an even stronger attraction pulled him into the section of hall that led straight ahead to the south.

From the blueprints, Jack knew this hall led to a door on the left that opened into Altmann's study. There was another door straight ahead that led into the three-car garage and to a large opening into the formal dining room on his right.

At the corner where the right wall gave way to the dining room, Jack stopped again to listen. But nothing called to him from that direction. The same could not be said of the study door to the left. Jack reached for the door handle and suddenly felt cold sweat bead his brow.

Jack stepped through the door and closed it behind him. He looked around the study through the IR goggles, its floor-to-ceiling bookshelves and twin reading chairs painted ghostly green, experiencing something he'd only felt once before in his life. The memory played so brightly on the theater screen of his mind that it froze him in place.

~ ~ ~

The wind howls through the high peaks of the Andes, driving the cold in through the chinks in the log walls of my command cabin and making me long to remove the heavy armor that siphons away my body heat. But that is not to be. Outside, in the frigid morning air, my mounted Spaniards await.

My desire drives me out into the pale winter sun, anxious to mount my horse and travel to meet with the Sapa Inca, Atahualpa. In truth, I care nothing for my puppet emperor. It is his silver staff with its golden crown piece that infects my dreams with unquenchable longing and unspeakable dread.

I know that Atahualpa will not part with it while he lives, and if my senior officers find out what I intend, some of them will try to stop me. But in this, I cannot be stymied. For even at the cost of my life, I must possess it.

CHAPTER 52

Having heard nothing as she stood silently on the pool deck, Janet turned and walked back inside, shutting the sliding glass door behind her. What the hell was going on with her head? She'd been dreaming and then awakened, convinced that Jack Gregory was here. She didn't believe in superstitious crap like that. She'd thought she heard something in the night, but the sound hadn't been repeated, even though she'd stood on the pool deck, watching and listening for several minutes.

What she needed was to go back to bed and get three more hours sleep before she started her day with a workout in Altmann's garage gym. But as she reached the door to her guest bedroom, she stopped. This felt wrong. She'd heard something, and no matter how much seeing Jack again had screwed with her head, she hadn't started imagining things. If it wasn't Jack, she had nothing to worry about. But if Jack had somehow slipped into the compound, he would go for Tupac. And that was something she couldn't allow.

Janet felt the weight of the Glock in her right hand. Now she understood what had to be done. She turned to her left, away from the bedroom door, and walked down the hallway toward the front of the house. She bypassed Altmann's office as the living room opened up before her. Just enough moonlight penetrated the high clouds to make the couches, coffee table, and easy chair visible against the large window that faced the helipad.

With the Glock held in a shooter's stance, Janet turned toward the east wing, passed the foyer on her right, the kitchen on her left, and entered the dining room. Turning left past the study, she entered the hallway that led to the master bedroom. But she wasn't headed there. Instead, Janet walked down the short hallway to her right and opened the door to the dark stairwell.

Ignoring the beckoning light switch, Janet stepped inside and silently closed the door behind her. Right now, the darkness was her friend. She'd been up and down these stairs so many times the last couple of days that she could see them clearly in her mind. Careful to step lightly, Janet descended the stairs, pausing briefly at the basement level to listen. She was tempted to continue on down to the dungeon level, but tactically this was the place that beckoned to her.

Here the landing opened directly into the basement. But to continue on down to the dungeon meant opening two ancient metal doors that creaked and groaned on their hinges. Altmann could have had repaired them, but he loved the way those sounds echoed down into the lower level, telegraphing the bad news of his coming to any guests who waited in the cells below.

Janet didn't think Jack had beat her down here. She would have heard those doors opening and closing. For now she didn't give a damn whether he came from above or below. This was the place he would have to pass if he wanted to get Tupac out.

Letting her memory of the large room guide her through the inky blackness, Janet stepped behind one of the support beams, aimed her Glock back toward the stairwell, and waited. In the perfect darkness, Janet didn't need to see the front and rear gun sights to know one thing. Even The Ripper couldn't get past her here.

CHAPTER 53

Jack roused himself from the vision that had momentarily paralyzed him, but the feeling remained. This room reeked of knowledge so old and terrible that something within Jack quailed in its presence. Believing he had to be imagining things, Jack nevertheless made his way past the reading chairs and over to the center bookshelf. Switching his gun to his left hand, Jack switched on the IR flashlight and began examining the titles on the bound volumes.

Most were old and written in German or Spanish, but neither of those languages presented a problem to Jack. The sight of an aging first edition of *Mein Kampf* would ordinarily have made Jack laugh, but right now he failed to see the humor in Conrad Altman's worship of the psychotic Führer. And it wasn't this book that bothered him. It was the thin, unlabeled binder next to it.

When Jack reached out to take it from the shelf, tension spread through his shoulders and neck, as if someone with a rope were desperately trying to drag him out of the room. If there was an effective counter to fear, it was anger, and this was really starting to piss him off. Gripping the binder, Jack pulled it from the shelf and laid it on the small round table that separated the two reading chairs. Fighting back the urge to drop the thing on the floor, Jack opened it. The hand-printed title page read *Excerpts from the Journal of Francisco Pizarro González.*

Jack popped open the binder's three metal rings, removed the pages within, and rolled the thin sheaf into a tube that he shoved inside his utility vest. He would investigate it later. He'd already wasted too much precious time on a weird feeling.

Shifting the IR flashlight to his left hand, Jack took a tactical grip, aligning the light beam with the H&K's barrel. Jack left the study and followed his gun back down the hall to the stairwell entrance. Silently opening the door, he cleared the stairwell and moved inside. Where before he'd sensed danger below, now all he could feel was the damn scroll tucked in his vest.

Jack had known for some time that he'd grown too reliant on his intuition. But tonight he'd have to do this the old-fashioned way and hope that whatever was screwing with his head wouldn't get him killed.

CHAPTER 54

Absolute darkness does strange things to your senses, making your mind generate ghostly images that flit across your peripheral vision. The longer you keep your eyes open in those conditions, the harder your mind works to compensate for the lack of visual stimulus, making the problem worse instead of better. The way around it is to focus your attention on your hearing.

There is a popular myth that the loss of a person's eyesight makes her hearing better. What it actually did was make Janet pay more attention to what she was hearing. Standing behind the concrete pillar in the basement's pitch-black darkness, her gun hand aimed back toward the stairwell landing, Janet had her attention firmly focused on her hearing.

She heard the door above open and close softly, heard very quiet footsteps begin the descent, imagined the man following his gun down those stairs. If she was lucky, he wouldn't be wearing night-vision goggles. But this was Jack Gregory, and those who opposed him didn't tend to be that lucky. So she would just have to rely on her judgment.

When she determined he was three or four steps from the opening, Janet spoke up.

"Hello, Jack. It's me."

CHAPTER 55

Janet's voice, clear and confident, echoed from the basement into the stairwell, bringing Jack to a stop just before he reached the corner that would have allowed him to peer into the large room where she waited. He should have sensed her presence, but since he'd tucked the rolled-up journal into his vest, its touch had infected him with an aching dread that he found both distracting and fascinating.

When he didn't respond, Janet continued. "I asked you to give me two weeks before you try to rescue Tupac."

"I said I'd think about it."

"Mind if I ask why you decided not to trust me?"

"For the same reason you didn't tell me why you needed the extra time."

Jack heard Janet pause and debated his next action.

When she spoke again, her voice had softened. "I'm going to walk to the wall and turn on the light. I'll appreciate it if you don't shoot me when I step out."

"I didn't shoot you at my house."

"New set of circumstances."

"They always are."

Janet's soft laugh tickled his ears, and Jack lowered the IR flashlight and his gun. She walked into his view, a shapely white ghost moving against a dark green background. As she reached for the light switch, Jack pulled the goggles from his face and squinted to avoid being dazzled. When the incandescent bulbs lit the basement, he was glad he had taken that precaution, but it still took several seconds before his pupils fully adjusted.

Standing ten feet away, Janet had turned to face him, her gun hand hanging at her side, a mirror image of his stance. A scene from *Gunfight at the O.K. Corral* leaped into Jack's mind, and it brought a grin to his lips.

Janet raised an eyebrow. "So what happens next?"

"That depends on what Tupac tells me."

"And if he says he wants to stay?"

Jack considered. "I'll tell you what. If he says he wants to stay here, I'll leave without him. But if he wants to go, I'm taking him with me. Can you live with that?"

A moment of silence hung in the air between them as she weighed the consequences of what he'd just asked her. When her eyes again met his, she nodded.

"If Tupac wants to go, my mission has already failed."

"I don't suppose you care to enlighten me on that mission."

"Not at the moment."

Jack nodded toward the door. "Okay, then. Lead the way. The clock's ticking."

Janet holstered her Glock, and Jack mirrored her action, clipping the goggles and flashlight to his vest. When she pulled on the door, the hinges creaked and groaned as if it hadn't been opened in years. Then Janet surprised Jack by stepping aside.

"Sorry. I can't go down there with you."

"Why not?"

"Tupac thinks I'm one of the bad guys. Since I've been waterboarding him, he's got damn good reason to think it. If he sees me with you, it'll blow my cover."

"Let me get this straight. You want me to walk down into the dungeon while you stay up here and guard the door?"

"You didn't have any trouble falling asleep on the couch with me watching over you."

Jack had to admit that she had a point. And that hadn't been the first time he'd put his life in her hands.

"What the hell."

Jack flipped the light switch just inside the door. A bare bulb illuminated ancient narrow steps and damp stone walls. As he descended, the stink of stale dungeon air entered his nostrils. When he opened another of the creaking doors at the bottom, the smell got worse. Finding another light switch, Jack turned it on, illuminating another series of bare bulbs that extended down the center of the arching dungeon passage. A groan from the second cell on his right alerted Jack to Tupac's presence.

When Jack stepped up to the bars, he saw the shaman struggle to a sitting position, his huge right hand held up to shield his eyes from the unaccustomed light. Even though Tupac had been held captive for only a week, to Jack's eyes, it looked like the man had been here for months. It didn't really surprise him. Jack had learned from personal experience what torture could do to a man.

"Hello, Tupac. Sorry it took me so long to come for you."

The stunned disbelief in Tupac's face transformed into joy. "Jack! What the hell are you doing here?"

"I'd love to tell you all about it. But first let's get you out of here."

Jack saw the expression on Tupac's face change as he leaned back against the far wall.

"You shouldn't have come. I can't go with you."

Jack stared into Tupac's dark-brown eyes and saw his jaw clench in determination.

"Why?"

"It's personal."

"Try me."

"Altmann has something that belongs to my people. This is my one chance to get it back."

Jack snorted. "And you're doing a damn fine job of it."

"Leave me and get out while you still can."

As Tupac lay down to rest his head on his wadded shirt, Jack's eyes were drawn to the tattoo on the shaman's chest. The bare bulb outside his cell cast stark shadows across Tupac's chest, making the image shift so that it appeared that the robed man held his staff out toward Jack. Again Jack felt himself pulled back into the waking dream he'd experienced in the study, but this time he angrily repressed it. He might be losing his damn mind, but he refused to do it here in front of this man.

Then the sound of a distant alarm siren echoed down the stairs and into the dungeon.

CHAPTER 56

Drawing his gun, Jack raced back to the stairwell, flipped the dungeon light off, and slammed the door behind him. When he reached the basement level, Jack was surprised to find the lights off. Switching off the lower stairwell light, he closed the door behind him. Unhooking the IR goggles, Jack slid them back on his head and switched them on, moving quickly up the stairs to the ground level.

As he stepped out into the hall, he heard Janet's yell from the foyer. "He went around the east side of the building. Don't let him get to the gate!"

As a thank-you for her efforts, Jack tossed a flash-bang grenade toward the foyer and then raced back into the master bedroom. Behind him, an explosion lanced the night, shattering the windows in the front part of the house. Not a very nice thank-you, but it would put her down for the remainder of this fight and protect her cover story. Reaching the open window, Jack glanced out. Crouched by the west wing were two more guards, their weapons aimed toward the spot where the flash-bang grenade had just blown out the sliding glass doors that opened onto the pool deck.

Jack fired four 9mm rounds into them, sending both men sprawling. One of their submachine guns chattered, raking the side of the house with bullets. Then Jack was outside, racing toward the spot on the north side of the pool where his hidden rope hung down the cliff face.

As he neared the rope, another guard peeked around the side of the electrical shed, his weapon firing wildly as it swung toward Jack. Ducking behind the hot tub's stone housing, Jack felt water splash down upon him as bullets chopped the water's surface. With his left hand, Jack grabbed a grenade, popped the pin free, and hurled it toward the gunner. The explosion pelted the pool and hot tub with shrapnel, but the submachine gun quit firing.

Throwing off his goggles, Jack moved to the edge of the cliff, snapped the rope through the carabiner on the left side of his rappelling harness, and took a wrap from the anchored end. Sliding his left hand into the rappelling glove, he grabbed the rope, leaned outward, and jumped, letting the rope race through his gloved hand as he plunged face first toward the ground a hundred feet below.

When the momentum of his outward jump carried his feet back to the cliff, Jack ran straight down, only slowing himself just before he reached the bottom, letting his weight stretch the rope so that his feet swung off the wall and onto the ground. Without slowing, Jack ran forward, letting the remainder of the rope slide through the carabiner until he was free. Then, as a smattering of gunfire from above slapped the nearby trees and rocks, Jack entered the dense woods and disappeared.

As he raced through the dark woods toward his distant vehicle, a new thought occurred to him. Despite all his preparation, Jack had nothing to show for his efforts but a rolled-up old journal that, for some crazy reason, scared the shit out of him. That and a whole new batch of questions.

When Jack stepped out of the woods at the sheltered spot where he'd parked, he stopped in his tracks, unable to believe his eyes.

Shit! Some worthless bastard had stolen his goddamn car.

CHAPTER 57

"What?"

Conrad Altmann's sudden fury burned so hot that he wanted to hurl the phone through the plate glass window. Renaldo's call had awakened him from a good dream to word of The Ripper's attack on his Cochabamba estate.

"Sir, the good news is that he failed in his attempt to free Tupac Inti. Janet Mueller intercepted him as he was headed for the stairwell. But he tossed a flash-bang grenade that knocked her out before she could get a shot at him."

"How the hell did he penetrate my compound?"

"It looks like he scaled the cliff behind the pool. Once up, he killed a guard and bypassed the alarm system before breaking into the house through your master bedroom window. Another of the roving guards found the dead one's body in the electrical shed and then removed the bypass circuit, triggering the alarm.

Once that happened, Janet Mueller yelled to the gate guards that Gregory was around the east wing. That's when the flash-bang grenade went off."

"How the hell did The Ripper get back out?"

"He fought his way out, killed three more guards, and rappelled down the cliff before the van arrived with our ten-man response force. They lost him in the woods. We've initiated a full sweep of the surrounding area."

"Get ahold of the Cochabamba police commander, Captain Lopez. Wake him up if necessary. Tell him I want road blocks set up all around the city. And tell him to keep his police out of my compound. I'll brief him on the situation personally after I get on the ground there. As for you, get ready for company. I'll be on my way in with reinforcements. I want The Ripper dead. "

"Yes, sir."

Altmann hung up and then dialed Dolf, who picked up on the first ring. Sometimes Altmann wondered if the albino ever slept.

"This is Dolf."

"The Ripper just attacked us in Cochabamba."

"Inti?"

"The Ripper didn't get to him. But he killed four of our people and got away."

"I thought Fraulein Mueller was supposed to put a stop to that."

Altmann felt his anger stir again. "You just focus on the job at hand, and leave her to me. Tell my pilot I want him ready to fly in fifteen minutes. Round up two dozen men, and get them loaded on a couple more choppers and on their way to Cochabamba. I want you there too. We're going to kill this son of a bitch before he manages to slip out of the area."

"Yes, sir."

"One more thing. I told Renaldo to call Captain Lopez, but I want you to alert the police commanders in Santa Cruz and here in La Paz to set up roadblocks coming into town from Cochabamba. We don't know what he's driving, but I want every incoming vehicle checked just in case he manages to get out of Cochabamba."

"I'm on it."

Altmann ended the call and set the phone on his dresser. Without bothering to shower, he dressed rapidly, pausing only long enough to brush his shoulder-length hair and beard. He wanted to be presentable when he looked into Janet Mueller's eyes and started asking her questions. And if her answers didn't satisfy him, he might just let Dolf have her.

CHAPTER 58

The sun had just peeked over the horizon, but Janet's head still hurt like hell. Although she'd slowed the flow to a dribble, her tissue-plugged nose hadn't stopped bleeding. She was pissed off at Jack for coldcocking her with a flash-bang grenade. What the hell had he been thinking? She'd been managing the situation just fine up until then.

Come to think of it, he'd had a wild look on his face when she'd encountered him in the basement. Janet had originally written it off as Jack being dazzled by the sudden brightness when she'd switched on the lights. But replaying it in her mind yielded something different. Although she wouldn't have believed it, Jack had looked spooked.

The sound of helicopters heading toward the compound got Janet moving toward the pair of twelve-foot-tall doors that formed the entry. The doors, with their decorative iron vines winding upward, stood closed, although their glass panes lay in shattered bits and pieces spread across the tile floor and out onto the front steps. Janet tugged the rightmost door open, feeling glass crunch beneath the leather soles of her black boots as she stepped outside.

As she stepped into the driveway, the smallest of the three helicopters settled onto the helipad, buffeting her with its rotor wash. The other two helicopters landed just outside the compound's main gate, spilling armed men as their wheels touched down. Beyond them, the flashing lights of parked police vehicles barred the road. The fact that no police had entered the compound, despite having arrived on the scene more than two hours ago, spoke volumes about the power and influence the neo-Nazi godfather wielded in certain parts of Bolivia.

When Conrad Altmann exited his helicopter, clad in white cotton pants, navy button-down shirt, and an off-white blazer, he made his way directly toward Janet, anger flashing in his eyes. That was fine with her. She wasn't in the mood to take any crap from this ass.

When he reached her, his eyes took in her paper-plugged nose and bloodshot eyes. Then Altmann launched his verbal assault.

"Didn't you tell me you were going to kill The Ripper when he came for Inti?"

"You weren't listening. I told you that The Ripper would come for Inti and I needed to be here when he did. I was here and he failed. The fact that I didn't kill him yet is irrelevant."

Janet saw Dolf step up beside his boss, towering over the older man.

"Irrelevant!" Altmann sputtered. "He killed four of my men. Look at my goddamn house!"

"Hire better men. As far as I could see, they're the ones who put all the bullet holes in your beloved home. The Ripper's flash bang just broke some windows. The other grenade just damaged your electrical shed and part of the outer fence."

Conrad Altmann leaned in until Janet could smell the spearmint chewing gum on his breath. "You want to tell me why he didn't use a frag grenade on you instead of the flash bang?"

"Isn't it obvious? I was too close, and he didn't want to risk killing himself with shrapnel."

"But you went down and The Ripper didn't."

"The flash bang went off right behind me, and you can bet he had hearing protection. Now are you done jerking my chain, or do you really want to piss me off?"

Dolf started to raise a hand, but Altmann put a hand out to stop him.

Janet eased the grip of her left hand on her belt knife, her eyes locking with the albino's. "Down, boy."

Altmann interceded. "Back off! Both of you."

Dolf turned toward his boss. "What do you want me to do with our men?"

"Tell Renaldo to get some vans up here to shuttle them down to the barracks. The other guards will just have to make room. But I want them ready to go as soon as The Ripper is located."

Dolf nodded and glanced down at Janet, the beginning of a snarl curling his lip. Then he turned and walked rapidly out through the gate.

Janet returned her gaze to Altmann. "When you find Gregory, I want to go with the assault team."

Altmann shook his head. "Not this time. You had your chance at The Ripper, and you missed. You're getting close to breaking Inti, and that's the priority. Right now, I want you to show me exactly what happened here. After that, we'll go to work on Inti."

For the next hour, Janet led Altmann through the compound, starting with the cliff where Jack had climbed up and eventually rappelled back down. Altmann emptied the backpack Jack had left, noting the extra rappelling harness and glove he'd left by the rope. Clearly, he'd been expecting Tupac to accompany him back down that rope.

From there, she showed Altmann each place where Jack had gone as he worked his way into the house and then toward the stairwell. The study surprised her, but not as much as it appeared to surprise and trouble Altmann. Although Janet hadn't noticed it earlier, Jack had clearly entered the study, taken a skinny binder from the bookshelf, removed the pages within, and left the empty binder lying on the reading table.

"Why wasn't I told about this?" Altmann asked.

"I didn't know The Ripper came in here. When I saw him, he was in the hall near the stairwell. He must have already left the study. What did he take?"

Altmann picked up the binder and closed it, sticking it back into the empty slot on the bookshelf. Janet noticed that the spine had no label.

"Just some historical notes. Nothing of value."

But when Janet looked in the godfather's face, it told an entirely different story.

CHAPTER 59

Dr. Bones McCoy hadn't slept or bathed in two days. When she got like this, everybody steered well clear of her private lab. The no-bathing thing probably had a lot to do with that. For the first time since she'd started working with the QB4096, it seemed stumped.

The quantum computer was by far the most advanced of its new breed, performing the same computation in a huge number of simultaneous variations, with thousands of entangled qubits operating in an unimaginably large number of simultaneous states. Nobel Laureate physicist Richard Feynman once said that if you think you understand quantum mechanics, you don't understand quantum mechanics. Bones had never deluded herself that she understood how the quantum computer her work had helped to make possible did what it did.

But as amazing as QB4096 was, it was also unimaginably stupid. In essence, it was the idiot savant of computers, capable of instantly solving problems that ordinary computers could never solve, yet struggling with tasks ordinary computers accomplished with ease. That was why the NSA had devoted one of their most advanced traditional super-computers to the task of serving as the system's front end. It was this machine that provided the advanced user interface Bones used to enter instructions and to receive results. It was this machine that figured out which parts of the problem to handle itself and which parts to pass along to the QB4096.

Because of this essential symbiotic relationship, Bones had come to think of the connected machines as one entity, which she called Cubee.

~ ~ ~

Even though Bones had originally only allocated a fraction of its processing power to the problem, the machine should have arrived at all possible solutions to the Incan Sun Staff's golden orb in a matter of seconds. But as time passed and little progress was made, Admiral Riles had ordered Bones to increase the priority given to this task until she had finally stopped Cubee from working on anything else. Incredibly, after three days of complete focus on the orb, Cubee had only now begun to make progress.

That progress had started when Bones had combined the 3D model of the silver staff with the 3D model of the orb. But the real breakthrough hadn't happened until she'd noticed an oddity in the original pictures of the golden orb. All of them had been taken with a high-definition camera that clearly showed the fine details of the intricate symbols on each ring as well as views of the internal clockwork mechanisms through the small gaps between the rings.

The symbols neither began nor ended on any ring, but extended onto the adjacent rings. And as any ring turned, the symbols combined with adjacent ones to form a different shape. Although that made the problem more difficult, such a mechanical device should have yielded a nearly instantaneous solution to Cubee. The fact that it hadn't was what had robbed Bones of sleep. She couldn't get it out of her head, and she didn't want to.

That was when a new idea had occurred to her. What if the problem wasn't with Cubee's processing power, but with the original 3D model of the golden orb? Other NSA computing systems had built that model from the photographs. But what if the model those other systems had produced wasn't good enough?

The key lay in the pictures themselves. The person who had taken them had done a very thorough job. The orb had been set atop a cushion, and a series of photographs had been taken from all sides of the object, including a set taken from above the orb. Then the orb had been turned upside down and the process repeated.

Anyone else but Bones might have missed it. It was, after all, the tiniest of variations, but when the orb had been turned over, a couple of the rings had rotated slightly from their previous alignment. That small outer change had produced a startling internal reconfiguration. It was as if Bones had suddenly stepped from a dark cave into the bright light of day.

Unlike a Rubik's Cube or Rubik's Sphere, it wasn't the externally visible symbols that gave the orb its complexity. It was the way the internal mechanisms arranged themselves at each movement of the rings. That internal state changed depending on the ring turned, the direction it was turned, the number of consecutive times it was turned, and a number of other factors she had yet to understand. And each movement not only changed the arrangement of the symbols on the sphere but the appearance of the symbols themselves.

This was no simple problem of correctly aligning the varied symbols. The order of the alignment was critical to the resultant configuration of the internal clockwork mechanisms, and that affected how the orb connected to the tiny gears on the top end of the silver staff. Together they formed not just a complex mathematical formula represented by the external symbols, but a mechanical device designed to do something, possibly even several somethings, depending on the code and the way it was dialed in.

If she only had the completed staff, she could hook it up to a robotic device under Cubee's control, and the solution would come easily. But she didn't have the actual artifact. She only had an imperfect 3D model, and that wasn't going to get the job done.

So Bones had ordered Cubee to cease work on the current problem and had instead fed in the raw digital images from the original photographs, instructing Cubee to analyze them and construct its own 3D model that extrapolated the actions and construction of the internal mechanisms. That completed model was what Cubee was now using as it attempted to solve the alignment sequences.

From the data Cubee was giving her, Bones could see that it had identified four possible paths to different solutions. And although Cubee had not yet arrived at a complete solution for any of the complex algorithms, they each got progressively more complicated.

Based on Cubee's nonlinear rate of progression, Bones figured that she should have the answers no later than tomorrow. In the meantime, the body odor in her private lab wasn't likely to get a whole lot better.

CHAPTER 60

Colonel Chumo Garcia studied the contents of the encrypted folder he'd just downloaded onto his computer. As good as the Cuban Directorate General of Intelligence was, the Russian FSB was better. Chumo liked the old KGB name and had never really gotten used to the new one. After all, it was essentially the same organization with many of the old familiar faces.

The FSB file on Janet Mueller was simultaneously more and less extensive than he had hoped. Her early life details were well documented and matched the information in the packet that General Montoya had said originated with the Golden Dawn. Middle-class German upbringing and subsequent Nazi radicalization while at the Technical University of Dortmund, where she obtained a degree in computer science. With dual German–American citizenship she had moved to Greece and had essentially dropped off the grid, with only vague references to her affiliation to Ammon Gianakos and the Golden Dawn.

Although the Golden Dawn file credited her with a number of assassinations, the FSB could find no specific evidence linking her to those hits. That could be because this woman was too good to be caught, or there might be another reason. Without exception, Chumo doubted any information obtained from Nazis. Neo or old-school, they were all the same.

Where things got interesting in the FSB file had to do with last year's Russian mafia attack on the Baikonur Cosmodrome. Although all the perpetrators of that terrorist action had eventually been killed, one of the sets of fingerprints recovered from the Baikonur control room in Building 92A-50 had turned out to be a match for Janet Mueller's prints in the packet Chumo had forwarded.

Interestingly enough, Janet Mueller's prints had been found close to a set of partial prints that had been traced to a dead CIA agent by the name of Jack Gregory. Although interesting, it was irrelevant to the background information General Montoya had requested. But one thing Colonel Chumo Garcia was famous for was his thorough attention to detail.

It was extraneous information, but it wouldn't hurt the quality of his report to include it. Having considered both sides of the argument, Chumo made his decision. What the hell? He'd let General Montoya cull it if he wanted.

CHAPTER 61

"Sir, we've intercepted a message from the DGI to General Esteban Montoya," said Levi Elias. "It concerns Janet."

Admiral Riles lifted his eyes to see Levi Elias standing in his door, once again having bypassed the NSA director's irritated admin. Riles waved her back to her desk.

"Come on in, Levi, and shut the door behind you."

Levi complied and then walked across the room to lay a small stack of printed pages on his desk. Riles liked it. Even though Levi had, no doubt, also pushed the files to him electronically, sometimes it was still easier to look at the hard copy.

As Riles studied the contents of the DGI report, spreading the pages out before him, he let Levi look on in silence. His top analyst knew him well enough that he didn't try to point out key information before Riles had formed his own impression of the material.

When Riles raised his eyes from the report, he worked to keep the concern from his voice.

"The Baikonur fingerprints could be a problem. Especially Gregory's."

"Yes, sir. Altmann's not stupid."

"But Montoya is. What are the odds that he forwards that part of the report?"

Levi shrugged. "He's lazy. He'll forward the whole thing. We need to get word to Janet."

Admiral Riles rose from his chair and walked to look out the window at the sunny winter day that failed to effectively pass much of its light through the NSA's dark glass.

"No. That's a one-time-use contact method, and we'll need it once Bones breaks the code. Janet's going to have to deal with this on the fly."

Riles saw the worry lines form on Levi's forehead. "Too many cracks are starting to appear in her cover."

True enough. But Riles didn't have any feasible alternative. "She's the best. I trust her to handle it."

A deep sadness settled in Levi's brown eyes. Then, as if shrugging off a heavy burden, he straightened, nodded, and walked out of the office.

Riles felt Levi's discarded burden settle on his own shoulders as he reseated himself in his chair. There was no doubt that Levi had good reason to worry. The weight of this entire operation hung from one end of a tightrope walker's balance pole, and the walker was Janet Price. With that weight getting heavier by the day, it was only a matter of time until it pulled her into the abyss.

Riles just hoped that day was not today.

CHAPTER 62

The old VW Rabbit was a diesel-burning, oil-belching piece of crap, but there were moments when car thieves couldn't be choosy. For Jack, this was one of those moments. On the plus side, it generated its own smoke screen. When he stopped at an intersection and then accelerated across, the car behind him disappeared in a black cloud thick enough to coat its windshield with soot.

Over the last couple of hours, the car wasn't the only thing Jack had stolen. He'd appropriated a long brown overcoat and a wide-brimmed floppy hat from a horse barn on the south edge of Cochabamba. That barn had also yielded a can of boot polish that Jack had used to stain his exposed skin dark brown. He'd passed through two checkpoints, but the police had barely glanced at him before waving him on.

The one-room cabin Jack had rented for a month had been advertised as a hiker's base camp. With a woodburning stove and an outhouse, it had all the comforts of home. Running water of the hand-pump variety emptied into a washbasin that doubled as a sink. Sitting back in the woods at the end of a two-mile stretch of dirt road, privacy wouldn't be an issue.

Jack parked the car inside the open barn that butted up against the house. From a minimalist construction point of view, the placement made sense, using the house's western wall twice. The roof lines didn't match, but Jack didn't think the homeowner's association was going to file a complaint.

As the morning sunshine had given way to a steady rain, Jack was glad the cabin's lone door opened from inside the small barn into the house. He guessed the builder couldn't imagine a day's work that didn't begin and end inside this barn.

Jack stepped inside, shed the overcoat, and surveyed his humble abode. A square wood table with two wooden chairs had an LED hurricane lamp and a battery-powered radio sitting in the center. In the far corner Jack had stacked two weeks of supplies along with an air mattress, sleeping bag, three changes of clothes, and a kitbag of tactical gear, weapons, and ammunition.

The stack of dry firewood by the woodstove would suffice for heating the beans and rice that would be his staples while he was here. As for cooking utensils, he had a metal pot and military mess kit. He didn't plan on staying that long, and for the most part, a can of cold pork and beans would do.

Jack wanted to drop off the grid, and this was about as far off the grid as it got.

For the first time since he'd rolled it up and stuffed it inside his tactical utility vest, Jack removed the journal, fascinated by the repulsion he felt at touching it, and placed it atop the table, next to the LED lantern. He almost expected the unlit lantern to suddenly flicker and the radio to turn itself on and start randomly changing stations. It had been that kind of night and morning.

Jack looked at the stove and then over at his sleeping bag atop the inflated air mattress. Was he more hungry or tired? He decided it was a toss-up and chose food. It wouldn't take that long, and who knew the next time he might get a meal. Besides, maybe a full stomach would help him sleep. In that area he could use all the help he could get.

The wood had been cut to stove length. Jack opened the iron door and mixed some charcoal lighter with the old ashes to form a paste, before loading the stove with wood. Striking a match, he tossed it onto the lighter paste. Seeing the flame spread beneath the wood, he closed and secured the door.

Outside, the rain was falling harder, the gusting wind pelting fat drops against the lone window and pinging the wood stove's metal chimney. The hiss and crackle from the stove as the flames bit into the dry wood made Jack drowsy, and he started to question his decision to eat first. Instead of giving in to fatigue, he set his pan on the stovetop, used a tiny military can opener to remove the top of the can, and dumped the pork and beans into the pot.

By the time the stove got hot enough to bring the liquid in the pan to a boil, Jack had shed the vest and T-shirt to stand bare-chested before the stove, letting the warmth splash against his bare skin. It was something he'd noticed many times, that the direct heat of a fire felt different on the lines of scar tissue that crisscrossed his chest and back than it did on the skin between those scars. His uninjured skin was much more sensitive to the heat than the nerve-damaged scar tissue. The net effect was that he felt both warm and cold at the same time, as if an ice spider had spun its cold web across his hot body.

Jack walked to his pack, grabbed the metal shower mirror, and set it by the sink. For some strange reason, he didn't want to go to sleep without shaving. He'd stained his arms, neck, and face brown with shoe polish, and that didn't bother him. But for some reason, he wasn't willing to eat and then crawl into his sleeping bag unshaven.

How screwed up was that?

~ ~ ~

Chop Chop Square. That was what the other international kids call Riyadh's central square. Sitting in the front row of chairs, my mother on my right, my brother Robert on my left, I know why I've been given the closest seat. This is my punishment.

As khaki-clad police look on, two men wearing traditional white Saudi robes stand on either side of a blindfolded, kneeling man whose hands have been bound to his ankles. The Saudi on the left pulls a great curved sword from beneath his robes as the other Saudi prods the condemned man's back with the tip of a knife. The kneeling man's involuntary response arches his back and extends his neck. With a quick up-and-down chopping motion that, to my eight-year-old eyes, seems to happen in slow motion, the long blade rises and descends. Horror floods my soul.

While blood spurts from the kneeling man's neck, his severed head rolls three feet toward me. Its motion shifts the blindfold up to reveal an open right eye. When the head finally comes to rest, that accusing brown eye stares directly at me.

My mother's and brother's wails echo from the columned buildings that surround the paved square, but I barely notice. I am frozen in place, unable to pull my eyes away from my father's dead gaze.

~ ~ ~

Jack opened his eyes, fought his way out of the confining sleeping bag, and stumbled through darkness to the sink. It took three full pumps before water spurted from the faucet so that he could shove his head into the stream. Jack continued pumping the ice-cold water over his head, neck, and back, letting it wash the remnants of the dream from his mind.

When he straightened, he mopped the water from his head and body with his hands, letting it drip onto the cabin floor. He didn't know what was happening to him, but this shit was getting old real fast.

He reached for the LED lantern and switched it on. Although it cast a circular glow, its illumination seemed concentrated on the stack of pages he'd removed from Altmann's binder. Well, he wasn't going to be going back to sleep tonight, so he might as well find out what the hell there was about this journal that had attracted his attention. But first he was going to heat up some coffee.

When Jack sat down, steaming metal mug in hand, he moved the short stack of papers toward him. With a strange mixture of anticipation and dread, he started reading. Halfway through the journal, Jack knew he was wasting his time. A half hour later, Jack found himself leaning over the journal, fully engaged. The change had come about when he'd turned a page to reveal a detailed drawing of an Incan Emperor holding an artifact that the natives called the Incan Sun Staff. Jack had seen this picture before, tattooed on Tupac Inti's massive chest. And he'd held the staff in his dreams.

In his journal, Pizarro had recorded many details of his conquest of the Incan Empire. The key had been the dispute between Atahualpa and his older brother as to who should become emperor, as their father had failed to specify his heir prior to his death. By right, the Incan Sun Staff, the symbol of the emperor, should have passed to the oldest son. But at Pizarro's urging and with the promise of Spanish backing, Atahualpa had stolen the staff and proclaimed himself the one, true emperor. Taking advantage of the resultant Incan civil war and helped by the spread of diseases brought in by the Spanish, Pizarro conquered the once-mighty empire in a matter of months.

But something about the staff and its legend had so enthralled Pizarro that he had betrayed Atahualpa, capturing and executing the puppet emperor he had helped install. Having come to believe that the staff had bestowed upon its wielder the power to build an empire, Pizarro took the object for his own. Pizarro also ordered that all the keepers of Incan high lore be brought before him so that he could acquire full knowledge of the artifact.

As Jack read Pizarro's words, he remembered his dream of Pizarro manipulating the golden orb crown piece and of the terror that had risen up within him as he felt himself compelled to twist its golden rings.

Staring down at the photocopies of the original script, Jack could remember penning those very words, the feel of the quill against his fingertips, the scratch of its tip on the paper. There was a connection between the Pizarro dream and the fear Jack felt as he continued reading.

The LED lantern struggled to push back the darkness that crawled around him. Jack shivered, feeling the need to get dressed, rekindle the fire, and make another pot of hot coffee. He had just started to push back from the table when it hit him.

He backed up a page, rereading the previous journal entry. In it Pizarro described what he'd learned from the last shaman to be brought before him, that the staff only granted its power to someone who correctly aligned the orb's mystic rings. In the grips of the torture Pizarro personally inflicted on him, the shaman had revealed the secret combination.

Paranoid that the secret might fall into the hands of others, Pizarro had committed it to memory, but not to his journal. That journal entry concluded with Pizarro's plans to perform the Sun

Staff ritual during the coming night's witching hour, when he would be alone in the poorly constructed shelter that served as his sleeping quarters.

Again Jack felt the written words stir his memory. The odd thing was that he had no such memory of the next journal entry, nor any entry that followed. Fascinated, Jack read all the subsequent entries, then reread the entire journal from beginning to end. The experience was unchanged. He remembered making the early entries, but after reaching that special one, it was as if someone had flipped his memory switch to the off position.

Jack leaned back until the wood chair balanced on its two rear legs, rubbing his temples in hopes that the pressure would relieve the throbbing pain in his head. The answer he was looking for was here, so close he should be able to see it, but it remained frustratingly elusive.

Why did his Pizarro memories suddenly stop with the entry just before Pizarro performed the Sun Staff ritual?

Wait. That was the last journal entry he remembered, but it wasn't his last Pizarro memory.

Although Jack had tried to push the sleepwalking memory from his mind, he'd been dreaming when that incident had occurred. In that dream Pizarro had been manipulating the staff and had been terrified of what he was doing.

That wasn't quite right. Jack focused on the memory. Something inside Pizarro had been terrified, just as something inside Jack had been terrified in Altmann's study. It was the feeling he had right now.

Jack leaned forward, bringing the chair's front legs back to the floor with an audible clatter. Not Pizarro's memories. Those memories had come from Pizarro's head, but they belonged to something else. On that winter night in 1533, Pizarro had done something that had expelled the Other from his mind.

Jack rose to his feet and walked out of the circle of lamplight, out the door into the barn, and then out into the raging storm. The wind-whipped rain drenched Jack's naked body as lightning crawled through the night sky overhead. With a sound like ripping cardboard, the leading edge of thunder crackled and then shook the ground with its fury. Legs shoulder width apart, his arms hanging at his sides, Jack raised his face to the light show in the sky. As brown shoe polish ran down his neck, onto his chest and back, a single thought filled his head.

Déjà vu!

CHAPTER 63

The timelines that stretched out before the mind worm writhed like dying snakes as Jack Gregory strode among them, chopping off their heads one at a time. Alexander, Cleopatra, Caligula, and the hundreds of other hosts that had fed Anchanchu their extreme emotional highs and lows all had one thing in common. They willingly imbibed the drug Anchanchu fed them, reveling in glory as the mind worm guided them to ever greater and more terrible experiences.

Anchanchu had seen infinity without man, and it had bored him. The human race offered him a thrilling escape from that boring hell. Above all else, the mind worm didn't want to lose what it now had.

But no matter how much Anchanchu opened the spigot, flooding Jack Gregory's mind with enticing and punishing impulses, the man continued to fight those urges. Although

Anchanchu was unable to directly influence Jack's thoughts, their limbic connection gave the mind worm the ability to transplant memories from previous hosts into Jack's dreams. Anchanchu had tried using raw fear to prevent Jack from taking certain actions.

But it wasn't working. None of it. Worse, the fear trick had actually caused Jack to do the opposite of what the mind worm wanted. A new thought occurred to Anchanchu. What if its interference was preventing this unique host from taking the steps that might protect mankind from those who had come before?

Anchanchu considered this idea and rejected it. As badly as Jack Gregory needed to be in control, Anchanchu needed it more. There was still time to fix this situation. And Anchanchu intended to do the fixing.

CHAPTER 64

Dolf finished reading the report he'd just downloaded from General Montoya, grinning as he printed a copy for Conrad Altmann. The Mueller bitch was dead meat. That she'd lasted this long had surprised him. Maybe his boss had a hard-on for the woman. The thought that Altmann might be losing his edge wormed its way into Dolf's mind. If that was true, strong new leadership might be called for.

Shaking his head, Dolf pushed the traitorous thought aside. Those who started thinking thoughts like that wound up dying unpleasantly. Dolf had seen it happen too many times not to have learned a crucial fact. Conrad Altmann had eyes and ears everywhere. And he never lost his edge.

Whatever his boss's reasons for ignoring Dolf's advice about Janet Mueller, Altmann couldn't ignore this. Only five months ago, Janet had been with Jack Gregory in Kazakhstan. The fact that she hadn't mentioned it said it all.

Rising from his desk, Dolf walked out of the bedroom-office that he regarded as his wing of Altmann's La Paz house. Occupying the far west side of the first floor, it was only slightly smaller than Conrad Altmann's master bedroom on the east side of the house. Although Altmann's bedroom had far more closet space and a much larger bath, those were two luxuries about which Dolf cared little.

The room's location gave Dolf rapid, twenty-four-hour access to the main floor, to the garage, and to the security center on the far side of the parking area. More important, it offered Conrad Altmann an extra layer of security inside his house.

Dolf entered the huge den, its twenty-foot-high windows providing a nice view out over the pool to the snow-covered Mount Illimani. Passing the kitchen, he tuned left and climbed the spiral staircase to the second floor. Bypassing the theater room, Dolf paused outside Conrad Altmann's office, removed his cell phone from his pocket, and placed it in one of the wall-mounted bins. He placed his right hand onto the security scanner and waited for the glowing green laser to image his palm. When he heard the click of the electronic lock, Dolf pushed the door open and stepped inside.

Conrad Altmann's office was spectacular. Tiled throughout, the Altmann house projected wealth. But the floor work in this office projected something else. Though it was subtle, the tile's reflectivity gradually changed as you approached Conrad Altmann's desk, making it feel as though you were approaching Olympus. Even though Dolf had no mystical inclinations, he still felt it . . . the Klaus Barbie effect.

Sometimes Dolf almost understood it. Altmann's father, the Butcher of Lyon, had passed to his son his sadism and his special ability to manipulate people. This room manifested Altmann's inheritance. It projected his incredible mind. He was the one man on this earth to whom Dolf could bend a knee.

Dolf had seen a picture of Klaus Barbie in his Nazi uniform, the iron cross boldly displayed at his throat. But if Klaus was the glorious image of Nazi Germany, Conrad Altmann, with his shoulder-length blond hair and graying beard, was the look of the new Nazi Party. Dolf had looked into his boss's eyes and seen the truth that blazed deep within those sparkling blue orbs. Something incredible was knocking at mankind's doorstep, and Conrad Altmann was about to usher it in.

Dolf stepped forward and reached out to lay the Janet Mueller file on Altmann's desk. When the powerful voice broke the silence, it startled him so badly he almost dropped the folder on the floor.

"Looking for something?"

Dolf swung around, surprised to see Conrad Altmann standing in the doorway, wondering why he hadn't been alerted to his boss's return.

Recovering his equilibrium, Dolf straightened, feeling the muscles tighten throughout his body as he rose to his full six feet seven inches.

"Just dropping off the latest intelligence report from General Montoya."

The older man's blue eyes narrowed as he stepped forward. "Show me what you've got."

Dolf nodded, spreading the contents of the file folder on Altmann's desk. "Sir, we now have conclusive proof that Janet Mueller is working with The Ripper."

Conrad Altmann studied the material spread out before him.

"Talk me through your logic."

"A week and a half ago, Janet Mueller insisted on accompanying us on the raid to capture Tupac Inti, and The Ripper was there. Two nights ago, The Ripper attacked our Cochabamba compound, and Janet was there."

Dolf pointed to one of the pages from the FSB report. "Now we learn that The Ripper's and Janet Mueller's fingerprints were both picked up at the scene of last year's terrorist assault on the Baikonur Cosmodrome. I don't believe in that many coincidences."

Dolf felt his boss's blue eyes lock with his.

"There's just one problem with your theory. The Ripper is trying to free Tupac Inti. If Janet was helping The Ripper, he would have escaped with Inti. Instead, The Ripper failed, and Janet continues torturing Inti on my behalf."

As usual, Altmann had seen straight into the heart of the problem, and Dolf found himself struggling to come up with a rebuttal.

"Maybe she's not torturing Inti as hard as she would like you to think."

Conrad Altmann laughed. "I've been present for her sessions, and the woman is a professional. Right now, Tupac Inti is so close to the breaking point that his body is starting to let him down. The big man shakes like he has the palsy, even when he's alone in his cell. You should be very glad that Janet Mueller isn't working on you."

"But how do you explain the FSB report that she and The Ripper were both present at the attack on the Cosmodrome?"

Altmann walked around behind his desk, seated himself, and leaned back, placing his hands behind his head.

"I don't know. But when I fly back to Cochabamba in the morning, I'll ask her."

"Sir, I'd like to accompany you."

Once again, Conrad Altmann grinned. "Granted. Maybe when you watch her work, you'll learn something more useful than breaking necks."

The comment made Dolf struggle to keep his anger from working its way into his face and eyes. It was only the thought of breaking one pretty little neck that counteracted it. With a nod, he turned and walked out of Altmann's office, closing the door behind him.

Even though he would have to wait awhile longer to teach that whore a lesson in what true suffering meant, Janet Mueller's time was slowly but surely running out.

CHAPTER 65

Stefan Rosenstein gazed out of his penthouse apartment that spread across the 38th and 39th floors of the Meier-on-Rothschild Tower in Tel Aviv, admiring the way the Mediterranean sunset cast long shadows from the shorter city buildings. But as beautiful as this winter evening view was and as happy as Stefan was to be reunited with his family, unfinished business called to him.

Stefan left the living area and walked across the parquet floor, past the small indoor swimming pool, and up the stairs to his private office, shutting the door behind him. Having detected his presence, the room lights came up automatically.

He had no doubt that The Ripper was still out there, working to free Tupac Inti, as he'd agreed. Having failed to finish the job so far, he hadn't been paid. Not that The Ripper hadn't earned his pay by once again saving Stefan's life, but that wasn't what drove the man. The Ripper couldn't stand losing, so he would try to recover and finish the job. Unfortunately, this was far too important to place all his faith in one man, no matter how good that man was.

Far across the Atlantic, forces were in play that might forever alter man's destiny. Although Stefan's source had only been able to forward him a portion of Klaus Barbie's research, before getting himself killed by Conrad Altmann, the intervening weeks of study had convinced Stefan that this was terrifyingly real.

Too bad it wasn't enough to convince the Mossad. But the Israeli intelligence service was preoccupied with less mystical threats, such as Iran's imminent acquisition of nuclear weapons. When your nation was only the size of New Jersey, the threat of nuclear attack from a sworn enemy took on a whole new meaning.

It took thirty seconds for his laptop to finish booting before Stefan could launch his browser and traverse to his e-mail account. E-mail was a completely insecure mechanism for transmitting information, but these days, even methods that promised security were vulnerable to the NSA and others. So Stefan had resorted to the old-style method of sending a message that anyone could see but which contained a phrase that had special meaning only to its intended recipient.

The message Stefan composed consisted of six words.

Home is where the heart is.

As the sinking sun proclaimed the Sabbath's eminent arrival, Stefan pushed "Send," launching his message out through the ether toward its targets in Bolivia.

CHAPTER 66

Having donned her winter jacket, Bones McCoy was about to go home, take a shower, and catch a few hours of sleep, when it happened. As she reached for the light switch, Cubee's holographic display changed, the virtual orb's golden rings twisting and turning as if spun by ghostly hands.

As the image came to rest, a digitized female voice broke the silence.

"Solution sequence one complete."

Before Bones's startled eyes, the holographic image rotated to reveal that from the base of the silver staff, a set of two-inch prongs had protruded, forming their own complex pin pattern.

Forgetting to remove her jacket, Bones slid back into her seat and issued a new command.

"Continue sequence."

The holograph rotated to focus her attention back on the golden orb, and once again the rings twisted and turned, this time in a more complex series of movements. So intensely was Bones's focus on the hologram that Cubee's voice startled her.

"Solution sequence two complete."

This time the hologram stayed centered on the orb. Bones could see the complex patterns of symbols had rearranged themselves into something that felt like a more satisfying equation, but she failed to discern its meaning.

One at a time the orb's rings turned, skipping around in a seemingly random pattern, back and forth. What took only seconds for the hologram to complete would have taken human hands several minutes. And that was if the person made no mistakes when performing the sequence. When Cubee announced the completion of the third sequence, there was no pause before it started on the last and most complicated set of manipulations.

"Final solution sequence complete."

Bones halfway expected some mystical event to happen, but it didn't. The image of the golden orb atop its silver staff merely stood in space before her eyes. It was beautiful, but except for the pin-like protrusions from the silver staff's base and the new arrangement of the golden orb's symbols, it wasn't significantly different from when she'd first beheld it.

Bones replayed the four solution sequences in her mind. Though it was unnecessary, she took the extra time to validate her memory against Cubee's recorded session. Then, in a voice that trembled with excitement, she issued a final command.

"Dump solutions to file name Sunstaff."

To Bones's tired mind, Cubee's response seemed fraught with satisfaction. "File Sunstaff save complete."

Bones leaned back in her chair and smiled. All her years of study and dedication had led to this one glorious moment of conquest.

Without her and her Cubee brainchild, this solution wouldn't have been possible. It was the code that would forever alter the world.

A tear leaked from the corner of her left eye to trickle down her cheek. Catching it on her index finger, Bones stared down at it in surprise. She hadn't cried since her mother's funeral, that dreary October day in Innsbruck. Today, her mother would have been very proud.

Bones rose to her feet and looked around her windowless lab as if seeing it for the first time. What time was it? Crap. Bones couldn't even remember what day it was. The only thing she was sure of was that she looked like hell and smelled worse. But filthy or not, Admiral Riles would be very glad to see her.

It took her seven minutes to close up her laboratory, verify the classified safes were properly locked and logged, sign the classified verification checklist, and make her way up to Admiral Riles's office. Only when she stepped up to Admiral Riles's administrative assistant's desk and looked out the windows did she realize it was daylight outside. The admin, Frederica Barnes, regarded Bones with a disapproving look.

"May I help you?"

"Admiral Riles will want to see me immediately."

"He's in a meeting."

"You'd better call him."

Again Bones saw Frederica's eyes narrow. But the tall woman pressed a button, spoke into the phone, listened, and then nodded at Bones.

"You may go in."

As Bones made her way past the desk, Admiral Riles's office door opened. Levi Elias ushered her in and closed the door behind her.

Admiral Riles fixed his gray eyes on her, his look expectant.

"Sir, the QB4096 just cracked the codes on the Sun Staff."

"And the orb?"

"It turns out that they work together. There are four separate solution sequences. Each sequence requires that the previous sequences have already been entered."

"And do we know what they do?"

"Only that the first one causes a number of pins to extend from the staff's base. Absent access to the complete staff, there's no way to tell what those codes actually do. I've made the solution files and recorded simulations available to you under the file name Sunstaff. You will find a link in your private messaging."

Admiral Riles rose to his feet, walked around his desk, and extended his right hand.

"Exceptional work, Bones."

"Thank you, sir."

Without releasing her hand, the admiral studied her face, a look of concern creeping into his eyes.

"How long has it been since you've been home and gotten some sleep."

"What day is it?"

Both Admiral Riles and Levi Elias laughed. The admiral released her hand from his grip.

"Go home. Get some rest. You deserve it."

Bones hesitated. His response to her next question would be critical.

"Sir, I would like your permission to take three days off. Not that I need that much recovery time, but I'm afraid I've fallen behind on a number of personal errands that require my attention."

Riles grinned at her. "It's Friday afternoon. I won't expect to see you back at work until Tuesday."

"Thank you, sir."

As Levi Elias opened the door for her to leave, Bones hoped she hadn't sounded too relieved.

"And Bones, one more thing."

She turned back toward the admiral, her heart catching in her throat.

"Yes, sir?"

The admiral's final order culled the worry from her mind.

"Take a bath."

CHAPTER 67

Nightfall found Janet Price sitting cross-legged on a brown leather couch in the living room of Conrad Altmann's Cochabamba house, with a laptop balanced on her lap, appreciating the fact that she wasn't outside in the lingering rain. She didn't care that the laptop was one that Altmann's foreman, Renaldo, had assigned for her use; didn't care that every keystroke was being monitored and recorded as she surfed the Web.

Going from news site to news site, Janet scanned the headlines, as she did at least once per day, looking for a single keyword phrase. When she found it on CNN's main page, Janet felt her breath catch in her throat. *Finally*.

For the last couple of days, she'd been worried that Tupac was approaching the end of his endurance, worried even that he might be headed for a complete nervous breakdown. Hope was a person's best defense against torture, but as torture wears someone down, time drags and hope fades. She had seen the hope fade from Tupac's eyes, and that sight left her cold.

Although she wanted to shut down the laptop and head directly down to the dungeon, Janet pushed that impulse aside, forcing herself to spend a full hour visiting all her usual websites, trying to lose herself in the fine details of the daily news feeds. When she finally put the laptop away, Janet made a routine security sweep inside the house, something the ceiling-mounted cameras had watched her do on every night since she'd been staying here, before heading for the shower and then bed.

Janet awoke to her alarm just after midnight, dressed in darkness, and stepped out into the hallway. Admiral Riles had posted the CNN message that meant Tupac's time was up. Now she had a one-hour window during which the NSA would maintain complete control of Altmann's Cochabamba security system, providing live feeds to the guards from cameras that didn't show Janet and providing loopback footage for any that could see her.

She turned right and walked down the hall to the living room. The only light came in through the large windows along the front of the house from the gate guard shack. That light would only serve to rob the guards of their night vision, insuring that they could see nothing happening within the lightless main house.

Janet passed the kitchen and dining room, reached the closed study, and turned left into the L-shaped hallway that would take her past the master bedroom and to the stairwell. She stepped through the door, closed it, and descended the stairs in total darkness, counting the thirteen steps that took her to the basement level.

Even though she knew for a fact that no one could hear it, the squeal of the iron-bound door on its hinges made her grit her teeth. Leaving it open behind her, Janet continued down, opened its sister door at the bottom, and stepped into the clammy tunnel beyond. Only after she'd closed it and let its groaning echoes die away into darkness did Janet flip the switch that lighted the string of bare bulbs that stretched away from her in a straight line down the curved ceiling.

Janet stood still, letting her eyes adjust to the sudden brightness, thinking that another owner could have turned these tunnels into a fabulous wine cave. But even the greatest wine aficionado could never have gleaned as much pleasure from that as Conrad Altmann got from its present usage.

Tupac's cell lay twenty feet down that passage, the first one on the right-hand side. Janet walked to the door and stopped. The man sat up, shielding his eyes with a huge right hand, his jaws clenched as he prepared himself for another go on the waterboard. Janet could feel the dread and determination in that gaze.

"Admiral Riles sends his regards."

Her words brought a sudden look of shock to Tupac's face, quickly replaced by distrust.

Janet knew what the man must be thinking, having heard the words he'd been waiting for come from the lips of the neo-Nazi bitch who'd spent the last week torturing him in Conrad Altmann's presence.

"Tupac," she continued. "I'm sorry for what I've had to put you through, but the NSA has broken the Sun Staff codes."

When he spoke, his voice was raspy. "You're NSA?"

"Yes. My name is Janet."

"Admiral Riles sent you?"

"Yes."

"To torture me?"

"To make sure Altmann didn't seriously injure you with his torture."

Tupac paused, taking several shuddering breaths.

"Do you have the codes? Do you know them?"

"No. But I will when the time comes."

Janet followed Tupac's gaze out through his cell bars to where the waterboarding table waited, slightly farther down the central tunnel.

"So. One more session?"

"The last one. We have to make it convincing."

"You mean I have to act scared?"

"I need you to resist for one more hour, possibly two. Do you think you can manage that?"

Tupac's laugh rumbled out of his throat, growing in volume until it echoed through the tunnel, carrying with it a note of hysteria. He was still laughing when Janet switched off the lights and closed the dungeon door behind her.

CHAPTER 68

When Conrad Altmann stepped off his helicopter, a soft leather valise in his right hand, the morning sun had just broken through the clouds, holding out the promise of a nice day. Accompanied by Dolf, he walked out of the rotor wash, surprised to find that Janet Mueller was not present at the helipad to meet him. Instead, Renaldo escorted them across the driveway and through the double doors into the foyer. Janet Mueller was visible across the open space that transitioned from dining room to kitchen, pouring herself a cup of coffee.

Janet turned toward him, her blond hair secured in a tight bun, looking like she hadn't slept at all. She raised her cup, inhaling the fragrance before taking a slow and apparently satisfying sip.

"Good morning, Herr Altmann."

The fact that she made no offer to pour him a cup further irritated Altmann.

"This was why you couldn't be bothered to meet me at my helicopter?"

She took another sip. "I'm not your footman. I meet you when it suits my needs. This morning I needed coffee."

Beside him he could feel Dolf tense. Altmann ignored him, switching his gaze to Renaldo.

"Renaldo, take a couple of men and prepare Señor Inti for our morning session. I would like to speak to Fraulein Mueller in my office."

Without comment, Renaldo stepped outside, raised two fingers to his lips, and issued a whistle that could be heard over the dying helicopter noises.

As Altmann turned toward the living room and the office door beyond that, he noted that Janet held her cup in her left hand. Though she appeared relaxed, she had the subtle posture of a highly trained killer.

Altmann entered his office, followed by Janet, with Dolf bringing up the rear. As Altmann seated himself behind his desk, Janet slid onto the rightmost of the two leather chairs that angled toward the desk. Watching Dolf's pale eyes follow her every move made Altmann uncomfortable. The last thing he wanted was to have Dolf's temper incite an unfortunate incident that might cause Janet Mueller to go for the Glock holstered beneath her left arm.

With a flick of his right hand, Altmann motioned Dolf toward the other chair.

"Have a seat."

Altmann removed a folder from the valise and flipped through its contents until he found the page he was looking for. Reaching across the desk, he held out the page. Raising an eyebrow slightly, Janet rose from her chair, stepped forward, and took the paper from his hand.

"I've had my people do some checking. It seems that Ammon Gianakos neglected to provide some important information when he sent me your file."

Janet glanced at the page as she took another sip of coffee. When she finished reading, she set the paper down on his desk and returned to her chair, crossing her right leg over her left.

"Ammon omitted many important things. He provided everything he deemed pertinent."

"And he didn't think your encounter with The Ripper at Baikonur was pertinent?"

"Why would he?"

"Because The Ripper is here."

Janet smiled. "I didn't learn The Ripper was here until I saw him in the jungle. If you remember, Ammon sent me to kill Tupac Inti, but you told me to wait. Say the word and I'll walk downstairs and cut his throat right now."

"Why were you and The Ripper both at Baikonur six months ago?"

"The Ripper was there to kill Rolf Koenig. Gianakos sent me there to kill The Ripper."

Altmann leaned forward so that his elbows rested on the desk. "Your failure in that regard is becoming a bad habit."

Janet shrugged. "The man is more dangerous than you imagine. Eventually, I'll kill him or he'll kill me."

She pointed toward Altmann's lieutenant. "In the meantime, I helped Dolf, over there, take Inti away from The Ripper. Two nights ago, I prevented The Ripper from taking him back. Maybe if you get off your high horse, we can go downstairs, and I'll make Inti tell you what you want to know."

If she meant to anger Altmann, she failed. The woman projected such complete self-assurance that it was going to be a real shame to kill her. For now, though, she remained useful. Altmann suspected Janet Mueller would retain some degree of usefulness right up until the end.

Locking a restraining gaze on Dolf, Altmann rose to his feet. "Fine. Let's go have our morning chat with Tupac Inti."

CHAPTER 69

The grinding squeal of the dungeon's outer door was something Tupac had spent the last several hours anticipating and dreading. He was almost through this hell. It would be great to throw up his hands as soon as Conrad Altmann walked into view and just give up. Unfortunately, that wasn't a good option.

The blinding lights came on. The footsteps echoed down the tunnel. Then, as his pupils fought to adjust so that he could see more than shadow figures behind the bars, the key ring rattled against his cell door.

Two men dragged him from his cell and once again strapped him to the table, pulled the cloth hood over his head, and applied the tilt that positioned his head lower than his feet. Then Janet's voice sounded close to his left ear, asking her questions, the same as every other day, but with a couple of small differences. This time he knew her name. This time the end was in sight.

When it started, he didn't have to fake it; his automatic drowning reaction was as bad as ever, possibly worse because the end was within reach, but he had to resist grabbing it. He was a drowning man, forced to avoid the lifeguard buoy that bobbed against him in the waves.

Knowing Janet's name, knowing that she was NSA, should have helped, but it didn't. She was far too good at what she did. While Altmann obviously got off on the torture, Tupac's mysteriously beautiful torturer pulled his sputtering screams from his lungs with clinical precision.

The time came when Tupac could go no further. With no air in his lungs and no strength left to struggle to inhale, he managed to utter a single word.

"Enough!"

The water stopped flowing. Someone jerked the hood from his head. Great glorious gulps of air filled his lungs. Tupac found himself sobbing uncontrollably and didn't care. It was a natural physical and emotional response that he couldn't have prevented if the world depended on it.

Tupac felt the bed being cranked back into a horizontal position. Then Conrad Altmann leaned over him.

"Are you finally ready to tell me where the silver staff is hidden?"

Tupac cleared his throat. "I have to show you."

"And the Altar of the Gods?"

"That too."

Altmann stepped away from the table, his strident command voice echoing through the dungeon.

"Clean him up, get him dressed, and get him fed. Dolf, start assembling the team. I want them fully prepped and ready to move out first thing in the morning. We'll be taking three helicopters."

"Yes, sir."

Dolf's heavy footsteps echoed loudly as they retreated to the exit. Then Altmann leaned over Tupac one more time, his voice a low growl.

"Make damn sure you don't disappoint me."

CHAPTER 70

Bones opened her eyes to the incessant buzz of her alarm clock, having slept through the night for the first time in recent memory. As much as she wanted to roll back over for a few more hours, she had a tight schedule to keep. She could catch up on her sleep on the two flights that would carry her to her final destination.

By the time she applied the black hair dye, allowed it to set, and rinsed, the clock's digital numerals told her it was already past 9:00 A.M. Bones dressed quickly in jeans, a navy turtleneck, and hiking boots, and then picked up her passport, holding it up in front of her as she carefully studied her appearance in the mirror. Not a perfect match, but what passport photo was? It was close enough to the Mary Davis passport picture not to arouse the suspicions of TSA or customs officials. Sliding the passport into the inner pocket of her handbag, Bones packed her toiletry travel kit and a change of clothes into her carry-on bag.

This trip she would be traveling light. With the exception of the internationally configured burner cell phone in her jacket pocket, she wouldn't be taking any electronic devices. And she didn't plan on switching on the phone unless there was an unforeseen emergency. Grabbing her keys from the wall peg, Bones slid into her winter coat, stepped out of her apartment, and locked the door behind her.

When the white Ford Fusion departed Columbia, Maryland, and merged onto I-95, headed toward the Baltimore/Washington International Airport, Bones felt her face flush with excitement. Because her breakthrough was about to change the world, it was only right that she be present to watch it happen.

CHAPTER 71

Jack stood outside the cabin, looking out toward the mountains that rose into the sky to the west. With the dawn of a brilliant new day, the smell of the mountain air clean and crisp after the recent rain, Jack finally felt like he was beginning to make some sense out of this mess into which he'd stumbled. It was a very good thing that the last two years of his special type of private consulting work had left him with very deep pockets, because so far this job was looking like a losing proposition. And that was assuming he didn't get himself killed trying to finish it.

Yesterday's covert trip to an Internet café in Cochabamba had yielded a plethora of historic information about Pizarro, the Incan Empire, and the Quechua people. In addition, Jack's special sources had delivered encrypted files concerning Klaus Barbie's research. What had become very clear was that this whole thing wasn't about Tupac Inti. It was about the staff shown in the tattoo on his chest. Apparently, the staff was close to being found after all the centuries since Pizarro had held it in his hands. Jack understood why Tupac would want it. It was, after all, a symbol of the Incan emperors, the knowledge of which had been passed down through a long line of lore keepers. The tattoo marked Tupac as a direct descendent and a designated keeper of those traditions, for which his birth had volunteered him, whether he wanted that destiny or not.

Why Conrad Altmann wanted the staff so badly was a mystery within a mystery, but Jack had enough secondhand information to make a poorly educated guess. Klaus Barbie had been interested in the artifact's history, and based upon the journal Jack had purloined from the Altmann study, Conrad Altmann had inherited his Nazi father's interest. But the effort Altmann was putting into his pursuit of the staff indicated that he valued the artifact far beyond what seemed reasonable. Of course, "Nazis" and "reasonable" didn't really belong in the same context.

The NSA's involvement was yet another mystery. For some reason they had made a deal with Tupac Inti that involved him allowing himself to be captured and tortured as the NSA stalled Conrad Altmann. Janet was with the neo-Nazis, which meant that she was deep cover.

A movement caught Jack's eye. Circling high above, its distinctive white underside highlighted by black, a king vulture looked down at him as if it was judging his likelihood of becoming dinner. It wasn't beyond the realm of possibility; Jack had to give the big fellow that.

What Jack should have been doing was getting the hell out of Bolivia. Tupac had refused to accompany him on his second rescue attempt. In the meantime, Jack had saved Stefan Rosenstein's life and rid the world of a few more Nazis. At this point, waving off this mission made total sense.

But this was no longer only about Tupac Inti. After studying Pizarro's journal and its relation to his own dream-memories, Jack found himself needing to put his hands on the Incan Sun Staff. It had freed Pizarro. It could do the same thing for him.

The idea was a foolish hope, one that lacked credible underpinnings. But it was a gut feeling, and Jack had always been a go-with-his-gut kind of guy.

Shifting his thoughts back to the present, Jack turned and walked back inside the cabin. Stripping off his shirt, he examined himself in the metal camping mirror he had propped on the sink. Having acquired better-quality dyes for skin and hair, it was time to wash off as much of the shoe polish as possible and take his native look to the next level.

If he was going to find out where the staff was hidden, he had to be watching Altmann's compound when Tupac finally told the Nazi where to find it. That still left the difficulty of finding out where Altmann's helicopter would take him after that. But the odds were decent that someone left behind at the compound would know where Altmann had gone, and there were ways to make such people talk. Especially if they thought you were flat-out crazy.

Applying the brown dye to his face and neck, Jack saw the familiar red reflection fill his pupils. That was okay. He could do crazy.

CHAPTER 72

Janet looked over the foreman's quarters toward the west, her eyes scanning the horizon without seeing what she was searching for. Conrad Altmann's three-helicopter flight was late arriving at the Cochabamba estate. Despite the sunny morning here in Cochabamba, La Paz sat at twelve thousand feet above sea level, and that extra four thousand feet made a big difference. One of those side effects, especially after a few days of rain, was morning fog. And flying helicopters through the high Andes in the fog wasn't conducive to living to fly another day.

The van arrived at the front gate five minutes before the scheduled 9:00 A.M. shift change, the stink of its diesel exhaust fumes scrubbing the fresh morning smells from Janet's nostrils. Ignoring the leers and loud voices of the six guards that climbed from the van as well as those coming from the men who strode toward the gate from their stations within the compound, Janet turned and walked back through the tall double doors into the tiled foyer.

She closed the doors behind her, shutting off the smell of diesel and all thought of the neo-Nazi guards. As Janet walked across the tile toward the sliding glass doors on the north wall, the click of her leather heels sounded preternaturally loud, drawing the glances of the two cooks in the open kitchen.

Feeling an undercurrent of irritation, Janet pushed the sliding door open and stepped out onto the deck, looking out over the infinity pool that was enfolded on three sides by the U formed by the house. Beyond that, the hundred-foot cliff dropped away, the same cliff that Jack had climbed during his assault on this facility. Here, away from the fumes and noise out front, Janet stood still, taking in the beautiful morning view of the valley west of Cochabamba, stretching away to the north and east.

For some reason, she felt odd this morning, her senses and nerves on edge as if something bad was headed her way. There was no doubt that this was the reason for her irritation. Jack Gregory was the seat-of-the-pants guy, not her. Janet relied on the superiority of her planning, the intricacies of her logic, and aggressive action to defeat her enemies. And when plans went wrong, as they almost always did, the detailed preparation that had gone into the original planning gave her the edge on making rapid adjustments.

Today was the day when the NSA's master plan would come into conflict with Conrad Altmann's, and violence would ensue. Even though Janet had not originally been a part of that plan, she'd been sent in to make sure that the train stayed on its rails. Just as she had done last year in Kazakhstan, she would play her role.

The sound of helicopters interrupted her thoughts. There they were, coming in low, just visible above the west wing's red tile roof. Janet turned, walked back through the house and across the driveway toward Conrad Altmann's helipad. In a virtual replay of the three-chopper arrival on the morning after Jack's attack, Altmann's helicopter landed inside the compound as the two larger birds settled to the ground outside the main gate.

Altmann, Dolf, and a dark-haired woman climbed out of his helicopter as two dozen men exited the helicopters outside the walls, all but Altmann's party armed with a mix of AK-47 and the more modern but smaller caliber AK-74 assault rifles. Interesting. For previous operations, they'd mostly carried 9mm submachine guns. To Janet, the Kalashnikovs meant that Altmann was anticipating longer-range conflict against opponents with increased firepower. Hardly a favorable development.

His voice reverberating loudly through the compound, Altmann directed his yell at one of the men by the gate. "Get these helicopters refueled. I want to be in the air in thirty minutes."

Seeing Janet, Altmann motioned toward the house. "Let's go get Inti."

Coming around the side of the foreman's house to the west of the helipad, Renaldo and two guards hurried forward, catching up with Altmann as he stepped into the foyer. Renaldo and his two men took the lead, followed by Dolf, Janet, Altmann, and the unknown woman as they made their way down the stairs to the dungeon.

Fully dressed in his original clothes, Tupac stood inside his cell, waiting for them.

"Step back from the door," Renaldo said as the two guards covered Tupac with their AK-74s.

When Tupac complied, Renaldo fitted the large key into the lock. With a clank and rattle, the door opened, and Renaldo stepped inside, expertly snapping a pair of stainless-steel handcuffs on Tupac's wrists, binding his hands behind his back, and then shoving him out of the cell. Beside Janet, Altmann nodded at the guards, and their guns suddenly shifted toward her.

As Janet started to reach for her Glock, Dolf's voice stopped her.

"Go ahead. Try it."

Janet shifted her head slightly, bringing the big man behind her into view, his Sig P226 pistol aimed directly at her head.

Conrad Altmann turned to face her, a wide grin on his face. "You won't be accompanying us. Carefully now, drop your weapon."

Feeling ice slide through her veins, Janet met his gaze. Slowly, she drew the Glock from her shoulder holster with two fingers and dropped it at his feet, the clunk of polymer against stone echoing through the chambers.

Altmann motioned toward the cell Tupac had just exited. "Put your hands on the bars."

As Janet did as she was told, Dolf stepped forward, kicking her feet back, more than shoulder width apart, so that if she released her grip on the bars, she would fall. Bending down, Dolf's huge hands removed her boots one at a time, throwing them and the small knives contained in each across the tunnel. His rough touch progressed up each leg to her crotch where it lingered while he thoroughly explored this region for more hidden weapons.

Her belt knife joined the pile of other weapons. As he finished groping her torso and breasts, Dolf noticed the six-inch-long, needle-sharp hairpin and removed it. Grabbing a handful of her shoulder-length hair, Dolf pulled her head back until his lips were close to her ear.

"Whether you admit it or not, this is how you like a real man to treat you."

Janet turned her focus inward, intent on allowing no emotion to show on her face.

"Enough," Altmann said. "Lock her up."

Grabbing Janet by the neck and left arm, Dolf hurled her into the cell. Janet felt the rough stone scrape her left shoulder before she rolled back to her feet, facing out. The door swung closed, the key rattled and clanked in the lock, and Conrad Altmann stepped up close to the bars.

"I'm disappointed. You Americans are so easily manipulated. Tell me, Fraulein Mueller—or whatever your real name might be—are you familiar with my family history?"

Stunned by his knowledge that she was an American agent, Janet made no response.

Altmann continued. "Do you know why the American intelligence organizations protected Klaus Barbie after World War II, why they employed his services for five years, why they helped him escape to Bolivia, and why, in October 1967, they again used his help to capture Che Guevara?"

Conrad Altmann's blue eyes gleamed in his shadowed face, his neatly groomed beard and shoulder-length gray-blond hair sparkling where touched by the bare bulb's harsh light. Janet was very familiar with hate. It had filled a significant part of her childhood. But the raw hatred that blazed in Conrad Altmann's eyes went beyond even that.

"Klaus Barbie's ability to infiltrate intelligence organizations was unmatched, and the Americans were smart enough to recognize it. Through the years, they used him repeatedly to infiltrate the Soviet, French, German, Bolivian, and Cuban intelligence services. What amazes me is how an agency that is smart enough to make such effective use of my father didn't realize that he would infiltrate their own ranks just as thoroughly."

Altmann gripped the bars and pressed his face so tightly against them that Janet almost expected his head to compress and stretch until the whole thing popped through.

"In the end, it was the Jews, not the Americans, who were my father's undoing. What they failed to realize was the extent to which he passed his brilliance, knowledge, and skills to his bastard son; how through the years that followed, I not only appropriated but expanded Klaus Barbie's connections, even compromising America's newly anointed god, the almighty, all-knowing NSA."

Stepping back, Altmann grinned. "All along, this has been about more than the possession of the Sun Staff. It's all about timing. Nothing could begin until I deciphered the clues that led me to uncover the golden orb. Without that, Tupac's knowledge of the silver staff's hiding place and the location of the Altar of the Gods was useless to me. So I left him locked up in Palmasola while I hunted for the orb, a search that took me considerably longer than I had anticipated.

"Even after finding it, I needed someone to unravel its secrets, something that only an organization like the NSA could accomplish. Of course, I couldn't just send them the orb and ask for help. But I didn't need to, did I?

"Don't get me wrong. Your cover was very good. I wasn't even sure you were working for the NSA. But I knew that once I had both the orb and Tupac, the NSA would attempt to gain access to the orb, because Tupac needed the answer just as bad as I did."

Turning to look at Tupac Inti, Altmann continued. "Didn't you, Tupac? After all, how were you going to relink the orb to the staff without those codes? How were you going to mount it to the altar? Wasn't that the deal you made with Admiral Riles? All because you believe that one of the staff's functions enabled Manco Capac and later Sapa Incas to unite the native peoples and create the Incan Empire. You wanted to restore what Francisco Pizarro took from your ancestors."

Once again Altmann shifted his gaze to Janet. "I know it must seem like I'm gloating, but we all need our little victory party, don't we? And thanks to the NSA, today I have reason to celebrate."

Altmann turned to Renaldo.

"Make sure nothing happens to our little NSA agent while I'm gone. I have days of questions for her, and upon my return I will pry their answers from those pretty lips."

Renaldo inclined his head in assent. "Yes, sir."

As Conrad Altmann, turned to go, Janet's eyes were drawn to the face of the woman who watched him so intently. In that moment, the realization struck Janet with such force that it startled her. This wasn't someone who just worked for Altmann. This woman worshipped him.

A moment later, the Altmann party departed, and the iron-bound door banged closed, leaving Janet alone in the black, her only company the occasional drip-plop of ceiling water landing in a shallow puddle on the cold stone floor. The knowledge of her mission's failure siphoned that chill into her core.

CHAPTER 73

At the foyer, Dolf watched as Conrad Altmann headed for the sliding glass doors to the pool deck.

Altmann motioned toward Renaldo and the two men who grasped Tupac Inti's arms. "Bring him out back and sit him down in a chair by the pool. We'll wait out there until the helicopters are all refueled."

As the men moved to comply, Dolf spoke up. "I'll check on things out front."

"Fine."

Dolf watched as Altmann followed Renaldo out onto the deck, accompanied by the woman they'd met at La Paz's El Alto International Airport earlier this morning. Dolf had heard rumors of a decades-old love affair that had produced a secret love child with a married woman. But Altmann's introduction of this woman as his daughter had caught Dolf off guard.

The resemblance was there, mainly in the intensity of her intelligent gaze. She was clearly thrilled to finally meet the man whose secret she had nurtured all these years. And Dolf had seen that Conrad Altmann had been excited to see her.

Bringing his thoughts back to the present, Dolf struggled with his next move. Instead of going out through the front doors as he'd said he was going to do, he turned back toward the stairs to the basement, feeling the thump of his heart against his chest. This was his one opportunity, and he couldn't let it pass him by.

It felt so different, descending the stairs to the dungeon alone, with someone other than the big native shaman waiting at the bottom. His thoughts were interrupted as he opened the bottommost door, hearing its squall announce his presence. Dolf reached out, felt along the wall for the light switch and flipped it on, grabbing the key ring from its hook beside the door.

He didn't have much time. By now the refueling truck would be close to finishing the second helicopter and shortly would move on to the third. That meant Dolf had ten minutes, max. But that was okay. He had no intention of engaging in foreplay.

From this angle, he couldn't yet see into the cell where Janet Mueller waited. That meant she couldn't see him either. She didn't call out to ask, "Who's there?" Instead, she waited silently for her mystery man to reveal himself.

Don't worry, baby, I'm coming.

At the cell door, Dolf put the key in the lock but did not turn it. Inside the cage, Janet stood at its center, her eyes reflecting a cold light. It was a hungry look. That was fine. It was exactly what he wanted. In a couple of minutes there would be a far different look on that face as he rammed his body into hers while he pinned her to the floor.

Dolf removed his shoulder holster and his shirt, folding the latter and setting it in a dry spot on the floor. Leaving his gun in the holster, he set it atop his shirt, stepped back to the door, and turned the key. From his pants pocket he withdrew a four-inch long stiletto, switching it open with an audible click.

Unlike the outer dungeon door, this one opened smoothly, and Dolf stepped inside, the glittering blade held low and easy at his side. Barefoot on the cold stone, Janet waited, six feet from where he now stood.

Then, to his utter disbelief, in one swift movement, she reached up and pulled off her turtleneck to stand bare-breasted before him. Without hesitation, she dropped the turtleneck on the floor and began unfastening her jeans, those intense eyes never leaving his face.

What the hell was happening here? Did she hope to seduce him into kinder treatment? No. She was much too smart for that. Was she stalling, knowing that there was a ticking clock? Wrong again. Shit. She was undressing faster than Dolf could have ripped off her clothes.

Then Janet stood naked before him. Cold eyes. Hard, sexy body. Unafraid.

She was the hottest thing Dolf had ever beheld. She was a want in his belly that he couldn't tamp down, a fire in his crotch that consumed him.

Dolf took one step forward. The woman in front of him didn't flinch, her posture as inviting as ever, her eyes liquid death. But she was small and hard, whereas Dolf was a Nordic god. The fact that she didn't fear him made him want to dominate her body and soul all the more.

"Kneel." The word rumbled deep in his throat, another god reference.

With her knees starting to bend, Dolf took another step forward.

The speed with which the woman spun gave him no time to react, her right heel striking the back of his right wrist with such velocity that it launched the stiletto into the stone wall, snapping the blade from its carved ivory handle. The two pieces skittered across the floor in different directions.

Although he'd been surprised by the speed of her attack, Dolf wasn't slow and he knew what her next move would be. Like every smaller opponent he'd faced, she would dance back after that first blow, attempting to counter his size and strength with her quickness. With the beginning of a triumphant grin forming on his lips, he lunged toward her, seeking to pull her into an embrace that would place her at his mercy.

Once again she surprised him, not dodging back but launching herself directly into him as he ducked in for the takedown, adding her forward momentum to his. Snapping her head forward, she executed a perfect head-butt, the crown of her head crashing into the upper bridge of his nose. With a crack, bone and cartilage exploded, the shock of pain and splatter of blood momentarily blinding him.

Dolf reacted automatically, doing exactly the wrong thing. Instead of hugging her body to his, he lashed out with his forearm, sending her rolling across the floor. Struggling to blink away the blinding tears, he saw her roll back to her feet and kick out, catching him directly on his right kneecap. The force of the blow would have been enough to tear the patella tendon of most men, but Dolf wasn't like most men, and it enabled him to grab her right ankle.

Squeezing her ankle, he twisted. She rolled to keep him from breaking her leg, ending up facedown on the floor. Before he could dive on top of her, Janet's left leg pistoned hard, catching him square in the groin and dropping Dolf to one knee. The sensitive nerve cluster exploded with sickening pain that pulled a ragged gasp from his lips, but he maintained his grip on her leg.

"What the hell is going on here?"

Shit. Somehow, in the midst of the struggle, he'd failed to hear Conrad Altmann's approach. Flinging Janet Mueller's body away from him, Dolf turned his head toward the sound. Despite the blurring of his vision, he noted the guns the three men with Altmann aimed into the cell.

Five feet away, Janet Mueller rose smoothly to her feet, her breathing easy, her voice soft and calm.

"Dolf was just giving me some pointers on hand-to-hand combat."

It was a struggle to regain his feet and remain there without wobbling, but Dolf managed it.

Conrad Altmann's lips curled to reveal his incisors. "Jesus, you're a goddamn disgrace."

For a moment, Dolf thought his boss was about to pull his gun and shoot him in the head. Instead, Altmann pushed the cell door open and held it.

"Pick up your weapons, put on your shirt, and get on the chopper."

Leaving a trail of blood that streamed from his nose and dripped from his chin, Dolf picked up the two pieces of his broken knife and then stepped out to retrieve his shirt and shoulder holster. As he headed toward the dungeon's exit, Dolf heard Conrad Altmann slam the cell door and twist the key in the lock. Dolf glanced back to see Altmann staring at the naked woman standing calmly in the center of the cell, much as she'd stood waiting for Dolf.

Then, without another word, Conrad Altmann turned and followed Dolf out of the dungeon, trailed by his three bodyguards.

Behind him the dungeon door screamed angrily on its hinges, a sound that Dolf felt like echoing. Even more than he dreaded Altmann's anger at what he'd just tried and failed to do, Dolf didn't like leaving the Mueller bitch alive at his back, even if she was securely locked in a dungeon.

He'd had her leg in his hand. A couple more minutes had been all he needed. Ignoring the stares of amazement from the other guards he passed, Dolf walked out of the house and climbed into the back of Altmann's idling helicopter. Ignoring the blood that still drained from his nose, he strapped in, knowing his mistake.

CHAPTER 74

Ensconced in his original sniper hide, high up on the mountainside overlooking Altmann's Cochabamba compound, Jack watched through the rifle scope as Altmann's group boarded his helicopter with Tupac Inti in tow. Jack recognized the big albino pretty-boy, although his face wasn't looking all that good right now. At maximum zoom, Jack could see blood leaking from a nose so badly broken it would never look quite the same as the first time he'd seen it.

A woman accompanied them on board the chopper, but it wasn't Janet. Jack watched, waiting for her to appear from inside the house. When Altmann's helicopter rose from the helipad, followed into the west by its two larger sisters, a new worry tightened Jack's throat. Janet had been left behind. That couldn't be good.

Right now, as he lay there watching, she might already be dead. Or she might be bleeding out somewhere inside the house.

If he was going to have any chance to do something about that, the time was now.

Jack counted the remaining guards. Two at the front gate, one each in the two towers at the northeast and northwest corners of the wall. Two more stood along the cliff on the south end of the house.

Jack sighted on the leftmost of these last two, centering the reticle just above the spot where the guard's neck met the back of his skull. From this distance and elevation, the bullet would strike two inches above his aim point. The man on the right would hear the thump of the bullet striking bone and brain before the loud rifle report reached him.

Stilling his breath, Jack squeezed the trigger, feeling the rifle's stock rock his shoulder back, letting his natural motion settle the sight on the second guard. Again he fired, shifted his aim to the next target, and fired again.

As the two dead guards plummeted outward over the cliff and down, his third bullet struck the man in the northwest tower, flipping his body out of the tower and down to the ground beside the foreman's cottage. To Jack's eyes, the other men moved in slow motion, the one in the northeast tower raising his submachine gun and spraying 9mm rounds wildly as he tried to decide where the shots had come from. Jack's next bullet ripped a hole in his throat and silenced his weapon.

The two gate guards were smarter and dived behind the cover of the high north wall, one on either side of the gate. From Jack's position, all he could see of them was the occasional arm as one or the other swung the muzzle of his gun out to spray bullets up in Jack's general direction.

Another man ran from the front of the main house, racing toward the spot where the two remaining guards crouched. In the scope, Jack recognized the foreman he'd watched on his previous stakeout. Jack followed the man's movement, letting him get within five meters of the cover he was seeking, before squeezing off the next round.

The bullet took the foreman in the center of his right thigh, sprawling him flat on the ground. Jack steadied the reticle on the kill zone, waiting for the bait to take effect. As he expected, the nearest of the hiding guards ducked out of his covered position to grab the foreman's outstretched arm. Jack's bullet dropped the hero's dead body atop the man he intended to rescue.

Then Jack was up, swapping magazines as he ran down the mountainside and through the concealing woods toward the compound.

CHAPTER 75

Janet finished dressing, noting the handprint bruise around her right ankle. She'd been sloppy, letting Dolf catch her leg like that. With one powerful squeeze he could have shattered her fibula, possibly even her tibia. But he'd been too focused upon raping her naked body to fully recognize his danger.

Suddenly aware of a sharp pain on the top of her head, Janet reached up and winced, feeling a wet stickiness in her hair. That was the problem with a head-butt. You had to be willing to accept the predictable consequences in order to inflict its punishment on your opponent.

As the adrenaline rush subsided, Janet felt a wave of weakness ravage her body. Reflexively, she felt her way through the darkness to the cell door and rattled it, despite having seen and heard Conrad Altmann lock it. As always, he'd hung the key ring on the wall peg by the outer door when he'd walked out.

Backing up against the wall, she allowed herself to sink down to a sitting position. She tried to stare through the darkness, but it was useless. The metallic stink of Dolf's blood mixed with the smell of stale water, giving the air a musty thickness that felt cold on her skin. The chilled stone pressed against her bare feet, her butt, and her back where she leaned back against it, leaching the heat from her body.

Her instincts cried out for her to get up, to move, to do something before depression could take hold. Her mission's failure bore down on her as much as her miserable circumstances. Altmann had Tupac, and he was going for the staff. Even though she knew that Tupac's Quechua people would be guarding it, they had been counting on her inside support to overcome the neo-Nazi assault. Now that wasn't going to happen, and there was no way to warn them.

Outside her cell there was a faint rustle, and then an almost silent chittering, the sound of one or more rats drawn to the smell of Dolf's blood. That was fine. So long as they left her alone, they were welcome to it.

There was a distant roll of thunder. Wait. Not thunder. Gunfire. The dungeon was so insulated from sound that Janet wondered if she had imagined it. She hushed her breathing and pressed her right ear against the stone wall. There it was again . . . and then again, the individual shots now answered with the barely audible staccato thumps of automatic weapon fire.

Taking a deep breath, Janet rose to her feet. That kind of action in the compound could only mean one thing. Jack.

Even Janet wouldn't have thought Jack would be wild enough to attack the Altmann compound twice in four days, this time in the bright light of morning. She pictured Jack in her mind, visualized how he would do it. Last time he'd come up the cliff in the darkness. This time he had waited until after

Altmann's three helicopters had departed, leaving only the day shift on duty here.

Janet had heard several shots, spaced closely together, before any answering gunfire had commenced. And even though Janet had broken Jack's CIA thousand-meter marksmanship record, it had been by less than a centimeter. Each of Jack's trigger pulls meant someone had fallen. The survivors would be crouched down behind whatever cover they could find, sometimes blindly spraying lead in hopes of getting a lucky hit when all they were really doing was waiting to die.

Returning to the wall, Janet listened. Nothing. She waited while the seconds combined to become minutes. Her left ear felt cold against the stone, and then it felt something else as a tiny bug crawled rapidly inside it. She pulled her head away from the wall, digging a fingernail deep within the ear canal, trying to scoop it out. She felt something squish between her fingers and hoped it was the insect instead of ear wax. Now that she had focused her attention upon her left ear, she felt an itch begin inside the right one.

Claustrophobic, she hated caves, especially the tight crawl spaces spelunkers always encountered, where the earth pressed down from above and below, where you had to slither forward on your belly, sometimes having to turn your head sideways to wriggle through a crack. Now Janet could add dark, musty dungeons to her list. She'd have to remember not to get herself locked inside one again.

A loud grinding clang brought her back to her senses. Then the lights came on. Through her squinted eyes, she saw a shadowy figure stride to her cell door, heard the clank of the key as it entered the lock, and saw the door swing inward.

It took several seconds until she could be certain that the dark-skinned man who stepped into her cell was Jack, but she recognized that special something in the way he moved. When he grinned, his teeth seemed to shine with a light all their own, but it was the red glint in his brown eyes that held her gaze.

It was stupid, but she couldn't help herself. Janet lunged forward, threw her arms around his neck, and kissed his mouth, her crushing embrace returned in full measure. She felt his lips caress hers, tasted the brief touch of his tongue. God she'd missed that. Would it always be like this, their embraces a celebration that life might continue for one more day? Janet didn't know.

And right now, she didn't care.

CHAPTER 76

Time froze. For an endless moment, Janet Price was in his arms, her parted lips pressed to his as they held each other close. It had been almost six months since Jack had felt her embrace, six months since he'd tasted her kiss. The moment lingered. And then it was over.

As Janet stepped back, Jack looked at her in the harsh glare of the naked bulb. She was wearing black jeans and a black turtleneck. Blood matted her blond hair on the top of her head. Her face was streaked with dirt. When she smiled at him, she'd never looked more beautiful.

"Looks like they left some of your things over there," Jack said, pointing to the spot where someone had tossed her boots, knives, and gun.

Janet walked to the pile of gear, sat down and began pulling on her socks and leather boots.

"I'm assuming we don't have to worry about the guards."

"They won't be bothering us. Altmann took most of the guard force with him, but I'd like to be out of here in the next couple of minutes."

"The guard shift changed just an hour and a half ago. Assuming they heard you, it'll take them fifteen minutes to crawl back out of bed, get geared up, and make the drive up here."

"How far away is their bunkhouse?"

"A mile and a half down the canyon."

"Then they heard me."

"It's a winding dirt road, so they can't go fast. The nearest police station is seven miles away in Cochabamba. On a Sunday morning they're not likely to be ready to respond, even if somebody calls in a report."

Janet finished strapping on her holster and returning her knives to their sheaths.

"Ready."

When they reached the foyer, Jack checked the driveway and helipad while Janet verified nobody was moving around on the pool deck.

"Front's clear," Jack said, reversing course, walking back across the dining room toward the study and the door on the south wall that led into the garage.

"I'll be right there. I need my kitbag."

Stepping into the dark garage, Jack flipped on the lights and pressed the button that started the segmented door rumbling upward on its track. He walked to the black Toyota Tundra pickup parked in the first spot, opened its door, and looked inside. It didn't surprise him to see the keys in the ignition.

Janet stepped up beside him, and Jack pointed toward the dead guards by the gate. "I'll open the gate. You're driving."

Without a word, Janet tossed her duffle in the back and slid into the driver's seat. Jack opened the driver's side back door and set the sniper rifle on the seat behind her. Shutting the door, he walked out of the garage toward the gate, stopping to retrieve an Uzi submachine gun and additional magazines from each of the two dead guards. As he pushed the button that sent the gate rumbling open along its track, Janet backed out and turned the truck toward him.

She stopped at the gate just long enough for Jack to climb into the passenger seat before accelerating out of the Altmann compound. Jack ejected the 32 round magazine from one of the Uzis, replaced it, and chambered a round before sliding the weapon onto Janet's lap. He repeated the process with his Uzi and settled back in his seat.

Beyond the gate, the pavement gave way to a dirt and gravel road that was better maintained than most of its Bolivian counterparts. Just beyond the cleared stretch of mountainside where the original Spanish landowner had built his fortress home and where Conrad Altmann's compound now sat, the road entered the forest and descended steeply. In a series of switchbacks that eventually led to the canyon bottom, it wound its way down the mountainside. From there, the road followed the canyon for four and a half miles until it connected with Highway 4 near the southwestern edge of Cochabamba.

At a maximum speed of thirty miles per hour, they had only progressed a half mile down the dirt road when a white van rounded the corner three hundred meters ahead.

Jack pointed to a wide spot where the road allowed passage. "Pull over and park there. They'll recognize the pickup. Lower your window, and let them recognize you. Let's get friendly."

Janet pulled out onto the wide spot on the right side of the road, put the pickup in park, lowered her window, and waited. Beside her, Jack moved the passenger seat as far back as it would go, inclining it until he was practically lying down, his Uzi hidden along his right side.

On his left, Janet angled the Uzi's muzzle up toward the driver's side window. She reached out and held up a hand toward the slowing van, leaning her head out the window.

The van rolled to a stop beside them. The driver spoke in heavily accented Spanish, his voice shrill with excitement.

"We heard gunfire. What happened?"

Janet replied in kind, her words rushed. "Another attack. Renaldo says The Ripper was hit. I have a badly wounded man in here who must get to the hospital immediately."

"Who is it?"

Jack's voice was low and sharp. "Now!"

Their guns came up in unison as Jack leaned forward, aimed from the shoulder, and pulled the trigger. The first bullets out of Janet's barrel killed the driver and the man in the passenger seat as Jack concentrated his fire on the back of the van, sweeping back and forth on full auto. In five seconds it was over; sixty-four rounds of 9mm Parabellum slugs had blown out all the windows and riddled the sides of the van with holes, some of which leaked blood from the dead men slumped against the interior.

The driver's foot came off the brake, and the van idled forward, left the road, and crashed into a tree. The flames started at a ruptured fuel line and quickly engulfed the vehicle, long orange tongues shooting out the windows, sending a cloud of black smoke up through the trees. A tire exploded with a loud bang, hurling burning pieces of rubber into the trees.

Jack slid his seat up and forward. "Let's go."

As Janet accelerated away from the scene, Jack again replaced the Uzi magazines, readying them to fire, even though he doubted they would be needed.

As they approached Highway 4, Janet looked at Jack.

"Where to?"

"South and then east to Oruro. Do you know where Altmann was going with Tupac?"

"No."

"To get the staff?"

Janet spared him a sharp glance. "How do you know about that?"

"You're not the only one with contacts."

"It doesn't do us any good. We can't catch them."

"Maybe not. It doesn't mean we can't take it away from Altmann later, though."

"We?"

Jack paused, rolling what he was about to say around on his tongue before he said it.

"It seems I'm going to need your help after all. And before this is over, I think you're going to need me too."

Jack watched her face as Janet kept her eyes fixed on the two-lane highway that stretched out before them. Whatever thoughts she might have had about his last statement she kept to herself.

CHAPTER 77

Levi Elias stared across the conference room table at Admiral Riles. His navy suit jacket bunched slightly at the shoulders as he leaned forward in his chair, resting his elbows on the table, his chin supported on his cupped fists. To the admiral's right sat Dr. David Kurtz, the gray hair of the NSA's chief computer scientist as wildly unkempt as ever, and Dr. Denise Jennings occupied the chair on the admiral's left, her hair pulled back in a severe bun. They were two opposite bookends sharing the same concerned look.

Admiral Riles's voice held a note of disbelief. "You're saying Conrad Altmann was playing us from the very beginning? And you believe he now has both the crown piece and the codes?"

"Based on the message we just received from Janet Price, Altmann arrived at his Cochabamba estate this morning with a woman Janet had never seen before. Although we weren't initially able to identify the woman, some additional information has just come to light."

Levi activated the view screen. "This is security checkpoint footage from BWI airport, recorded Saturday morning."

Levi clicked a button, and the video froze, showing a clear view of Dr. McCoy's face as she placed her carry-on bag on the X-ray conveyor belt. Despite her newly black hair, the image left no doubt as to her identity.

Turning his attention back to Riles, Levi continued to lay out the bad news. "Airline records indicate that she checked in with a passport under the name of Mary Davis on a flight connecting through Miami to La Paz. That flight arrived in Bolivia early this morning. I had our people check Dr. McCoy's apartment. It shows evidence of a hasty departure."

Riles leaned back in his chair. "Do you mind telling me how Bones McCoy is connected to Conrad Altmann and how we missed it?"

"As we've experienced before, background checks aren't as complete as we would like to think. I've asked Dr. Jennings to initiate a high-priority correlative search to see if she can identify any links."

Admiral Riles turned to Dr. Jennings. "And?"

"And I've got Big John looking into it. So far he hasn't come up with anything."

"It."

"Pardon me, sir?"

"Not 'he.' *It* hasn't come up with anything. Big John is a neural network, not a person."

Levi felt the weight of Admiral Riles's gaze shift back to him. "Where is Altmann now?"

"We don't know, sir. He flew out of Cochabamba with Tupac Inti on one of three helicopters headed west. We know he didn't go back to La Paz."

"Then how did Janet contact us? Isn't she with him?"

The news wasn't getting any better, and Levi didn't enjoy being the messenger. But he earned his paycheck by giving his boss his best estimate of what was really happening, and it wasn't his nature to dodge the tough facts.

"No, sir. Altmann locked her in a cell before he left Cochabamba. She doesn't know where he was headed."

"Then how did she contact us?"

"Jack Gregory busted her out. Together they fought their way out of the compound."

"She's still with Gregory?"

"Right now they're holed up together in Oruro, awaiting instructions."

Levi didn't expect an emotional outburst from Admiral Riles, and he didn't get one. But the admiral's icy stare clearly communicated his mood.

"Is Jack Gregory on board with us for this?"

"Janet says he is."

"What do you think?"

Levi paused. He'd been debating this very thing since he'd read Janet's message. The Ripper had aided Janet six months ago. But after that operation he'd walked away despite Admiral Riles's offer to let him lead the NSA's top-secret cleanup team, of which Janet was a key member. At the time, Levi had been glad that Gregory had walked away. But that didn't mean they couldn't use him right now.

Levi looked up from his study of his hands. "I think Gregory has his own agenda, but Janet's going to need his help if she's going to have a shot at repairing the damage that's already been done."

The admiral stood up, and the others at the conference table echoed his movement.

"Fine. We know that Tupac Inti is taking Altmann to the staff. Figure out where, and get Janet and Jack moving to intercept them."

At the door, the admiral turned back to face them.

"The one thing Conrad Altmann couldn't possibly do in all of this was break the codes on the Sun Staff. So how the hell did he con us into doing it for him? Find out! We're the damn NSA, for God's sake."

CHAPTER 78

They'd been on the ground for five hours. In the lead, Tupac reveled in the feel of the high mountains of the Yungas beneath his feet and the fragrant smell of the thick vegetation as the aroma of the cloud forest filled his lungs. His leg muscles ached with exertion, and that too felt wonderful. Now he had the Nazis on his turf, and with any luck at all he would be the only member of his present party to walk back out of the deep canyon.

Here in these steep, densely wooded canyons, just miles from the North Yungas Road, helicopters were useless, as were vehicles of any type. In this rugged country, even mules and donkeys had great difficulty getting around. And where Tupac was leading Conrad Altmann, the dark-haired woman, and the thirty armed men who accompanied them, foot travel was the only option.

He glanced at the woman. At just over five feet, she was slender. If she hadn't worn such a severe countenance, she would have been quite pretty. Besides Tupac, she was the only unarmed member of the party, unless you counted her six-foot-long walking stick as a weapon.

Uncuffed, Tupac had a ten-foot-length of rope tied around his waist to keep him from escaping, the other end secured to the big man Altmann called Dolf. The Nazis needn't have bothered. Tupac had no intention of escaping, not until he took the backpack containing the golden orb from Altmann's dead body.

Tupac paused at the edge of a fifty-foot drop, searching for good footing to cross a spot where the trail had been washed out by water that cascaded down the verdant cliffs high above. Here in the cloud forest, man-made roads and trails didn't last long if left untended. And this trail had been untended for quite some time. At the base of a tree that leaned into the slope on his right, a broken branch reached out, offering the false security of a compromised handhold. Ignoring it, Tupac ducked under, pushed his way through dense brush, and again picked up faint traces of the narrow trail.

Behind him, the sound of rolling rock was followed by yells and curses as one of Altmann's men almost fell from the ledge.

A tug on the rope brought Tupac to a halt. He turned to face Altmann, who stepped up by Dolf.

"How much longer until we get there?"

Tupac looked up at the mountains that rose on both sides of the narrow canyon, pretending to search for landmarks. What he really wanted to see was some sign of the Quechua fighters who should be awaiting his arrival. But if they were out there, his trained eyes failed to spot them. Odd. He felt worry's sharp knife edge nick the corner of his mind.

"An hour. Maybe two, if your men continue having trouble keeping up."

"You'll go at the pace I want you to."

"So do you want me to wait, or should I keep moving?"

Altmann's blue eyes flashed, but his anger did not make its way into his voice.

"Keep moving forward until I tell you to stop."

Tupac turned and pushed his way through the undergrowth and vines that sought to obscure the path. Ahead, the trail descended, widening until two could walk abreast. Although Tupac only felt a slight breeze, dark clouds slid along the opposite side of the canyon, the curtain-like undulating ridge lines appearing and disappearing as the gray vapors scudded past. It was mid-afternoon, but the high clouds overhead and that drifting, smoke-like fog made it feel much later.

Tupac tilted his head up to sniff the air. For a moment he'd smelled it, the fetid odor of a dead animal wafting away on the damp breeze. One of the moving clouds crawled along the steep hillside toward him, extending misty fingers that brushed Tupac's skin, dropping the temperature noticeably. Again he caught the smell, much stronger this time. But it wasn't an animal corpse that he smelled. It had that unique stink of gases released from a human body that was just beginning to decompose.

Tupac slowed, pushing aside a branch that blocked his view of the treeless stretch where a rockslide had carved a path through the trees. This was the spot where it was supposed to happen. Tupac could sense what no white man could, and this was his plan. So why the hell was he feeling so wrong about it?

Once again the wind changed direction, coming from behind him now, carrying that horrible smell away with it.

"What's wrong?"

So intently had he been focused on the slide zone ahead that Altmann's voice surprised him. Tupac considered his response and decided to go with the truth.

"I smelled something."

Altmann's laugh did nothing to alleviate his growing concern.

"Quit stalling."

Tupac nodded and stepped out onto the slide. Ahead, fifty meters of jumbled rock and shale separated him from the next tree line. Stepping from boulder to boulder, he weaved up and down on the steep slope, avoiding stones that threatened to slip and slide under his weight. Three-quarters of the way across, he glanced back.

All thirty-two Nazis were now out in the open, moving slowly and carefully to avoid triggering a fresh rockslide. Any second now a dozen machine guns should open up, firing from covered and concealed positions on both sides of the slide area, cutting down everyone but Tupac. Basilio, the best marksman of all of the Quechua men, would take out Altmann with a head shot, taking great care not to damage the orb the Nazi leader carried. Tupac had been very specific about that part of the plan, knowing that Conrad Altmann would never trust anyone but himself to carry the orb.

By the time Tupac was ten meters from the trees, his worry had turned to fear. Why hadn't the shooting started? Where were his men?

Then he saw the body, sprawled face first across the trunk of a fallen tree. The man's face was turned toward Tupac, his forehead obliterated by the bullet's exit wound. But the prominent nose and staring eyes left no doubt as to the man's identity. It was Basilio.

Tupac stopped, fighting down the retching impulse that flooded the back of his throat with burning bile. From the state of the partially eaten body, it had lain here for at least two days.

"A friend of yours?" Conrad Altmann's voice carried the sneer that curled his lips.

The fear Tupac felt drained away, leaving only sorrow in its wake. The signs were clear. His oldest and most trusted companion lay dead before him, shot in the back of the head by someone he had put his faith in. Now the meaning behind the lack of gunfire became clear. There would be other bodies scattered nearby.

Tupac turned his gaze on Conrad Altmann, noting that Dolf stood ready to intercept him should Tupac give in to his desire to leap forward and snap Altmann's neck.

A noise in the brush to his right redirected Tupac's eyes deeper into the trees. Five native men stepped forward, their assault rifles held in a relaxed posture, barrels pointed toward the ground. Tupac knew each and every one of them. His hands clenched so tightly that both sets of knuckles cracked, but before he could move, Tupac felt the rope around his waist pull tight.

Again Conrad Altmann spoke. "Most people have a price. It's only a matter of negotiation."

Finally words formed on Tupac's tongue. "If you already owned these people, why did you need me to lead you here?"

"I didn't. But I dearly wanted to see that look on your face. Even though your friends can show me to the cave, they have been unable to find the staff's hiding place within it. And only you can take me to the altar."

Tupac looked into the Nazi's face, noting the pleasure in those blue eyes. Tupac considered his remaining options. He could take a suicidal leap as he led them toward the staff. But that would merely delay the inevitable. With enough manpower, Altmann would find it and, eventually, the Altar of the Gods. That would mean that everything Tupac had endured had been for nothing, that his loyal friends had sacrificed their lives in vain.

The decision made itself. He would take Altmann to the staff, would escort him to the altar. It was the worst-case contingency for which Tupac had prepared.

CHAPTER 79

Jack sat on the couch in their hotel suite, cleaning weapons and watching Janet Alexandra Price. Upon arriving in Oruro, Janet had procured a new laptop and the dye that had returned her hair to its natural brunette color. Having also ditched the blue contact lenses, she focused her gaze on the laptop while she waited for her hair to dry.

It was unusual for a field operative to have a degree in computer science. When the CIA had recruited her from the University of Maryland, they had planned to train her as an analyst. But her trainers had soon realized that keeping the two-time NCAA women's triathlon champion behind a desk wasn't feasible.

Jack knew that Admiral Riles had stolen her from the CIA to join a top-secret team he had created to augment the NSA's electronic intelligence collection mechanisms. So Janet had left a budding career as a CIA agent, adopting an NSA-provided cover that she'd found religion and would be doing international missionary work.

Jack chuckled at the thought. *Right*.

Janet looked up from her laptop and arched an eyebrow at him.

"What?"

"Nothing. Just thinking about old times."

She shook her head. "And Baikonur struck you as funny?"

"Not Baikonur." He decided to change the subject. "Any word from the NSA on Altmann's location?"

"Not yet. Apparently he's not in any of Bolivia's ten largest cities, and he hasn't left the country. Admiral Riles has retargeted a number of national collection assets to try to track him down."

"Aren't you worried about your communications being intercepted?"

"Not really. It's a new laptop that I personally wiped and then downloaded and installed some of the NSA's latest tools on. Except for standard WiFi, it's not emitting any extraneous radio frequency signals."

"I did that in Santa Cruz, and you found me," said Jack.

"The stuff you were using was dated."

"You gave it to me six months ago."

"Like I said, dated."

Janet pushed her chair back from the small table and turned to look at him.

"I need you to tell me how you found out about the Incan Sun Staff and what you learned."

Jack finished wiping down his H&K P30S and slid it back into his holster.

"Share and share alike?"

This time Janet hesitated, her brown eyes studying his face.

"Okay. You first."

Jack stood up, walked over to his kitbag, grabbed the journal pages from an inside pocket, and set them on the table beside the laptop.

"I took that from Altmann's study in Cochabamba."

Janet glanced at the title on the cover page. "So this is what used to fill the empty binder."

"An extract from Pizarro's journal. It mentions the Sun Staff prominently."

"But what prompted you to take this in the first place?"

Jack rose, walked to the small refrigerator, and popped the top on a can of diet soda. There was no way he could tell her about the dreams. She already thought he was crazy.

"You've seen the tattoo on Tupac's chest."

"What about it?"

"It got me curious, and I did some checking. One thing led to another until I finally ran into a reason that Conrad Altmann might be interested in Tupac. It was rumored, but never proven, that Klaus Barbie smuggled the crown piece out of Germany after the war and that he may have been attempting to reassemble the entire Sun Staff. I looked through Altmann's study, hoping to find some confirmation that he shared his father's interest in the artifact, and I think I did. I think he's using Tupac to find the missing silver staff."

"For what purpose?"

"You tell me. I think you owe me a complete rundown of the deal the NSA made with Tupac and what Admiral Riles is trying to accomplish."

Jack studied Janet's face, but it remained impassive, a mask that revealed no sign of what was going on within her head. It didn't give him a lot of confidence in her forthcoming reply.

"I'm not fully read in on the operation."

"Bullshit. They sent you here, so you had a need to know."

"They only sent me here because you were trying to free Tupac. I was pulled out of Africa and sent here to make sure that didn't happen."

"You're telling me that you don't know anything about what the NSA wants from Tupac?"

"No. I'm telling you I'm not fully read in. I know Altmann believes that if the fully assembled staff is placed in something called the Altar of the Gods and if the correct code sequence is dialed into the crown piece, it acquires some mystical power that could restore the master race."

Jack didn't like where this was going. Not that he believed any of that Thule Society crap, but it was striking a little too close to his somnambulistic visions.

"And Admiral Riles believes that?"

"I doubt it. But I know he's very interested in obtaining the complete staff for study. His deal with Tupac was that the NSA would help him recover it, thereby returning the holy Incan artifact to its rightful owners. In return, Tupac agreed to loan the Sun Staff to the NSA for a short period of time so that they can study it."

"And why would Riles want to do that?"

"Again, he didn't tell me. But I gather that the NSA scientists are puzzled at how the ancient Incans could have created such an intricate, durable device almost a thousand years ago."

Jack took a sip from the cold soda can.

"One thing doesn't make sense. Why the delay? Why have Tupac endure days of torture before agreeing to take Altmann to the staff?"

"That was part of Tupac's demand. He wanted the NSA to break the Sun Staff codes and deliver the answer to him first. It took longer than expected."

"Why?"

"I don't know."

"You delivered the codes to him?"

"No. I told him the NSA had deciphered them, but Altmann locked me up before I could pass them along."

"But you have them?"

"Now I do."

"Damn it, Janet. You're not making sense. You just told me that Tupac needs the codes and that Altmann needs the codes, but the only organization capable of deciphering them is the NSA."

"When he locked me in that dungeon, Altmann claimed to have infiltrated the NSA. Maybe he got the codes before I did."

Jack stood up, drained the last of the soda, and crushed the can in his hand. Tossing it in the trash, he glanced down at Pizarro's journal, a disconcerting rumble starting in his gut.

"If that's true, we better hope that the NSA's right and Altmann's wrong about what that damn thing can do."

CHAPTER 80

The appearance of the cave surprised Altmann. It was no wonder that very few people even knew of its existence, the opening little bigger than a blue whale's blowhole. He was amazed that Tupac Inti and Dolf Gruenberg managed to worm their way inside. But once inside, everything changed almost immediately.

This was no mammoth cavern with stalactites and stalagmites. This was the entrance to an interconnecting network of lava tubes from a long extinct volcano. "Tube" was an excellent description of the tunnel through which he now moved, following close behind Dolf and Tupac Inti. The lights of dozens of flashlights bobbed and weaved along the red walls, ceiling, and floor that continued fairly, but not quite, straight ahead until darkness again reclaimed supremacy.

It made Altmann think of nineteenth-century coal miners making the long walk back to the surface at the end of a long day's work, their bobbing lanterns as impotent as fireflies, pushing the endless dark back a tiny bit, only to have it slide in from behind as they passed.

Though tubular, the walls weren't smooth. In places water had leaked in, carving its own structure, augmenting the naturally occurring nooks and crannies with side passages of its own. It was into one of these steeply descending, narrow slots that Tupac Inti led them. Forced to tromp through a foot of swiftly flowing water, Altmann's feet ached with the cold, but it could not dampen his mood. From nearby the silver staff called out, its sweet song summoning its soul mate, the golden orb crown piece.

Here in these underground halls the water splashed and echoed with a mystical rhythm, each drip a note thrumming within Gaia's womb. Altmann laughed out loud, the sound drowning the more subtle noises that had so enchanted him. He hadn't felt like this since he'd been a boy, since he'd made his first kill.

It was only a cat. A sickly, scrawny one at that. What he'd done was a kindness, although he hadn't intended it as such. He'd meant to drag it out, to extend the animal's sweet suffering until it screamed and yowled for the release that only death could bring. But like a young man with that first woman's hand on his crotch, his excitement had exploded too soon, terminating his pleasure long before he'd wanted it to end.

Tupac Inti stopped ahead, turning to stare back at Altmann with a questioning look on his face. Dolf had turned to look at Altmann too. Something in those looks pissed him off.

"Keep moving."

Five minutes passed, and then ten before the passage suddenly stopped descending and the tunnel widened. Here, the cold water became more than waist deep, forcing the men to hold their weapons and flashlights above their shoulders. Even Altmann removed his Sig P226 from his shoulder holster to keep it dry.

The ripples produced by their passage sent shimmering waves of reflected light skittering across the tunnel's red walls and ceiling. The chill Altmann had previously regarded as pleasant agony now made his teeth chatter, threatening hypothermia.

Altmann glanced at the adult daughter he had first met at the airport this morning, smiling at the thought of how she'd corrected him when he'd called her Priscilla. Bones was what she wanted to be called, a nickname she didn't bother to explain. Although the water rose almost to her shoulders, she made no complaint, seeming to endure its chill with less distress than he was feeling.

From behind, low mutters and curses reached Altmann's ears, but he ignored his men's grumbling. He would endure the cold and discomfort to get what he wanted, and they would because Altmann demanded it.

The tunnel rounded a bend, and Tupac Inti scrambled up onto a rocky outcropping on the right, forcing Dolf to provide slack in the rope to avoid pulling the native man back into the water. Dolf climbed up, stopping on a ledge as Inti squeezed sideways into a crack in the wall.

Altmann grasped a rocky handhold, wet and slippery from the passage of the other two men, and clambered up, hearing Bones splash out of the water close behind him. When Altmann stood erect on the ledge, he saw Dolf vanish around a bend inside the crevice. His lieutenant's voice, tinged with excitement, echoed out into the larger tunnel.

"We're here!"

"Do you see the staff?"

"Yes."

"Don't touch it. I'm coming in."

Altmann holstered his gun and turned to help Bones up onto the ledge. Then, seeing the first of the others start to follow her up, he directed his flashlight into the man's face.

"The rest of you wait where you are."

The prospect of waiting rib-deep in the icy water brought a fresh round of German and Spanish curses from the long line of armed men.

Removing his backpack, Altmann stepped up to the crack, turned sideways, and shuffled inside. What had been a very tight fit for Inti and Dolf only gave Altmann the occasional jab from a protruding rock. Three meters in, an opening yawned before him. Altmann stepped out into a room the size of a London double-decker sightseeing bus, formed by an ancient lava bubble.

Then he saw the silver staff, glittering in the glare of Dolf's flashlight beam, lying atop a narrow ledge on the far wall. With excitement palpitating his heart, Altmann walked forward, directing his own flashlight at the object he'd desired for so long.

As he drew close, Altmann saw that the staff wasn't actually resting on the ledge. It had been lovingly placed atop twin mounts of carved wood that supported the artifact an inch above the ledge so that no part of the metal touched the stone. In its own way, the staff was as beautiful as the golden orb that occupied the waterproof top pocket of his backpack. Perfectly cylindrical, it looked to have been precision machined and polished bright. Judging by the age of the wood mounts upon which it rested, it had lain in its current position for at least a decade. But despite the passage of time, it bore no trace of tarnish.

The finely engraved symbols twisted and intertwined their way up the staff from its base all the way to the top, where the golden orb had once been fastened. Now, for the first time in five centuries, both pieces of the Incan Sun Staff occupied the same room.

Bones's voice at his left shoulder caused Altmann to glance at her.

"So perfect."

She leaned her walking stick against the wall and stepped forward. Altmann was struck by the reverence in her gaze as she reached out both hands to gently lift the legendary object from its resting place, rolling it on her fingers as she examined its symbols. Then Bones turned to face him, extending her arms as if she was offering the staff in tribute.

Cool to the touch, the staff's surface was incredibly smooth, making the edges of the runes etched into its surface feel even sharper than they were. Repeating the movements that he'd just watched Bones make, Altmann rolled the staff across his palms, the motion animating the symbols as if he were rapidly flipping the pages of a cartoonist's sketchbook.

A gentle longing in the pit of his stomach made him want to remove the orb from the backpack, place it atop the staff, and enter the code that would cause them to interconnect. But this was not the place.

Altmann nodded at Bones, and she retrieved her walking stick from where it leaned against the cave wall. She twisted the top, and it came free, revealing a padded, hollow compartment within. Altmann carefully guided the silver staff into its new carrying case and then let Bones seal the protective cap back in place.

When he looked up, he caught Tupac Inti's gaze, the man's dark eyes glittering ominously in the flashlights' glare. Altmann understood the hatred in that look. After all, Inti had just handed the Quechua people's most sacred artifact to one of their sworn enemies. Even worse, Tupac understood the legend of the Sun Staff's true power as only a direct descendent of its original keepers could.

Altmann grinned and then nodded at Dolf.

"Let's go."

It was time to bring the legend to life.

CHAPTER 81

Levi Elias looked up from his desk to see Dr. Denise Jennings standing in his door, her graying hair pulled back so tightly that she'd never need a face lift. He motioned her to a chair and watched as she closed the door behind her and took a seat. His nose caught the faint hint of her shampoo, one of those herbal scents he found mildly unpleasant. Then again, Levi wasn't a big fan of scented anything. Thank God she didn't wear perfume. Some aging men and women started applying smells as heartily as teenage boys who had seen too many body-spray commercials.

"You're in awfully early. What have you got for me?"

"Big John texted me at four this morning."

"Texted you?" His voice carried with it the concern her statement triggered. "From where?"

"No need to worry. Big John used an embedded encryption that only the node stored on my device could decrypt."

"And its content?"

"Altmann probability, 0.83."

Levi felt the first glimmer of hope he'd felt in the last twenty-four hours.

"Should we bring Admiral Riles in on this?"

"That's your call, but I think it's too early. Big John identified communications activity between high-ranking military officials who are known to have taken bribes from Altmann. Nothing specific, but it implies that Altmann may have contacted key figures there."

"Do we have any indication of the subject of those communications?"

"The military received a bomb threat against the Tiahuanaco archeological site. They have temporarily closed the site in response to the threat. However, the closure may be completely unrelated to Altmann and the Sun Staff."

"When was the threat received?"

"Late last night."

"Do we know its source?"

"The message claimed to be from a communist rebel group affiliated with the Shining Path."

Levi considered this new information. None of it was specific to Altmann or the Sun Staff, and right now he had received no updated reports of Altmann's location. The man had taken Tupac Inti and a couple of dozen armed men, departed his Cochabamba compound yesterday morning aboard three helicopters, and hadn't been seen or heard from since. The available satellite imagery had been of no use either.

Levi turned his attention back to Dr. Jennings. "Thank you, Denise. Let me know if Big John comes up with something more specific."

The computer scientist nodded, rose from the chair, and walked out of the office. Levi watched her go and then began composing an encrypted message to Janet Price. It wasn't much to go on, but he'd rather have Jack and Janet check it out than have them sit idle in Oruro. The trip would take them a few hours.

There was a clear connection between the legend of the Sun Staff and those old Incan ruins. That didn't necessarily mean that was where Altmann would go. But at the moment, it was the only thing he had. Decision made, Levi picked up the phone and placed a high-priority intelligence request to retask the next available satellite for a fresh batch of high-resolution imagery of the Tiahuanaco site.

As he'd agreed to join Admiral Riles in breaking the rules, it was time to go all in.

CHAPTER 82

The laptop speaker issued its new-message alert, redirecting Janet's attention from Jack to the display.

"We've got a lead. Time to pack up and hit the road."

As she started to shut down the laptop, Jack stopped her.

"Hold on. Let me check to see if any of my connections have come through with anything."

Janet stood and stepped away, letting Jack slide onto the seat she'd just vacated. She looked over his shoulder as he logged into an e-mail account named WatfordElephant87654@gmail.com and checked for new messages. There was only one, and it contained just a single line of text.

Home is where the heart is.

Jack deleted it, logged out, and shut down the laptop.

Janet caught his eye. "What was that about?"

"Just a friend offering his help."

"A friend?"

"Stefan Rosenstein."

The name caught Janet by surprise. "The Bolivian senator? How do you know him?"

Jack's smile held a hint of the old cockiness. "You mean there's something about me the NSA doesn't know?"

Janet ignored the jab. "What kind of help?"

"We'll find the answer at his house in La Paz."

"Alright. That's on the way to where we're going."

"Which is?"

"The Tiahuanaco ruins."

Janet saw the surprise flash in Jack's eyes; then it was gone, almost as if she'd imagined it. Only Janet didn't believe it had been her imagination. It wasn't unusual that Jack would recognize the name. Tiahuanaco was a famous Bolivian site situated fifty miles west of La Paz. But the look she'd seen in Jack's face had been more than recognition. It was a strange mixture of excitement and dread.

"What makes the NSA think Altmann's headed for Tiahuanaco?"

"They just said they want to investigate unusual activity there. It may be nothing."

Jack surprised her by not arguing the tenuous nature of the NSA lead. He merely nodded, rose to his feet, and began rapidly packing his gear. Again Janet felt the reluctant excitement in his movements, as if Jack were fighting an internal duel, simultaneously winning and losing.

Shrugging aside the disconcerting insight, Janet began her own preparation for departure. If something was waiting for them at Tiahuanaco, they would deal with it when they got there. On the way, they'd see just how much help Jack's friendly senator could really provide.

CHAPTER 83

By the time they reached La Paz, the sun was already sinking low in the west, painting the snow-covered slopes of Mount Illimani pink. At twenty-one-thousand feet, the peak was often shrouded in clouds, but not this evening. Except for a narrow swath along the western horizon, the skies were clear.

Somehow Jack could feel that tonight was the night he'd been unknowingly seeking for almost two years. Somewhere out there, Conrad Altmann had the Incan Sun Staff in his possession, and Jack was going to find him. There would come a moment when he would have his chance to grasp the staff, just as Pizarro had done in his dreams. And like it had for Pizarro, that touch would free him of the entity that threatened his sanity.

There was no way Jack could tell Janet that part of his plan without her concluding that he'd already lost his mind. Perhaps she would be right to think it. After all, hadn't he had the very same doubts?

Approaching their initial destination, Jack turned the car into the entrance to Stefan Rosenstein's mansion, stopping at the closed front gate. Unlike his previous visits to the house when Stefan had been in Bolivia, this time Jack planned to park in the driveway near the front door. Jack lowered the window, pressed the call button, and waited.

A moment later he heard the smooth voice of Stefan's butler, Ricardo Hernandez, through the speaker.

"Quién es?"

"Home is where the heart is." The phrase from Stefan's message rolled off Jack's lips in English, exactly as he'd received it.

There was a short delay, and then the electric gate swung open to allow them admittance. Jack pulled forward, progressing counterclockwise around the looping driveway, coming to a stop before the front door. Seeing Janet place her hand inside her leather jacket, Jack shook his head.

"Easy. We don't want to spook him."

"Stefan?"

"No, his butler."

Jack climbed out of the Tundra and Janet did likewise, both of them approaching the double doors together. The leftmost door swung inward, held open by the tall, traditionally clad butler.

"It is a pleasure to see you again, Señor Gregory. Please step inside, both of you. The others are waiting in the parlor. May I take your jackets?"

Jack, familiar with Ricardo's strict adherence to the formal rules of his profession, didn't offer to shake his hand or to introduce Janet, merely extending the standard greeting.

"Thank you, Ricardo, but no."

Jack led the way through the foyer and then turned left into the parlor. Inside, four high-backed chairs were arranged in a semicircle before an unlit fireplace, the center two occupied by the two men that Jack had expected to find here, both puffing on thick cigars. They smiled up at him but only bothered climbing to their feet when they saw Janet.

Beside him, Jack saw Janet smile at the oddly archaic courtesy these men suddenly felt compelled to render. He stepped forward to shake the hand of the nearest of the two, a fair-skinned, curly-headed man who stood an inch shorter than Jack.

"Janet, this is Stefan's cousin, Efran Rosenstein. A good man who can't drive worth a damn."

Janet merely nodded. "Nice to meet you."

"My pleasure," said Efran.

"And this," Jack said stepping forward to shake the hand of the second man, "is Pablo Griego, a man of big deeds but few words."

After Janet and Pablo exchanged pleasantries, Pablo and Efran returned to their seats while Jack and Janet took the two chairs that bracketed them. Cigars were offered and refused. Then they got down to business.

Jack glanced at Janet, sitting with her legs crossed, leaning back in the chair opposite his. Her brown eyes glittered in the light of the sunset that filtered in through the tall, western-facing windows. For a weird moment, it seemed that she picked up the same red eye-shine that was a common trait of his.

He turned his attention to Efran, who had just taken a deep pull on the cigar, blowing out a blue cloud of smoke that drifted upward toward the twelve-foot ceiling.

"Tonight I'm going to finish the job Stefan hired me to do. I need to know what help you've come here to offer."

Efran moved his arm to the armrest, a movement that threatened to drop a half inch of ash on Stefan's fine hardwood floor.

"Not much, I'm afraid, at least not in terms of active support."

Jack felt his jaw muscles tense and forced them to relax. "Then what's this all about? Why did Stefan bother to message me if you're not going to help."

"Let me remind you that Stefan hired you to do this, not us."

"Then why waste my time with this little side trip?"

Efran crushed out the stump of his cigar in the free-standing ashtray beside his chair and stood.

"To show you this."

Efran nodded at Pablo, who rose from his chair and walked across the room to open the door to a standard-sized coat closet.

A low whistle escaped Janet's lips and she stepped forward as Jack rose from his chair.

Efran shrugged.

"It's not a huge selection, but considering the short notice Stefan gave me, it was the best I could round up."

Jack looked on as Janet ran a loving finger over the weapons and satellite communication gear stacked inside.

"I take it," Janet said, "Stefan wasn't your typical Bolivian senator?"

Efran laughed, his curious eyes studying Janet.

"Help yourself to anything you want."

Jack found himself adjusting his previous ideas of how he and Janet might deal with Altmann at some location where he was protected by two to three dozen heavily armed fighters.

"Don't you think we'll be a little conspicuous hauling that stuff out front and loading it into the bed of the Tundra?"

"No need. The van I used to pick you and Tupac up at Palmasola is parked in the second garage. I know a chop shop that will be happy to get rid of your pickup."

Janet turned to Efran. "I need to connect my laptop to the Internet to download the latest update on Altmann."

Efran's quizzical eyes shifted to Jack.

"It's okay," Jack said. "Otherwise, she wouldn't be with me."

"There is high-speed WiFi throughout the house."

As Janet, assisted by Pablo, retrieved their kitbags from the Tundra, Efran spread a protective mat on the floor. By the time she had set up her laptop and received log-in instructions, Jack had already begun pulling equipment out of the closet and laying them atop the mat.

What they were taking wouldn't win World War III, but it would certainly go a long way toward getting it started.

CHAPTER 84

As the sun sank below the long line of clouds, low down on the western horizon, Conrad Altmann watched the red sky bleed out. After all these years of patiently working toward this night, his patience had finally worn thin.

For most of the day he and his men had waited as the Bolivian Army units secured the site, clearing all the archeological teams, even evacuating people from the surrounding farms and villages. To complete the fiction they were creating, bomb search and disposal teams scoured the ruins before progressing to the nearby hotels and hostels.

Now all he waited for was the passage of twilight and the deeper darkness that followed. The light of the quarter-moon wouldn't bother him. His men would blend in with the activity of the preceding daylight, the continuing work of a bomb squad that had identified suspicious materials and the security team that had been put in place to keep others away from the implied danger.

Three meters to Altmann's left, Tupac Inti sat stoically, his hands securely cuffed to a belly chain, his legs shackled at a length that would limit him to something slightly less than a normal walking stride. Standing beside Tupac, ever watchful, stood the tall form of Dolf Gruenberg, a pale specter in the deepening twilight.

Altmann's daughter stood at his side. Although he would have loved to have known Bones while she was growing up, her mother had done a marvelous job of home schooling the child, preparing her for the role she would play in her father's master plan. Tonight, here at the Temple of Kalasasaya, that plan would reach its glorious objective. Klaus Barbie would have been very proud of his son and granddaughter, had he only been alive to see this.

Altmann turned back to Dolf.

"Position the men, then hustle back here. I want to be ready to move out in half an hour."

Dolf glanced down at Tupac and then strode rapidly away, gathering Altmann's men to him as he went.

With the purple remnants of the sunset at his back, Altmann knelt beside Tupac Inti to look directly into the whites of the shaman's eyes.

"Can you feel it? Can you sense the power I am about to unleash?"

Tupac made no sign that he had heard, but Altmann continued.

"For the first time in history, the Sun Staff will perform the task it was designed to do. Your ancestors knew the staff held the power to recall the old gods, but until now, no one has had the key to unlock that power. It wasn't their fault. Until now, the technology to unravel the codes didn't exist."

Altmann clapped a hand down on Tupac Inti's shoulder.

"Be happy. Tonight, with your help and that of my daughter, I will turn the dreams of your forefathers into a reality."

CHAPTER 85

Admiral Riles was more angry than he could ever recall being. Conrad Altmann had pissed in his oatmeal. Now Riles intended to use the full arsenal at his disposal to help Janet Price and Jack "The Ripper" Gregory burn Altmann's little empire down around him.

The NSA War Room was in full operation, something that rarely happened without the president's direct authorization. This was no circle of generals sitting around an oval table staring at digital maps showing the layout of forces or incoming and outgoing missile tracks. It was more akin to the NASA mission control center in Houston.

In a glass-walled room that overlooked three tiers of workstations, Admiral Riles stood beside Levi Elias, absorbing the scene that spread out before him. On the curving far wall, high-resolution displays summarized the activity of the assembled group of cyber-warriors that Admiral Riles had nicknamed the Dirty Dozen.

The NSA War Room was a construct Riles had created. Although it was true that most of the best programmers and hackers preferred to work alone, at heart they were gamers, and the very best enjoyed being recognized as such. The only way to prove who was the best was to dominate in a competitive game environment. So Admiral Riles had come up with a way that, when the most difficult cyber-attacks had to be carried out under tight timelines, his current top crop of CWs could be thrown into an environment that drove them into a competitive frenzy.

Inside the war room, the hacking targets were clearly defined and prioritized. The cyber-warriors were awarded or penalized points based upon the speed and progress of their attacks. They were allowed to team up or to attack targets individually. At the end of every war room battle, the overall ranking of each CW was adjusted and publicized throughout the NSA's CW community. The reigning CW top gun was a twenty-year-old black MIT prodigy named Jamal Glover, who went by the nom de guerre "Ace." Riles considered recruiting Jamal to the NSA as one of his best feats—right up there with stealing Janet Price from the CIA. If he managed to land Gregory, it would complete the hat trick.

As always, tonight's action had started with the posting of the target list, most of the targets in the Bolivian military, but some designed to blind or delay other international agencies from being alerted to what was happening in Bolivia.

The room in which Riles stood was the op-center. It was where a mixture of analysts, linguists, and communications experts gathered to exploit the target systems that the Dirty Dozen hacked. As Riles watched targets pop out of the red queue and into the green, he managed a smile.

"Levi. Do we have solid confirmation that Altmann's group is at Tiahuanaco?"

"Yes, sir. The next batch of satellite imagery will start coming in on the downlink in three minutes. We're picking up low-priority Bolivian military comm-link chatter. They are referring to Altmann's group as Bomb Squad Zero. Apparently, it is causing quite a chuckle among the rank and file that some bozos are searching for explosives in the dark."

"Are Janet and Jack on-site?"

"Their last contact was from La Paz. We're monitoring the encrypted satcom link Janet said she'll be using."

"Wait for it. We don't want to distract the military police until we know exactly where Janet and Jack plan to assault."

"Yes, sir."

As the long target list continued to transition from red to green, Admiral Riles watched with satisfaction. Very soon now, it would be show time.

: CHAPTER 86

Tupac Inti led the way toward the Kalasasaya Temple ruins, one of the many architectural wonders of this ancient site, but the only one he was interested in tonight. Behind him he could hear the crunching footfalls of Conrad Altmann and the select group of eight who accompanied the Nazi boss to the altar cavern, their flashlight beams lighting the ground but killing their night vision. He tried to keep his eyes averted from these bright spots with only partial success.

Although he'd dreaded the moment that would forever rob the Quechua people of their most sacred artifact, he found himself anxious to get it over with. Altmann wanted to be shown to the Altar of the Gods, and Tupac would make sure he got there. It was the only way to forever end the threat that Altmann posed.

He approached the Kalasasaya Temple from the east, initially heading toward the gate before turning northward along the outer wall. Tupac held out his left hand, counting the precision cuts in the stone blocks as he moved slowly northward. Such was his rising excitement that he momentarily forgot his shackles, almost tripping and falling as he lengthened his stride.

Suddenly he slowed, his count having reached the magic prime. Forty-seven. Feeling up and down the wall with both hands, he traced the edges of the blocks and found the two spots he was looking for. It was an engineering marvel from the past. The whole place was, but this place in particular.

How many hundreds of archeologists had examined every facet of these stone walls as they sought to uncover the ancient secrets that lay buried in these ruins? The walls of Kalasasaya grew more interesting as one progressed toward the temple's interior. But the entrance to this temple's greatest secret had been hidden on the outside, in the most visible but least likely spot.

Tupac gestured toward Altmann, pointing at two stones that jutted out slightly from the wall.

"I need strong men here and here."

Altmann gave the command, and two men stepped forward until they could touch the dark wall.

Tupac guided their hands into position beneath the head-sized stones.

"When I say lift, put your backs into it and push straight up. Do not stop until I say to do so."

As Conrad Altmann stepped forward to observe, Tupac positioned himself between the two men, thrust his fingers into two holes that seemed to be mere cracks between stones, and gave the command.

"Lift now."

The men to his left and right grunted, and though the weight of the edifice would have seemed to make such a thing impossible,

Tupac felt a slight shift in the stone before him. Grasping his handholds, he levered himself up, placed his feet against a large stone, leaned back, and pressed with all his might.

Deep within the wall there came a sound of rolling stone, followed by a grinding, sandy sound as the stone against which his feet pressed moved ever so slowly inward.

"My God!" Conrad Altmann gasped.

Tupac ignored him, increasing the effort he was directing into the stone.

"Lift harder on the right side," he gasped.

Dolf stepped forward to place his hands under the other man's and lifted, grunting with effort. The smaller man's bones cracked, and he screamed, but the stone started moving again. This time it did not stop until it rolled inward to reveal a one-meter-wide opening.

"Release the stones," Tupac hissed.

Dolf and the other two complied, one cursing and cupping his injured hands to his chest.

Altmann's voice rang in Tupac's right ear. "Quick. Jam something in there to keep it open."

Tupac pulled his legs back out of the hole and righted himself, struggling to catch his breath.

"No need. The passage will remain open until we again lift the two stones and release the counter balance within."

Conrad Altmann pushed through, thrusting his head and shoulders into the hole, his flashlight pushing back the interior darkness. He backed out.

"The air smells bad."

"It is old air," Tupac replied. "But it will not kill you."

I will do that. The thought came unbidden to his mind.

And then, one after another, they squeezed through the hole and scrambled inside.

CHAPTER 87

Two kilometers east of Tiahuanaco, Jack killed the headlights, turned off of Highway 1 onto a dirt road, and pulled into a concealed parking spot. In the dim light of the quarter-moon, he looked across the van at Janet, feeling the familiar rush of adrenaline that approaching danger and her presence fed him. Tonight the adrenaline spigot was cranked wide open.

As was always the case when that happened, Jack felt his natural intuition amped up disproportionately, leaving no doubt in his mind that his enemies were close by. Still, it paid to spend some time gathering whatever intelligence the NSA could provide. So he would muzzle the hound that howled within and give Janet a chance to do her thing.

It took her fifteen minutes to set up the secure satellite data link, running a cable from the vehicle battery to the inverter that would power the rig. Seated on the floor in the back of the panel van, she powered the system on, giving Jack direction as he worked outside, adjusting the satellite antenna for maximum signal strength.

When she was satisfied, Jack moved to the side of the van where he could see her work while he maintained a lookout for any unwelcome visitors.

The sound of her fingers hitting the laptop keys mimicked the staccato beat of a soft drumroll.

"We're in," she said. "Altmann has two dozen of his men in firing positions around the Kalasasaya Temple. A military police platoon has set up road blocks just east and west of the ruins, but most of their men are at a temporary headquarters they've established at one of the hotels in town."

"Any chance your NSA buddies can provide some satellite imagery?"

"I'm downloading one now. It's big, so it'll take some time."

"How long?"

"Fifteen or twenty minutes for the first one."

Jack didn't like the sound of that. "Cancel the download. We can't afford to wait that long. Have them reduce the resolution and crop the image so that it only covers the Kalasasaya Temple and the firing positions that surround it. In the meantime, they can send us the coordinates of each firing position, the roadblocks, and the police headquarters. We'll have to do this the old-fashioned way."

As Janet sent the request, Jack pulled his kitbag out of the back of the van, extracted a waterproof map case containing a one-to-fifty-thousand scale map of the area, and spread it on the floor of the van next to Janet. The glow of the laptop gave enough illumination that he didn't have to turn on a flashlight.

A minute passed before Janet responded.

"Got 'em."

Taking a grease pencil from a pocket on the map case, Jack marked each position on the map as she read off the coordinates.

A new message popped up on Janet's screen.

"The NSA has hacked into the military police communications network. They are ready to cut the communications between the Bolivian MPs and their headquarters."

"Can the NSA team spoof the MPs and substitute their own commands on those channels?"

Janet entered the message, receiving an immediate response.

"Yes. And they're sending the cropped image now. We'll have it in just over a minute."

Jack reoriented the map to north and pointed at a spot along Highway 1, ten kilometers southwest of the ruins.

"Have the NSA command all the nearby MP units to intercept a rebel force that has been seen near this intersection."

Janet nodded and sent the message.

"Also tell them to block all of Altmann's communications."

"The NSA won't be able to interdict short-range radio communications. No local jamming assets."

"I'm betting Altmann's team is talking to each other on cell phones. Regardless, if Altmann goes underground, he'll cut himself off from outside signals without anybody else's help."

"And you think he's going underground?"

Jack felt the memory of his waking Pizarro dream take him and nodded. "Count on it."

He watched as Janet sent this additional request and got back an affirmative response. A minute later she turned to look at him and grinned.

"We've got the image."

Jack leaned in closer as she displayed it on the laptop, zooming out and then in on each of the firing locations. Although the resolution wasn't great, they could still make out the pixelated forms of the pairs of men that occupied each of the dozen positions. The image confirmed what Jack had marked on the map. Each firing position was separated from its neighbor by at least a hundred meters.

Hearing the distant sound of diesel truck engines starting, Jack folded the map case and stepped out of the van.

"What about a distraction?"

"I told Admiral Riles to give us five minutes before he works his magic. Help me disconnect everything we have from its battery."

"What are they going to do, hit us with an EMP burst?"

"The next best thing."

"Even the night-vision goggles?"

Janet removed the battery from her laptop and moved on to her cell phone. "Better safe than sorry. We'll have to carry batteries for anything electrical we take with us."

Jack mirrored her actions and then opened the van's hood and disconnected its battery cables. Stepping back around the side, he saw Janet stacking equipment by the sliding door.

"Time to gear up."

CHAPTER 88

Bones McCoy slid through the small opening with an ease none of the others who accompanied Conrad Altmann managed, thrusting the walking stick into the tunnel ahead of her. When she extricated herself, she found herself in a descending natural tunnel that men had long ago widened so that two could walk abreast. Ahead of her, Conrad Altmann directed his flashlight beam back toward her. Beyond Altmann, Dolf Gruenberg stooped beneath the two-meter-high ceiling, aiming his flashlight forward toward the spot where the ceiling rose to allow Tupac Inti to stand erect.

When the first of the men behind Bones worked his way in and rose to his feet, Altmann spoke to him in a commanding voice.

"Leave two men here to guard the entrance, and take up positions with the other two farther down the tunnel. Kill anyone who tries to get past you."

"Yes, sir."

Without waiting for the other men, Altmann continued on down the tunnel, motioning for Dolf and Tupac to do the same. The man-made entrance gave way to a taller and wider natural passageway that wound its way forward in a series of turns and switchbacks before branching right and then left. Tupac crossed these two intersections, continuing to lead them forward down the main passage.

Although she'd managed to control her excitement up until now, Bones felt her hands begin to shake. Maybe she was absorbing some of Altmann's emotion. It didn't really matter.

Five paces in front of her, Tupac Inti came to a stop at the entrance to a large cavern. Altmann and Dolf stepped up beside him. The sight that confronted Bones as she joined them filled her with awe. A glance to her left told her that Altmann shared her feelings as emotions twitched the muscles at the corners of his eyes and mouth.

Against the rightmost wall of the cavern, a three-tiered, golden altar rose from the floor to a height of two meters. Its intricately carved and inlaid surface channeled and amplified light, reflecting the harsh flashlight beams back into her eyes as if the altar were angered by their ungentle touch. Bones started to have a fingernails-down-the-chalkboard feeling that made her want to smash the flashlights.

Altmann turned and grabbed one of the torches from its sconce on the near wall, applying the flame from his lighter to it. As the torch sputtered to life, he gestured at Dolf.

"Light the torches, all of them. And turn off that damned flashlight."

Grabbing another torch, Dolf held it up to let the flame spread from Altmann's to his, then began making his way methodically around the irregularly shaped, twenty-meter-diameter cavern until smoky flames from all but one of the six torches licked the darkness. The metal sconce that held the torch nearest the altar crumbled at Dolf's touch, its frame shattering as it struck the stone floor, sounding as loud in the still cavern as a bell in an enclosed church steeple.

Bones couldn't shake the feeling that a sacrilege had just occurred in this ancient tomb. A crazy thought occurred to her. She doubted that another such occurrence would be tolerated.

CHAPTER 89

"Five minutes from now, Janet wants a distraction. The best we can do."

Admiral Riles nodded at Levi and then pressed a button and looked into the camera. Outside the glass op-center, the heads of the Dirty Dozen rose in unison as Admiral Riles's visage filled the giant wall displays, his voice of a volume and timbre that commanded their full attention.

"Listen up. At the top of all displays, a five-minute countdown timer has started. When that mark hits zero—and not one second before—I want to hit every connected device within a five-mile radius of Tiahuanaco. If it has an alarm, I want it blaring. If it has lights, I want them flashing. If it has a ringer, I want it ringing. Music blasting, TVs blaring, horns honking, engines racing. Speakers at max volume. Displays at max brightness. You now have four minutes and thirty seconds to hack as many devices as possible."

Riles paused for two seconds.

"I want them all!"

Riles's face disappeared from the wall displays, replaced by the cyber-warrior scoreboard for this new game. Above them in the op-center, Riles turned his attention to Levi Elias.

"Game on."

CHAPTER 90

Conrad Altmann stepped forward, pausing at the base of the altar to motion Bones forward. Carefully setting his backpack on the stone floor, he opened the waterproof compartment that held the golden crown piece and lifted it out. The torchlight licked its surface and then crawled through the cracks between rings into the intricate interior, where dark shadows reared and plunged, struggling to avoid the torchlight's fiery touch.

For a moment, Altmann found himself transfixed, unable to take his eyes away from the beautiful orb. His daughter stepped up beside him, looked at the orb cupped in his hands, and gasped.

"So beautiful."

Altmann barely heard her whisper, so intently was his attention focused on the artifact. His touch lingered as if he were afraid to break the spell it cast. Then inexorably, he turned his gaze upon the two-meter walking stick held tight in his daughter's right hand.

"Remove the staff."

Bones started. For the first time, Altmann noted how closely the color of her blue eyes matched his own. Whether it was the gravity of the moment or the awe that filled his soul to be this close to his lifelong goal, his senses were so attuned that he noted the muffled rustle of her clothes against her skin as Bones lowered the walking stick and unfastened the cap. Her delicate fingers grabbed the end of the silver staff and pulled it carefully from the padded compartment that had cradled it.

Holding it in both hands, Bones stepped up onto the altar's first tier, Altmann at her side. Although he'd read nothing about such ceremonial choreography, their matching movements as they climbed onto the altar felt right. They took another step, and Altmann tried to calm his pounding heart. Together they mounted the topmost tier, the high priest and priestess performing a ritual that none had ever before performed, not in its entirety.

Missing the torch on the wall in front of them, the light from the other five torches cast moving doppelgangers of their shadows across the altar and onto the far wall. The top of the altar upon which they stood was a highly polished gold rectangle, approximately two meters wide and one deep. In the exact center, a not-quite-circular hole the size of the silver staff's base appeared to have been machined into its surface.

Bones knelt, tilted the staff erect, and attempted to slide it into that hole. It took Altmann a moment to realize that it fit, but not precisely, so that the staff wobbled slightly within the hole. Bones rose to her feet, and together they inspected the opposite end. It was clearly designed to mate with the orb.

Altmann puzzled over this. Every aspect of these objects had been crafted with impossible precision. For the staff to have such a sloppy fit into its altar slot made no kind of sense. Could Tupac have deceived him, brought them to the wrong altar? He glanced across the cavern toward Tupac, who had shuffled back away from the altar into a shallow alcove, his face a dark mask of dread. That look could mean only one thing. This was the right place.

Cradling the orb in his palms, Altmann returned his gaze to the staff, wobbling slightly in the hole as Bones slowly twisted it back and forth, seeking that perfect fit.

If this was truly the Altar of the Gods, then what the hell was wrong?

CHAPTER 91

Janet tracked the countdown in her head as she and Jack ducked low, moving silently through the knee-high desert grass and scrub brush toward the stone remnants of outer ruins where they had chosen to launch their assault. They had just over a minute remaining of the five she'd asked Levi to give her. She could tell that Jack sensed it by the way he increased the pace.

They both carried the short M89SR Israeli sniper rifles with suppressors that reduced the sound of their shots to no louder than what Janet's sandal made when she slapped it against the ground to dislodge some beach sand. Besides the rifle, Janet had her Glock, night-vision goggles with battery, two knives, and a mix of flash-bang and fragmentation grenades in pockets or clipped to her utility vest. Jack was similarly outfitted.

She'd thought about bringing the sat-phone, but it was too damn bulky. Besides, it wouldn't work underground, and though he didn't say how he knew, Jack was certain Tupac was taking Altmann into an underground cavern system. If they didn't make it that far, the phone wouldn't pull their asses out of this fire.

The pile of cut stones was little more than rubble, one of the portions of this site that had been looted for paving stones prior to coming under the protection of the Bolivian government. But as Janet took up a firing position on the left side of the pile, with Jack on her right, she had to acknowledge that she was glad these stones were still here.

And then the night was rent asunder. From all around the ruins, dozens of cell phones lit up, warbling out ring tones, playing music, or sounding wake-up alarms as the waiting men struggled to silence them. Vehicles rumbled to life and headlights stabbed the night while horns and radios blared. Farther to the west, in the adjacent town, a competing cacophony arose. Pure bedlam.

Janet heard Jack's rifle spit, centered her reticle on one of Altmann's men and squeezed the trigger. Twice more she fired, and each time a man sprawled to the ground. She had no doubt that each of Jack's shots was finding its mark as well.

Then they were up and moving, short, crouching rushes that took them from ruin to ruin, with brief pauses between to scan for more targets. Along the front wall of the Kalasasaya temple, a man poked his head out of a hole, and Janet put a 7.62mm slug through it, leaving his body slumped in the opening.

Then Jack was up and running toward that spot as Janet lay still, providing the cover he was counting on her to give him. A man aimed a weapon around the north corner of the wall, but Janet's bullet sprawled him backward, his machine gun chattering as the death grip on its trigger sprayed tracer rounds into the night sky.

Janet moved, her running feet bringing her to Jack's side at the wall. With a quick motion, he pulled a pin on a flash-bang grenade and tossed it over the corpse and into the hole. Janet leaned back against the wall, covering her ears and eyes, and waited for the detonation. When it came, she felt the vibration in the cold stone.

When Janet opened her eyes, she found herself crouching alone in the darkness, with only a corpse to keep her company.

CHAPTER 92

Bones McCoy closed her eyes against the flickering torchlight, shutting out her father, Dolf, and Tupac. She brought her great mind to bear on the problem, visualized the staff and the altar slot, felt again the imperfection of the fit. Bones had turned it full circle inside the altar hole, had tilted the staff this way and that, but the female receptacle had refused to allow the male piece to slide smoothly inside.

Unbidden, her mind pulled forth the image of a medieval knight desperately struggling to unlock a maiden's chastity belt. But he lacked the key.

Suddenly the answer blossomed in her mind.

Not the key. The combination.

Bones opened her eyes, feeling the grin part her lips. Altmann saw it too.

"What?" he asked.

"The altar won't accept the partial staff. We must first attach the crown piece."

Removing it from the slot, she planted the bottom of the five-foot silver staff on the altar, holding it erect as Altmann carefully slid the glittering golden orb on the top. It didn't surprise Bones when the orb failed to lock into place.

"Carefully now," she continued, "as if you were looking up from the bottom, turn the bottom ring slowly counterclockwise until I say to stop."

With infinite care, she guided Altmann's movements, and despite his obvious excitement, his hands remained rock steady, a tribute to her father's iron-willed self-discipline. Completing the first step, Bones moved him up three rings, then down two, sometimes moving the same ring forward a partial turn before reversing its direction.

Suddenly, within the orb, gears continued moving after Altmann stopped, as if father and daughter had finished winding up a toy that could now perform its function. Something clicked and the orb locked itself solidly atop the silver staff.

Bones heard Altmann exhale. When he turned his gaze on her, his voice was filled with elation.

"We've done it."

Bones shook her head. "Only the first of four steps. By far the simplest."

A broad smile spread across Altmann's face. As her father looked at her, Bones saw just how beautiful this man could be, his sky-blue eyes sparkling in the torchlight.

"You and I are about to do something Hitler couldn't even imagine."

Altmann lifted the Sun Staff and set the tip of its base gently into its altar slot, allowing it to settle into place. With the crown piece at face level, Altmann shifted his hands carefully up to frame the golden orb, almost caressing, but not quite touching it.

His voice was little more than a husky whisper, but it sent chills crawling up Bones's spine.

"Shall we continue?"

At that moment, a noisy chorus from the cell phones of the guards they'd left back at the entrance echoed through the tunnels and into the cavern. The noise migrated to Dolf's and then to Altmann's cell phone, a pattern Bones immediately recognized. Even though they couldn't reach directly below ground, the NSA was walking a Bluetooth chain through the tunnels as they hacked their way from device to device.

Altmann's beatific smile froze on his face, transforming into a death mask of fury.

"Kill that damn noise!"

Stepping back from the staff, Altmann pulled his phone from his pocket and hurled it into the cavern wall, ricocheting plastic and metal pieces across the cavern floor and bringing to an end the shrill notes of his ring tone. Twenty feet away, Dolf crushed his phone in a massive hand. Turning, he shoved the cuffed and shackled Tupac Inti in the chest, sending the native man tumbling against the cavern wall and onto the floor. Delivering a hard kick to the downed man's unprotected ribs, Dolf spun and ran back down the tunnel toward the entrance, his strident yells preceding him.

As he disappeared around the nearest bend, a distant explosion vibrated the walls, the sound echoing through the cave tunnels. Despite the ringing in her ears, Bones heard Altmann's deep-throated growl rumble through the chamber.

"The Ripper."

CHAPTER 93

With his hands cuffed to the belly chain and feet shackled, Tupac was unable to catch himself as he tumbled backward under the force of Dolf's shove, barely managing to turn so that his shoulder, instead of his head, struck the wall. He was not quite so lucky when his face hit the cavern floor. The stone opened a one-inch cut on his forehead, sending a warm stream of blood over his eyebrows and into his eyes. He never saw the steel-toed boot that broke at least one of the ribs in his right side.

Awash in pain, Tupac struggled to draw breath and then wished he hadn't. As the pale Nazi disappeared around the corner, Tupac rolled to a seated position, back against the rough cavern wall, less than a dozen feet from the rock outcropping he wanted so desperately to reach.

The sound of the explosion that echoed into the altar chamber surprised Tupac. He blinked, trying to clear the blood from his eyes, but it was no use. Dimly visible through the red blur, Conrad Altmann stood atop the altar, the small woman at his side, both staring down the tunnel from which the sound had come. Just beyond them, the Sun Staff had been inserted into the mounting hole in the altar's center.

The fact that they had successfully attached the crown piece to the staff scared the hell out of the shaman. When Altmann and the woman turned back toward the staff to resume their work, their action fanned the flames of his fear.

Tupac looked to his right. Where the tunnel entered this cavern, the outcropping jutted out into the room, leaving a small alcove that could not be seen from the altar. And at the top of a pile of rubble within that alcove, hidden behind a rock, rested the explosive device Tupac had placed here when he'd first made his deal with the NSA.

The trouble with big intelligence organizations was that you could never trust them. You could try to use them to your own advantage, like he'd done, but you had to be realistic and realize that they might beat you. In that case, you had to have a failsafe.

When Conrad Altmann had subverted the shaman's own people, he'd crushed Tupac's plan beneath a Nazi boot. Now the failsafe was all Tupac had left to prevent Altmann from achieving his goal.

Sick to his soul with what he was about to do, Tupac gritted his teeth. He had no doubt that the Sun Staff had been brought here by beings whom his ancestors had considered gods. As the shaman looked across the room at the pair working atop the altar and then back at that rubble pile, pain and blood loss dimmed his vision. Hurt as badly as he was, he wasn't sure he could make that climb up to the hidden bomb. Even if he did, Tupac had no idea how he would activate the timer, with his hands chained at his sides.

Nevertheless, he would have to try.

CHAPTER 94

With the sound of the blast still ringing in his ears, Jack scrambled across the corpse and into the hole. In front of him, a disoriented man tried to raise his gun, but Jack's first bullet caught him center of mass, impacted the man's body armor, and slammed him back into the wall. The second shot punched out his right eye. Up ahead, he heard more cell phones continuing their squawking and saw a flash of light from around a bend. Then with a crunch, the light went out.

From much deeper in the tunnel, the loud yells of a running man echoed through the cave, just as Jack heard a familiar chink followed by the bouncing clang of a rolling grenade. Reacting instinctively, Jack ran forward, catching it on the second bounce. With a quick sidearm motion, Jack flung it back where it had come from as he dived against the right wall.

The blast showered Jack with stone chips and then with fist-size rocks as a section of the ceiling gave way ahead of him, filling the tunnel with dust. Pressing himself back against the wall, Jack kicked his legs free of rubble and grabbed for the night-vision goggles. The feel of shattered glass and plastic told him the bad news. He wouldn't be gaining that advantage tonight.

Suddenly Janet was at his side.

"Are you hurt?"

"Just some scrapes and bruises. But my NVGs have had it."

"Give me a second while I put the battery in mine, and I'll have a look around."

Jack heard her unclip the goggles and then soft rustling, snapping sounds before she spoke again.

"We've got a new rubble pile, but it looks like there's a place we can climb through at the top."

Jack climbed back to his feet.

"Good."

"I don't think it's a good idea to toss any more grenades down here."

In the choking, dust-filled darkness, Jack grinned, feeling a shooting pain in his jaw. When he placed a hand on his chin and mouth, it came away wet.

"That wasn't my grenade."

As Janet started scrambling up over the rubble, her reply brought another grin to his bloody lips.

"Just sayin.'"

CHAPTER 95

The mind worm felt an incredible rush of excitement, anger, and fear as its host's timelines converged and then branched wildly. But with each passing moment, Anchanchu grew more and more troubled. Something eluded it, something that hovered at the edge of awareness. Despite all the centuries of experience manipulating the human condition, Anchanchu had just experienced another example of Jack Gregory's unpredictable nature.

The man had scrambled into the tunnel, pulled by an adrenaline-fueled battle frenzy, and been injured just enough to whet that fury to a knife edge. But Jack's former lover had thrown him a lifeline, pulling him back off that ledge with her calming words. That restoration of some semblance of emotional balance was the greatest threat that Anchanchu now faced.

Almost five centuries had passed since another of Anchanchu's hosts had entered this subterranean vault. Back then, although the artifact was the same, humans had not had the technology to solve the full sequence of codes required to fully activate it. But even the entry of the simple combination that had separated the crown piece from the staff had sent a shock through the mind worm's system that had somehow destroyed Anchanchu's limbic connection, freeing the host from its influence.

Up in the cavern that lay ahead, two humans worked to activate a beacon that would summon beings capable of altering humans to such an extent that they would no longer be capable of experiencing the emotions of lust, hate, love, and fear upon which Anchanchu fed. It would not allow that to happen. The staff had to be eliminated, and only the entry of a specific code sequence into the golden orb could cause it to self-destruct.

Until now, Anchanchu's attachment to this fascinating host had prevented it from applying the force that might kill Jack Gregory or render him completely insane. But if that was the price to be paid to protect all of Anchanchu's future playthings, so be it.

It was time to open the floodgates.

CHAPTER 96

As Dolf rounded the first of the bends in the tunnel, the torchlight from the altar cave faded behind him, forcing him to slow and fumble for his pocket flashlight. The distinctive bang of a stun grenade echoed through the labyrinth, followed by the sound of distant gunfire. A larger explosion, accompanied by the rumble of falling rock, pulled him up short.

What the hell was happening at the entrance? If he didn't hurry, the idiots guarding the tunnel were going to end up sealing the only exit.

He paused at the next corner, aligning his flashlight below his gun hand to lead him around the bend. Dolf was halfway across the thirty-foot section leading to the next bend when two men backed around the corner, their weapons aimed toward the spot where the last explosion had originated.

"Where the hell are you two going?"

Hearing Dolf's voice, the two guards turned to face him. Suddenly, as if he had heard a new sound from around the bend, the rightmost guard spun and raised his weapon, just as a bullet took off the side of the man's head. With a look of horror on his face, the remaining guard ducked behind the cover of the wall.

"With me, now!" Dolf rasped, leading the startled survivor rapidly back toward the entrance to the altar cave. "Let The Ripper come to us."

CHAPTER 97

Conrad Altmann heard his daughter's clear voice tell him to slowly turn the center ring clockwise. As she said to stop, the orb quivered in his hand, and for a second time, he felt something within it unwind. Altmann looked down and saw the base of the staff deform ever so slightly. Then the staff slid six centimeters down into the slot and locked firm.

An electric thrill coursed from his fingertips to his scalp, standing the fine hairs of his arms on end. A movement at the periphery of his vision turned Altmann's head toward the spot where Tupac Inti had been knocked flat. With a look of horror on his face, the big shaman was attempting to slide his injured body along the wall and behind an outcropping that would hide him from the altar. It was as if he thought hiding behind a rock wall would protect him from the Sun Staff's wrath. It was as pathetic as it was laughable.

Altmann started to say something to Bones, but gunfire and a second explosion echoed out of the tunnel and into the altar cave, interrupting his thoughts and causing him to return his attention to the orb.

"Give me the third sequence! We need to go faster."

"But if you make a mistake . . ."

"I won't!"

Altmann's breathing deepened, his heartbeat slowed, and one by one the sounds of violence fell away. Right now there were only two things worthy of his attention: the orb and his daughter's methodical voice. Time dilated so that instead of coming faster, her instructions and his motions seemed to slow to a crawl as he precisely manipulated the rings.

When Dolf reentered the room with a guard and they positioned themselves to take advantage of the protected firing positions the cavern's opening provided, a tiny part of Altmann's mind made note of it before he walled away this new distraction. The sequence ended, and for a terrifying moment Altmann thought he must have made a mistake. Then, from within the altar, a vibration started, so small that at first he thought he was imagining it, that perhaps it was the muscle tension in his own body producing the feeling.

In an attempt to verify that the sensation was real, Altmann grasped the staff with both hands. Now he was certain. The staff hummed with an energy that felt vaguely electrical. No. That wasn't quite right. It reminded Altmann of the feeling he got when he tried to touch like poles of two powerful magnets together, an invisible, repulsive force that seemed almost magical.

A wave of dizziness assaulted him, as if Altmann were caught in a vortex that threatened to tear his mind from his body. For a moment his view of the cavern blurred and distorted so that he seemed to be in a very different place. Then, before he managed to get a clear view of what he was seeing, he was back.

Altmann gasped and released his hold on the staff. He would have tumbled from atop the altar had not Bones reached out to steady him. Recovering his senses, Altmann straightened and shook off her helping hand, once again reaching for the golden orb.

"Tell me the final sequence."

The worry lingered in her voice.

"Shouldn't you rest a second?"

Altmann raised his right hand to slap her but managed to still his rage, noting the shock in his daughter's blue eyes as he clenched his hand.

"Tell me the final sequence. Don't make me say it again!"

When she spoke the next instruction, Altmann heard the faint quiver in her voice. Good. His daughter's education was just beginning.

CHAPTER 98

Tupac lay on his face, having slid most of the way back to the bottom of the rubble pile that sloped up to the top of this rocky alcove. He moved and felt something like a hot knife slide deep into the right side of his chest. A wet cough bubbled to his lips and he spat, splattering the rock beside his face with blood.

He longed to lie there, to just give up and die. One way or another that last thing was going to happen. Tupac's thoughts turned to that last glimpse he'd had of Conrad Altmann, standing atop the altar with his hands on the crown piece, twisting the golden rings as the small woman dictated her instructions. He'd watched as they had successfully connected the orb to the staff and then mounted the Sun Staff to the altar. Any lingering hope he'd had that Altmann might not possess all the codes was now gone.

Dolf Gruenberg reappeared, his glance taking in Tupac and the blood he'd just coughed out on the rocks. With a sneer, the albino turned his back on him and knelt behind the outcropping, hidden from anyone that might step through the cave entrance. Tupac heard Dolf tell someone else to cover the passage from the far side of the door, but was unable to see whom he was talking to.

Tupac knew that if he was going to do something, it had to be now. He hadn't suffered so much for so long only to abandon his calling without one last effort. Resisting the next cough he felt coming, Tupac forced himself to take a deep breath. As he visualized what he was about to attempt, tightening the muscles in his massive arms, shoulders, and chest, one thing became crystal clear.

No matter what he told himself, this was really going to hurt.

CHAPTER 99

Jack followed Janet, scrambling up the pile of rock that had partially blocked the passage, sliding up beside her as she scanned the passage ahead through her night-vision goggles.

"Anything?" he asked.

"Just a guy who took the brunt of the grenade blast. What's left isn't pretty."

"I'm going to make a move to the next corner. Cover me."

"Ready."

Jack unclipped his flashlight and cupped it against his gun hand, aligned with the H&K's gun barrel. But he didn't switch it on. If things got hot, a press of the button would dazzle his enemy, whether that person was wearing night-vision goggles or not. Besides, Janet would kill anyone that tried to aim a weapon around that corner before Jack got a chance to light him up.

Jack wriggled over the top of the pile, bumping his head against the stone ceiling in the process. *Damn.* The blast had damn near sealed the tunnel. When he reached the cavern floor on the far side of the pile, Jack slid left until he felt his shoulder bump the wall. He moved forward along the wall in a shooter's crouch, blinking hard to clear the film of dust that coated his eyes, trying to identify anything that moved in the inky blackness that stretched out before him.

He took one silent step. Then another. The next one took him from the dark tunnel into the sleepwalking dream-memory he'd experienced in Santa Cruz. But this time Jack was himself, not Pizarro. He stood at the same spot in the tunnel where he'd been standing a moment before, although instead of a Heckler and Koch pistol, he now held a flaming torch in his right hand.

Jack's head swam in a roiling sea of disorientation. He spun, looking back toward Janet. Only she wasn't there. Neither was the pile of rock from the cave in, just an empty torchlit passage leading back toward the entrance. As a fresh wave of fear released an adrenaline rush that robbed Jack's limbs of strength, his mind struggled to cope with the new situation.

What the hell was happening to him?

For the third time in the last two weeks Jack had stepped across the boundary into crazy land, each trip worse than the last. This time it had happened when he could least afford to lose control. Jack squeezed his eyes closed and concentrated.

Come on. Breathe deep. Focus.

The sound of the stuttering torch, the feel of its heat against the skin of his face, pulled his eyes open. Back in the direction from which he'd come, the passage stretched away undamaged, the orange light of his torch sending shadows crawling along the uneven walls. Jack spun to face forward, his sudden movement making the torch sputter and hiss as it whipped through the still, musty air.

With his heart hammering his rib cage, Jack resumed his forward motion. Inside his head something whispered to him.

Hurry . . . hurry . . . hurrrrry!

Though he fought the urge that pulled him forward, Jack found himself walking faster and faster, feeling the time in his hourglass drain away with each step. Somewhere up ahead was the terrible thing that must be destroyed. But first, just as Pizarro had done, Jack needed to touch the golden orb and feel its delicate rings twist in his hands.

Only then could he truly be free.

CHAPTER 100

Janet watched Jack squeeze through the tight opening and scramble down the far side of the rock pile, his body glowing white hot in the green glow of her night-vision goggles. She watched as he moved along the passage's left wall toward the bend in the tunnel thirty feet ahead.

Suddenly Jack froze, as if he'd heard something. Janet's shifted her gaze back and forth but saw no sign of movement or any sign of body heat signatures. What Jack did next stunned her.

Where before he had moved along in a trained shooter's crouch with his pistol and unlit flashlight clutched in a two-hand grip, he now straightened, his left hand falling to his side as he stared at the gun in his right hand, as if he'd never before seen such a thing.

Then Jack spun back toward her, his eyes glowing brighter than the rest of his face in the NVG display. Though she knew he couldn't see anything in this dark place, Janet had the strong impression that he was looking at something behind her. The feeling became so intense that she lifted her head from the weapon and turned to look back, her motion loosing another shower of dust from the ceiling one foot above her. Absolutely nothing had changed in the passageway behind her since she had crawled up to this spot.

Shifting her gaze back to the front, Janet gasped. Jack was on the move, but not in a tactical way. Instead he strode rapidly down the center of the passage holding his gun at shoulder height, at such an odd angle that he almost seemed to be holding something else. Then, without waiting for her to join him, without even pausing to listen or look ahead, Jack walked around the corner and disappeared.

"Shit!"

Janet crawled through the opening, pushing the rifle ahead of her. Once through, she climbed to the bottom of the rock pile with all the speed she could muster without taking a dangerous fall or starting a fresh slide. At the bottom, she righted herself, readying the weapon to fire as she quickly followed Jack.

Janet stopped at the corner, just as Jack should have, and listened.

Dolf's distant yell echoed down the passage.

She swung the weapon out and around. Twenty feet in, a side passage opened on the right. Beyond that opening, one of Altmann's men stepped into view, his head turned back toward the spot where Dolf's yells had originated. Then, sensing Jack's approach, he spun and raised his weapon, just before Janet put a bullet through his head.

Again she heard Dolf yell, although she still failed to make out his echoing words.

As if unaware of the chaos around him, Jack continued down the middle of the main passage, as if he was on a stroll beneath the noonday sun. Without slowing, his long stride carried him out of view around the bend. Janet felt her breath coming in gasps. What the hell was wrong with Jack? She hadn't bothered to check him after the explosion and cave-in. He'd been bleeding from the mouth and chin, but it hadn't seemed serious.

Janet knew that concussions sometimes did strange things to people. Whatever the cause of his bizarre behavior, if she didn't do something quick, Jack was going to get himself killed.

Driven by a deep dread that at any second she would hear the echo of gunfire, that she would find Jack's bloody body sprawled across the cavern floor, Janet dropped the sniper rifle, drew her Glock, and sprinted toward the spot where Jack had disappeared.

She burst around the corner to see Jack, who had dropped his gun, walking toward a narrow opening into a large torchlit cavern, his long shadow stretching back toward her. A man swung a gun out from behind the wall on the right, but Jack blocked her line of sight, leaving her no shot.

With memories of her two NCAA national triathlon championships flashing through her head, Janet closed the ground between them, knowing that she was already too late.

Suddenly, as if he'd just been hit by a passing truck, Jack spun, and Janet saw blood spurt from high up on his left shoulder. Then, with the amazing quickness she'd come to recognize, Jack's spinning elbow impacted the man's forearm, sending the gun flying away and leaving a bloody white shard of bone jutting out through the Nazi's skin. Relief washed through Janet's mind. Jack was back with her.

Then Janet saw Dolf step out from behind an outcropping, his gun hand rising toward the back of Jack's head as Jack plunged his knife into his opponent's armpit.

Launching herself through the air, Janet hit Dolf's arm with all the momentum her shoulder could deliver, her speed and Dolf's surprise at her unexpected arrival knocking the gun out of the big man's hand as it discharged harmlessly. Janet landed in a shoulder roll that brought her back to her feet, but this time Dolf reacted faster, his fist catching the side of her head as she tried to duck away.

As the star-filled night sky twinkled all around her, Janet felt her body spinning weightless through empty space. Then the blackness took her.

CHAPTER 101

Tupac Inti watched Dolf crouch behind the outcropping that shielded them both from the view of those at the altar or standing in the cavern entrance, the albino's gun held in a two-hand grip by his face, pointed straight up toward the ceiling. The gunshot from around the corner was surprisingly loud in the enclosed space, but the sound that followed it was unmistakable—the sharp crack of a breaking bone accompanied by the gurgling scream of the injured man.

Dolf swung around the corner, aimed his gun at someone, and started to pull the trigger. Suddenly, a woman catapulted her body into the albino's arm, causing the gun to discharge harmlessly as it was knocked out of Dolf's hand and clattered across the cavern's stone floor. When she rolled to her feet, Tupac saw that it was the female NSA agent.

Before she could completely recover, Dolf lunged forward, delivering a glancing blow to the side of her head that sent her body spinning through the air to sprawl limply on the cavern floor. Instead of running across the cavern to retrieve his gun, Dolf stooped, picked up a rock the size of a soccer ball, raised it high above his head, and stepped toward the spot where Janet's unconscious body lay face up.

From somewhere near the cavern entrance, Tupac heard Jack's rage-filled scream.

"No!"

Then The Ripper launched himself into view, hitting Dolf in the right kidney with a shoulder. Driving with his legs, Jack lifted the bigger man, slamming him into the cavern wall with an impact that would have normally broken bones. But although he looked surprised, Dolf wasn't stunned and grappled the smaller man into his powerful arms.

Tupac inhaled deeply, ignoring the pain in his ribs, and stood erect. If he was to have any chance, now was the time. Turning away from the death match playing out before him, Tupac faced up the rubble slope and put a lifetime's strength into the chains that bound his wrists to his sides. At first, his only reward was an explosion of agony as his damaged ribcage cracked and shifted. Then with a loud pop and rattle, the chains parted and his arms were free.

Tupac exhaled, spat bloody foam, and forced himself to pull another painful breath into his lungs. Grinding his teeth, he climbed. With the sounds of hand-to-hand combat continuing behind him, Tupac reached the top of the slope. A fresh rush of panic threatened to rob him of his remaining strength. The bomb wasn't here.

Then he saw it, the corner jutting out from behind a stone that had shifted in front of it as Tupac had scrambled up. The shaman removed the rock that blocked his access and stared at the bomb. It sat atop a flat ledge exactly where he'd left it two years ago. The boxy device was crude but effective. A single switch would power it on and start the two-minute digital timer. Once started, the bomb could not be stopped. If someone moved or tampered with it, a silver blob of mercury would roll from one end of its tiny tube to the other, instantaneously triggering the detonation of the two kilograms of rust-orange Semtex that rested within the case.

Having studied engineering and explosives at West Point, Tupac had chosen this enclosed spot with care. Just as Sampson had done to the Philistines, it would collapse this cavern beneath hundreds of tons of rock.

Tupac was glad for the two minutes. With his internal injuries he could never make it out of the cave in that amount of time, but it would allow him to move to a place where he could get one last look at the Incan Sun Staff he had tried so hard to keep from the hands of those who would abuse its power.

Tupac flipped the switch and watched the red digital counter start at 2:00.

Then the countdown began.

One last look would have to be enough.

CHAPTER 102

Conrad Altmann heard the shots behind him, saw Bones turn to look, and hissed, "Finish the sequence! Don't look away again."

When she returned her attention to the orb, Altmann could see his daughter's genius shining in her eyes as she picked up where she had left off, not needing a pause to recollect her thoughts.

Behind him, Dolf was fighting The Ripper, hand to hand. No matter how good The Ripper was, he had no chance in such a contest. Altmann pushed all thoughts of it from his mind, reprimanding himself more harshly than he'd done with Bones. Right now, any distraction was intolerable.

As he progressed up and down the golden orb, precisely turning rings this way and that, something amazing was happening. With each turn of a golden ring as the complex sequence progressed, the orb caught torchlight, so that the light seemed to coalesce into glittering droplets that crawled across the surface and into the cracks between rings. To his amazement, with each droplet of light that the orb absorbed, the room around Altmann darkened perceptibly.

The low hum he'd felt during the entry of the previous sequence deepened to a barely audible thrumming that emanated from the altar, traversed up the length of the staff, and entered the orb. Altmann felt a tremor in his fingers and took a deep breath. But the tremor would not be stilled.

Seeing it, Bones glanced up at him, her look carrying an implied question. *Do you need a break?* Altmann scowled and she continued. He wanted to ask her how close they were to the end of the sequence but dared not break what remained of his concentration to do so. Amid this cacophony of distractions, he would persevere. For all he knew, the next turn might complete the combination. And that would unleash the power that rumbled beneath his feet, powering an interstellar beacon, recalling the master race that had found humans unready on their last visit.

Right here and now, he and Bones stood ready. Whether the rest of humanity was or was not, Altmann couldn't care less.

CHAPTER 103

A sudden sense of imminent danger shifted Jack out of the mind trip that had held him just in time to see a man swing out from behind the right edge of an opening into a larger cavern, a gun clutched in both hands. Jack spun away from the gun's aim-point, felt the bullet graze his left shoulder, and whirled. When his left elbow impacted the man's right forearm, Jack felt the bone break before he heard it, saw the gun spin away across the floor as a sharp spear point of white bone jutted out through skin, leaving the hand that had previously held the gun dangling uselessly.

Pulling his knife from its sheath, Jack plunged it into the Nazi's left armpit, giving it a hard twist as he watched the life drain from his enemy's blue eyes. The rage that went into that final knife twist betrayed Jack as badly as the knife's manufacturer, snapping the blade off at the haft.

His reemergence from the mind trip had left Jack shaken and disoriented. In the past he'd relied upon his intuition and his strange ability to sense what his opponents were about to do, to give him an extra edge in combat. But tonight his senses had betrayed him completely. Even now, conflicting compulsions buffeted him, leaving Jack desperate to use the Sun Staff to free himself from the demon that threatened his sanity, though another part of him just wanted to destroy the artifact.

Behind Jack, another shot rang out, spinning him around in time to see Dolf's blow hurl Janet's limp body across the stone cavern floor. But once again the scene before Jack's eyes faded, replaced by the dream version. Jack stood alone in a cavern lit by torches mounted in six wall sconces. To his right, mounted atop a golden altar, the Sun Staff gleamed brilliantly.

"No!"

With frustration stoking his rage to a white heat, Jack forced his head back into the present.

Ten feet away, Dolf lifted a heavy slab of rock above his head and took a step toward the spot where Janet's unconscious body lay. The Ripper moved. Every muscle in his legs fired Jack forward, eliminating the distance that separated him from the big man he was about to kill. As Dolf prepared to hurl the stone down into Janet's skull, Jack's shoulder hit him just above waist level on the right side.

Jack wrapped his arms around the giant and continued driving his legs as he levered Dolf's body upward. Behind him the rock smashed harmlessly to the ground as he slammed Dolf's body into the wall with bone-jarring force. Unfortunately, nothing broke. Worse, the impact stood Jack up, enabling Dolf to wrap his massive arms around Jack's shoulders, crushing him face first into Dolf's chest.

Bringing his right knee up hard into Dolf's groin failed to loosen the hold. The realization that Dolf had worn a cup eliminated that area as a future target. With a wide grin, Dolf slid his embrace down to pin Jack's arms at his sides. The albino hitched Jack up, lifting his feet off the ground, a move that enabled Dolf's encircling arms to slide lower. With his fists cupped in the center of Jack's back, Dolf squeezed harder, the tremendous pressure threatening to break Jack's back and arms at the same time.

Jack struggled to draw breath, his muscles so taught that it seemed they might rip through his skin as he sought to resist the irresistible pressure Dolf applied. The realization that this man was going to kill him and then walk over, pick up the rock, and bash Janet's beautiful head into red and gray mush pulled forth a hate that Jack had only felt for one other man. The adrenaline rush that accompanied that feeling misted his vision red.

The head-butt Jack attempted failed to reach high enough to impact Dolf's nose, but it broke Dolf's front teeth off at the gum line, sending them out through his lower lip. Still Dolf's grip strengthened.

Jack threw his head forward once again, and Dolf lifted his chin to avoid a repeat. This time Jack tilted his head to the side, opened his mouth wide, and sank his teeth into the right side of Dolf's throat. Ripping and gnashing, Jack tasted the blood that gush into his mouth as its coppery odor filled his nostrils.

With a scream, Dolf released his hold and reached up to thrust him away. But Jack wrapped his arms and legs around Dolf's torso and held on, as his jaw muscles powered the teeth that ripped and chewed through flesh and cartilage.

A mighty thrust of Dolf's arms tore Jack free, sending him tumbling to the floor. In flight, Jack whipped his legs, rolling into the crouch that would launch him back at his injured opponent.

Five feet away, Dolf stood still, eyes wide and staring as his big hands sought to staunch the flow of blood from the wound in the side of his neck. Jack knew he hadn't been able to bite deep enough through all that neck muscle to fatally injure Dolf, but the look in the big man's eyes said that he was scared shitless.

Jack launched himself at Dolf, feigning a left-hand blow at Dolf's bloody throat and then dropping into a side kick that transferred all of Jack's adrenaline-amplified strength into Dolf's right kneecap. Through the sole of his boot, Jack felt the bone and tendons give way.

The pain would have left a lesser man rolling on the floor in agony, but Dolf merely dropped to his knees, holding his neck. With one last burst of will, the giant albino raised his eyes to lock with Jack's, angry defiance shining in the pale orbs.

Jack kicked him in the teeth. The blow toppled Dolf's body backward, his head striking the rock he'd tried to use on Janet, producing a sick crunch that sounded like a dropped melon. Standing over the dead Nazi, Jack spit the mouthful of Dolf's blood and flesh onto the corpse and then turned away.

At that moment, Jack's eyes were drawn up to the spot where Tupac Inti slid down a shale-covered rubble pile. Clearly visible on a small ledge above Tupac's head, on the front of a shoebox-sized case, a red LED timer counted down. Jack had seen enough bombs to know exactly what that countdown meant.

With the current count showing 1:23, Jack moved to kneel at Janet's side. Pressing a finger to the side of her neck, he breathed a sigh of relief. Her pulse was strong, and her breathing was steady. Suddenly Jack's eyes were drawn to the Sun Staff mounted atop the altar on the far side of the cavern. Conrad Altmann and the petite woman stood in front of it, both focused on Altmann's manipulation of the shimmering orb.

Jack found he had taken two steps toward the altar before he could stop himself. He had just enough time to grab the staff and escape the cavern, but not enough to come back for Janet. He looked back at her sprawled body, his thoughts flashing to that first night in Prague, to those two amazing weeks in Crete. Then his eyes flicked up to the red LED numerals on the bomb case. He now had fifty-eight seconds.

Moving quickly, Jack turned and knelt beside Janet. Grabbing her flashlight, he cradled Janet's limp form carefully in his arms and rose to his feet. Striding rapidly back toward the cave entrance, Jack saw Tupac Inti lying on his side, blood bubbling from his open lips. In that noble face, his dark brown eyes stared across the room at the Incan Sun Staff and the two Nazis desperately working it.

Ignoring his frustration and the rage-filled scream that echoed deep in his head, Jack hugged Janet's body to his chest, switched on the flashlight, and ran.

CHAPTER 104

Tupac Inti lay on the floor just beyond the place where a jutting section of the cavern wall blocked the bomb from Conrad Altmann's view. He coughed again, felt the rib that had punctured his lung shift within his chest, and spit blood onto the stone. Pushing aside the pain that threatened to drive him into unconsciousness, he saw Jack Gregory pick up Janet and head for the exit. As the killer strode past his prone form, Tupac caught his gaze, saw the sadness and frustration within that look, and then watched Jack break into a run out of the cavern.

Tupac understood that look. From the time he'd first met the strange man, he'd seen the raging passions within Jack and his inner struggle to control them. Here, in this cave, Jack had failed to accomplish the mission he'd been hired to do, namely saving Tupac's life. Failure wasn't something the man who people called The Ripper could tolerate.

Tupac had endured many failures in his own life, but tonight wasn't going to be one of them. A quick glance up at the ticking timer brought a bubbling laugh from his throat, but Tupac managed to suppress a fresh bout of wet coughing. Shifting his gaze to the spot where Klaus Barbie's bastard son and granddaughter worked so feverishly with the orb atop the Sun Staff, Tupac raised his voice so that it echoed through the altar cave.

"Altmann!"

The woman's eyes briefly shifted to Tupac.

"Stay focused!" Conrad Altmann rasped.

Again Tupac laughed. He no longer felt any pain. It had grown so intense that his nerves and brain could no longer process the impulses.

"Did you really think I would bring you to the altar without consequence?"

Again he saw the woman flinch. Both her cadence of instruction and Altmann's manipulation of the orb increased in speed as the thought that something was seriously wrong occurred to both of them.

Tupac continued speaking, though he briefly shifted his glance to the timer and its red LED numerals that counted down toward zero.

"How does it feel to be this close to your dream, to your destiny, only to have it snatched away from you in the last thirteen seconds?"

Tupac saw the realization of the meaning behind his last words dawn in Conrad Altmann's face.

"Faster!" Altmann commanded.

Tupac tried to speak, but blood filled his throat and mouth. He spat a foaming mouthful onto the cavern floor. As he watched the older Nazi's hands twist the rings, the speed and precision of his movements were simultaneously impressive and impotent.

This time when Tupac began laughing, he found that he couldn't stop, even when it changed to a loud, sputtering gurgle in the back of his throat.

As the timer ticked to three, then to two, Tupac managed two last, joy-filled words that distorted Conrad Altmann's face into a snarling mask of fury.

"Time's up!"

Then the world came apart around him.

CHAPTER 105

With a mental count ticking down in his head, Jack again felt the dimensional shift that placed him back in a past that wasn't his. But this time he was ready. He'd just learned that rage could pull him back to the present, and right now rage was in plentiful supply.

Jack took another step forward, thought about the woman he could no longer see or feel in his arms, thought about the being that was trying to make Jack sacrifice both their lives, and let that liquid red rage take him. Around Jack, the tunnel shifted so that it was once again dimly illuminated by his bobbing flashlight beam. When he rounded a corner with Janet Price held in his arms, his mental count now stood at thirty.

Ahead, the rock pile from the cave-in rose almost to the ceiling. Jack stumbled, shifted Janet's body over his right shoulder, and scrambled up.

Twenty seconds.

At the crawl space that would take him to the other side, Jack lay Janet down and squeezed through. Turning he reached back, grabbed her arms, and roughly pulled her through. Only then did he notice that he'd dropped the flashlight on the far side.

Shit!

Ten seconds.

Jack grabbed Janet's limp body and again slung it up over his shoulder as he scrabbled down the rubble pile. When he reached the bottom, he ran blindly, hit the wall with his left shoulder, and staggered to his knees. As he tried to climb back to his feet, the floor of the passage lurched. The shockwave propagating away from the altar cave impacted the blockage, causing another section of the roof to give way behind him.

Jack stumbled forward blindly with Janet in his arms, keeping his left hand on the wall. Thick dust swirled through the passage making it impossible to draw breath without coughing. For a moment, the rumble behind him grew in volume and then subsided as Jack rounded a last bend and halted. Far ahead there was a feeble glow of light from the outside world, a sliver of moonlight that sliced through the swirling dust.

The dead man's corpse still lay sprawled through the entrance. Jack's next step felt oddly squishy, and he realized that his foot now rested on another man's corpse. Then, from outside, he vaguely heard voices and froze, his battered brain struggling to cope with this new complication. As he gently lowered Janet to the ground and readied himself for the action he felt coming, a tired thought edged its way past his natural defenses.

Christ! Can this night get any better?

CHAPTER 106

Janet felt something sting her cheek, tried to brush it away with her hand, and then felt it again, this time more painful than the last. Then she remembered. Dolf had hit her on the side of the head. Now he must be beating her while she was down.

She lashed out with her hands, but he caught them. As Janet started to kick, the voice that had been speaking finally registered. Jack's voice.

"Easy, Janet. It's me."

Janet stiffened, opened her eyes, and saw nothing but darkness. She tried to take a deep breath, but inhaled more dust than air, and succumbed to a fit of coughing. When it abated, she spoke, her voice a hoarse croak that echoed in the darkness.

"Jack?"

"Yes."

"Is it over? Are we safe?"

He paused.

"I wouldn't be waking you if we were."

She struggled to a sitting position, the pain in her skull so intense she thought she would puke her guts out. But she could do that later. Right now she needed to know where they stood.

"What's our situation?"

"Ahh, let's see. We have no guns, no night-vision equipment, no flashlights, and no working communications gear. An explosion has collapsed the tunnel behind us, trapping us against the entrance we crawled through to get in here this evening. It's still open but I hear men moving around outside. I'm thinking bad guys."

"Jesus, Jack! You woke me up to tell me that?"

"You asked."

Janet rolled to her knees, fought off another bout of nausea, and managed to climb to her feet, guided by Jack's hand on her right arm.

"So what's the plan?" she asked.

"This is Bolivia. It looks like Butch Cassidy and the Sundance Kid for us."

Janet knew he was trying to use levity to help clear her head, but it wasn't working. Another memory returned, elevating her heart rate. The last time she'd seen Jack, he'd walked like a zombie right into a Nazi ambush in the altar cave, almost getting them both killed. She couldn't really assume he was functioning normally.

Jack continued.

"I checked the dead guy here at my feet for weapons and found some full magazines and a knife, but nothing else. I want you to help me search the rest of the passage to see if we can find any guns that he or others may have dropped during the initial fight."

"And if we don't find any?"

"Then I'm going to try to drag the dead guy lying in the opening back inside without getting killed. He has a weapon in his holster."

Janet took a breath, coughed again, and tried to blink the crustiness out of her unseeing eyes. Then, angry at the situation and angry at Jack for making it worse, she lowered herself to all fours and began searching the floor around her. Her voice left little doubt about her mood.

"Let's get started. I don't have all goddamn night."

CHAPTER 107

"Jack, are you in there?"

The voice echoed through the opening and down the passageway to where Jack groped through the darkness on his hands and knees, gradually working his way methodically back toward the entrance. At first he thought he had imagined it. Then he heard Janet's urgent whisper from beside him.

"Who is calling for you?"

The voice called out again, louder this time.

"Yo, Jack. Can you hear me?"

Jack's reply reflected the mixture of surprise and relief he felt at hearing the familiar Hebrew accent.

"Efran? Is anyone with you?"

"Just Pablo."

"You sure about that?"

"Except for some scattered dead guys, we're it."

Jack heard Janet rise to her feet, and he did likewise. Janet reached the opening two steps ahead of him, crawled over the corpse and out of the hole, taking the dead man's gun as she exited.

"That guy looks better than you two," Efran said as Jack climbed out through the hole and stood in the pale moonlight.

To Jack's left Pablo crouched at the southeast corner of the Kalasasaya ruin's outer wall, rifle at the ready.

"You didn't see any other Nazis when you got here?"

"They were here, but when the explosion collapsed part of the inner wall, they hauled ass back toward town."

As glad as he was to see the man, Jack spoke the accusation anyway.

"I thought you told us that you two wouldn't give us any active support."

Efran laughed. "I said not much."

Janet interrupted. "How about we cut the small talk and get the hell out of here?"

Efran shook his head. "I'd love to offer you a ride, but our vehicle crapped out about a mile from here, and we had to abandon it. Same story with our cell phones."

Jack pointed east.

"Our van's parked a couple of kilometers that way, and it still works."

Efran's grin revealed teeth that looked whiter than normal in the light of the quarter moon. He unholstered an H&K P30S, handing it and two extra magazines to Jack.

"Just in case."

Despite Efran's assurance that they were alone at the ruin, Jack ducked low, moving from cover to cover in a zigzag pattern that turned the two kilometers into three. When they reached the van, Jack reconnected the battery and closed the hood. Janet started to climb into the driver's seat, but Efran stopped her.

"Pablo can drive. Hop in the back, and I'll take a look at that head wound."

Janet shrugged, tossed the darker man the keys, and followed Efran into the back of the panel van. Jack came last, sliding the rear side door closed behind him. When the engine rumbled to life, Jack breathed a sigh of relief and sat down on the floor next to Janet, leaning back against the driver's side panel.

For an hour and thirty minutes, Pablo drove along rutted dirt roads, without headlights, maintaining enough speed to make Efran's attempts at first aid less than perfect. By the light of a red lens flashlight, Efran cleaned and bound Janet's and Jack's wounds, and even though the bandages didn't look pretty, they were effective.

Finally the van turned off onto a rocky trail across the high desert and then slowed as Pablo parked it inside an abandoned barn. Efran slid the side door open and stepped out, switching on his flashlight. Following close behind, Jack's nose filled with the smell of dust and old hay. As Efran swept the flashlight beam around, Jack noted the partially fallen roof, broken stalls, rotting leather scraps, and rusted blacksmith tools scattered about. Seeing boxes piled next to one of the stalls, Jack stepped forward to take a closer look.

"Military rations and water?" Jack asked.

Efran spread his arms welcomingly.

"This is as close to a safe house as I can do. Help me unload your stuff from the van. You'll be staying awhile."

Janet tested a pile of straw with her boot, a movement that sent two large rats scurrying away into a dark corner. When she turned back toward Jack, her head swathed in red-stained bandages, she spoke just one word.

"Outstanding."

CHAPTER 108

Jack Gregory's battle beneath the Tiahuanaco Ruins had drained Anchanchu, an altogether new experience in the infinity that comprised the mind worm's existence. Panic had forced it to try to take control of its human host. The destruction of one host's mind to prevent the alien device from being used to recall the Others was a sacrifice worth making. But despite the mental battering Anchanchu had delivered, Jack Gregory had somehow managed to reassert self-control at the critical moment.

More startling, Jack had resisted his own desire to use the staff to free himself of his immortal rider, something Francisco Pizarro González had accomplished five centuries earlier. Instead, Jack had yielded to an irrational emotional urge to save the human female.

Despite the explosion and the resulting collapse that had prevented the humans from completing the activation sequence,

Anchanchu knew that no amount of falling rock could destroy the Sun Staff or its altar. As it evaluated the probabilities associated with the changed timelines that spiraled outward from this event, Anchanchu remained troubled. Jack Gregory had chosen to allow the native priest to bury the artifact instead of using the staff to destroy itself.

Anchanchu shuddered at the knowledge that humanity's chances of survival had just dwindled. Yet at each future inflection point where human survival remained possible, Jack Gregory danced. Apparently, it was a dance that Anchanchu was destined to share.

CHAPTER 109

Admiral Riles stared through the op-center glass at the ongoing activity in the war room. After more than six hours, the NSA's unauthorized nighttime cyber-attack on a backwater section of Bolivia continued. As expected, in addition to the direct tasks posted on the game board, a number of much more difficult objectives had arisen, designed to mask this evening's NSA activity from other intelligence services, foreign or domestic.

Once again Jamal Glover was leading the game board, much to the dismay of his closest rivals. But they still had time to overtake him. Regardless of how Janet came out on the ground, Riles planned on tightening the cyber-vice throughout the night. When he pulled the plug just before 5:00 A.M., he'd let the Bolivians decide whether the disruption had been caused by solar flares, Shining Path rebels, or evil spirits. In the meantime, his crew would keep them so screwed up that they would have no hope of mounting a coordinated response to the assault Janet and Jack had initiated.

Levi Elias stepped to his side.

"Sir, we've just received an encrypted satcom message from Janet Price. During the battle inside the altar cave, Tupac Inti triggered a suicide explosion that also killed Conrad Altmann and the woman we believe to be Dr. Bones McCoy. I'm sorry to report that Janet believes that the Sun Staff was also destroyed when the ceiling of the altar cave collapsed."

Riles gritted his teeth and looked away in an attempt to hide his bitter disappointment at this news. An operation into which he'd invested significant resources and three years of detailed planning had failed to recover the Sun Staff. That meant the NSA would never get the chance to study an artifact so intricate in design and manufacture that it was impossible to imagine how the Incas had made it.

Conrad Altmann and Klaus Barbie had been so fascinated by the Incan Sun Staff and the legends surrounding it that they had come to believe it was of alien manufacture, that the solution to its symbolic codes would somehow trigger a beacon that would summon its makers back to earth where they would restore the master race.

That was, of course, complete bullshit, but apparently Tupac Inti had also believed it. It was one more thing Riles had overlooked. How could he have seen that Tupac would destroy his people's most sacred artifact, all to prevent Altmann from doing what? Calling E.T.?

Admiral Riles swallowed hard, thrust the bitterness from his thoughts, and shifted gears to something he could do something about.

"What about Janet and Jack?"

"They both suffered minor injuries but have established a temporary base of operation at a remote safe house."

"Do we have their location?"

"Yes, sir."

Riles took a deep breath and turned to look directly into his chief analyst's hawkish face.

"Okay, Levi. Keep the War Room going until five in the morning, then shut it down. In the meantime, I want an exfil plan for Janet and Jack on my desk by noon."

"And if Jack won't come?"

"I'm betting he will."

As Admiral Riles walked out of the op-center and back to his office, he tried to find a bright spot in this whole disaster. But the way he felt right now, if there was one, he just couldn't see it.

CHAPTER 110

Stefan Rosenstein walked into the Meier-on-Rothschild tower, nodded at the security guard, and took the private elevator directly to the penthouse apartment that occupied the 38th and 39th floors. Unbuttoning his black cashmere topcoat, he hung it in the coat closet and walked directly to his office.

Since Miriam had taken their daughters to visit her sister in Jerusalem, Stefan had the apartment to himself for the next two days. That was good because he had much to do. Last week's events in Bolivia had not gone as he had wanted, but what in this life does? News of Tupac Inti's death had saddened him greatly.

Stefan thought about going to his office, but instead walked to the wet bar and filled a glass with Chivas Regal 25. Stopping to stand at the floor-to-ceiling windows that looked out over Tel Aviv to the Mediterranean Sea, he swirled the amber liquid below his nose, and sipped, letting the Scotch spread its warm glow from his esophagus down to his stomach.

Bolivian officials had released a statement saying that the army had successfully interdicted an attack by Shining Path rebels on the historically valuable Tiahuanaco ruins. Although a number of people had been killed during the attack and a small part of the ruins had sustained damage, the heroic actions of the Bolivian military and police units had defeated the rebels and prevented them from destroying the ancient site.

There had been no mention of UJC or other neo-Nazi involvement, but a separate story reported multiple attacks on Conrad Altmann's Cochabamba estate by a rival neo-Nazi faction. Conrad Altmann himself was reported missing amid growing suspicion that he had been kidnapped by the same rival group and executed.

Despite the propaganda spread by the Bolivian government, news of Tupac Inti's death and his role in killing Conrad Altmann had leaked out. Stefan's man, Pablo Griego, had made sure of it, and the senator couldn't have stopped the loyal Quechua man if he had wanted to. The Quechua people deserved to have Tupac's heroism confirmed. They would mourn the loss of their charismatic shaman, but his uniting influence on the indigenous peoples would linger alongside his legend.

Stefan's thoughts turned to the Nazi hunters who had spent so many years tracking down Klaus Barbie, finally arranging his arrest and extradition to France, where he'd died in prison. It gave Stefan great satisfaction to know that, by hiring The Ripper, he had played a significant role in stamping out the Butcher of Lyon's undead agenda. And by so doing, Stefan had helped free many Bolivians, both native and of German descent, Jews and Gentiles, from a ruthless neo-Nazi godfather's yoke.

It troubled Stefan that The Ripper had refused to take payment for this job. Though it was true that The Ripper hadn't managed to save Tupac Inti, he had accomplished the underlying goal behind that task, something worth far more than the amount Stefan had offered him.

As he watched the bright winter sun sparkle off the Mediterranean Sea, Stefan shook his head. It was nice to know that an archaic sense of honor lingered in one exceptionally rare individual. Of course, in the end, it would get him killed. Such unrealistic attitudes always did.

CHAPTER 111

Sitting at a small table outside one of the many cafés that lined Miami's South Beach, Jack sipped his cappuccino as he awaited Janet Price's arrival. The two weeks that had passed since that night Tupac had blown up the altar cave had healed most of his physical wounds. The mental trauma was taking a bit longer. That was the difference between winning and losing. Though they'd stopped Conrad Altmann, this sure hadn't been a win. Not for Janet and not for Jack. Jack wasn't used to losing, and he didn't like it.

But it wasn't just the mission's outcome that had put the chill in Janet's eyes whenever she looked at him. Something else had come between them on that Bolivian night. Jack wished he didn't know what that something was, but he'd had plenty of time to review the events leading up to the battle beneath the Tiahuanaco Ruins.

The being that screwed with Jack's head had almost brought him to his knees in its determination to make him destroy the Incan Sun Staff. And Jack had made things worse through his failure to enforce self-discipline, all in the hope that the artifact could set him free. Not only had he almost gotten himself killed, his loss of self-control had almost killed Janet.

When Janet walked up, she slid onto the chair opposite Jack, and he felt the chill spread from her chair to his. Janet had set up this morning's meeting at Admiral Riles's request. She was right about one thing. The admiral was a hard man to say no to. The offer she had forwarded in advance of this meeting was almost the same one Jack had said no to in Crete, but something had been added and something taken away.

Come work for Riles as part of a very special, off-the-grid team, and have access to the intelligence resources only the NSA could provide.

In Crete, Riles had offered Jack the team lead. That part of the offer had now been removed.

But it was the sweetener Riles had added that got Jack's attention. Jack could keep his role as an independent contractor, and the NSA would pay the same fee he would charge any other client for the same job. He was free to accept or reject any mission without prejudice. But there would be other team members as well as Janet.

Jack watched her watch him as he took another sip, regretting the doubt that he saw reflected in her brown eyes. What he said next was driven more by a desire to remove that doubt than by a change of heart when it came to working for the NSA.

"Riles's offer sounds acceptable."

Janet abruptly slid back her chair and stood. "Good. I'll pass that along to the admiral."

As she started to turn away, Jack gently placed a hand on her arm. Janet turned to look down at him.

"You don't seem thrilled," Jack said.

"You're not my choice."

"That's not what you said in Crete. What changed?"

Janet hesitated but did not take her gaze from his face.

"Inside that passage, when you took the lead, for a while there you lost it, went suicidal."

Jack laughed, even though he failed to feel true humor.

"I've got to be a little crazy to do what I do."

Janet's face tightened.

"Is that what that was? A little crazy? Because I think it might be more than that. And Jack, that scares the hell out of me."

When he failed to respond, she continued.

"Does it scare you, Jack? Do you ever wake up scared?"

Her words knocked the wind out of him. For a handful of seconds, Janet continued staring down at him. Then she turned her back and walked away. Knowing that she'd never hear his whispered response, Jack answered her anyway.

"Every day, babe. Every goddamn day."

ACKNOWLEDGMENTS

I would like to thank Alan Werner for the hours he spent working with me on the story line. Thank you to my editor, Clarence Haynes, for his wonderful work in fine tuning the end product, along with the outstanding editorial and production staff at 47North. I also want to thank my agent, Paul Lucas, for all the work he has done to bring my novels to a broader audience. Finally, my biggest thanks goes to my lovely wife, Carol, for her loving support throughout our many years together.

ABOUT THE AUTHOR

Richard Phillips was born in Roswell, New Mexico, in 1956. He graduated from the United States Military Academy at West Point in 1979 and qualified as an Army Ranger, going on to serve as an officer in the US Army. He earned a master's degree in physics from the Naval Post Graduate School in 1989, completing his thesis work at Los Alamos National Laboratory. After working as a research associate at Lawrence Livermore National Laboratory, he returned to the army to complete his tour of duty. Today he lives with his wife, Carol, in Phoenix, Arizona, where he writes science fiction thrillers.